BUTCHERY OF THE MOUNTAIN MAN

BUTCHERY OF THE MOUNTAIN MAN

WILLIAM W. JOHNSTONE
with J. A. Johnstone

PINNACLE BOOKS

Kensington Publishing Corp.

www.kensingtonbooks.com

PINNACLE BOOKS are published by

Kensington Publishing Corp.
119 West 40th Street
New York, NY 10018

PUBLISHER'S NOTE
Following the death of William W. Johnstone, the Johnstone family is working with a carefully selected writer to organize and complete Mr. Johnstone's outlines and many unfinished manuscripts to create additional novels in all of his series like The Last Gunfighter, Mountain Man, and Eagles, among others. This novel was inspired by Mr. Johnstone's superb storytelling.

If you purchased this book without a cover, you should be aware that this book is stolen property. It was reported as "unsold and destroyed" to the publisher, and neither the author nor the publisher has received any payment for this "stripped book."

All Kensington titles, imprints, and distributed lines are available at special quantity discounts for bulk purchases for sales promotions, premiums, fund-raising, educational, or institutional use. Special book excerpts or customized printings can also be created to fit specific needs. For details, write or phone the office of the Kensington special sales manager: Kensington Publishing Corp., 119 West 40th Street, New York, NY 10018, attn: Special Sales Department; phone 1-800-221-2647.

PINNACLE BOOKS and the Pinnacle logo are Reg. U.S. Pat. & TM Off.
The WWJ steer head logo is a trademark of Kensington Publishing Corp.

ISBN-13: 978-0-7860-2005-8
ISBN-10: 0-7860-2005-9

First printing: December 2013

10 9 8 7 6 5 4 3 2 1

Printed in the United States of America

First electronic edition: December 2013

ISBN-13: 978-0-7860-3327-0
ISBN-10: 0-7860-3327-4

PREFACE

In 1923, which is two years before this writing, I undertook the task of putting together a scholarly tome on the Vanguards of Western Expansion. Heroes, Trappers, Indian Fighters, Explorers, Scouts, and Adventurers were to be my subjects, but I faced the immediate problem of deciding who should be the focus of my study. I had many to choose from: Kit Carson, John C. Frémont, James Bridger, Jedediah Smith, Arthur "Preacher" Gregory (though the last name is uncertain), Kirby "Smoke" Jensen, Matt Jensen, Ian MacCallister, his son Falcon MacCallister, a cousin, Duff MacCallister, and John "Liver-Eating" Jackson. Most will agree that all warrant their own book, and in many cases those books have, indeed, already been written.

But the decision was made for me when I realized that as of October 1923, the time I began the project, one of the most storied of all the aforementioned heroes, Smoke Jensen, was still alive. Furthermore, my initial investigation led me to the inescapable fact that Smoke Jensen and

John Jackson were not only friends, but shared the incredible adventure of Liver-Eating Jackson's personal war with the Apsáalooke, or, as they are more popularly known, Crow Indians. The decision was made. I would write about Smoke Jensen and John Jackson. I contacted Smoke Jensen and brought him to the University of Colorado, where, by making use of the magic of voice recording, I was able to extract the story herein presented to the reader.

Mr. Jensen proved to be an excellent storyteller, and I apologize to those readers who must absorb this account from the printed page while I was able to actually hear the story from his own mouth. And, because of the transformative power of Mr. Jensen's spoken words, I was miraculously transported back in time to actually witness the events described here.

Discerning readers will soon realize that Jensen possesses the knack for noting and relating details, which is the prime ingredient of the storyteller's art. He has preserved a detailed picture of how things were in the century previous. The varied roles he played during his active career involved him in so many different activities that his own life story constitutes a fair approach to an encyclopedia of life on the American frontier.

Quite apart from its informational value, Smoke Jensen's story provides grand entertainment for the general reader. The scholar, however, intent upon reconstructing accurately the life of the past, will naturally ask how faithfully Smoke Jensen has recorded it.

Smoke Jensen's memory is quite detailed and astonishing. He can recall all the interesting experiences of his own eventful life, and the day and date of almost everything that has happened in the mountain region within the last sixty years. I have included in this book Jensen's verbatim accounts, recalled from his personal participation, as well as his recollection of stories relayed to him by his friend John Jackson.

I have also included, at various places through the book, editorial inserts if I believe that I have ex cathedra information that will enhance the readers' appreciation of the story herein told.

> *Jacob W. Armbruster, Ph.D.*
> *Professor of History, University of Colorado*
> *Boulder, Colorado*
> *April 9, 1925*

CHAPTER ONE

Office of the President of the University of Colorado—
September 1923

"I have taken your proposal to the Board of Regents," Dr. Norlin said. "And, I might add, I did so with my own, heartiest recommendation that it be approved."

"And?" Professor Armbruster said.

Dr. Norlin smiled, then slid the papers he was holding across the desk. "The approval was unanimous. You will be given the time, the resources, and an intern to help you with your project. What are you going to call it?"

"I'm going to call it *Vanguards of Western Expansion*."

"And it is our understanding that you plan to publish it?" Dr. Norlin asked.

"Yes, Runestone Press has agreed to publish it. In my proposal, I offered thirty percent of the royalties to the university. They were okay with that?"

"Well, they do have a counterproposal," Dr. Norlin replied. "They thought that because you would be researching and writing this book on university time, as well as using university assets, that a fifty-fifty split would be more appropriate."

Professor Armbruster stuck his hand across the desk. "Agreed," he said.

Dr. Norlin chuckled. "You had actually planned that all along, hadn't you?"

"Yes. I figured if I offered thirty percent . . . but agreed to giving up half, that the Board of Regents would feel a sense of accomplishment."

"I'll never say a word," Dr. Norlin replied with a smile. "What is your first step?"

"My first step is to invite Kirby Jensen to come to the university for interviews, and hope that he agrees."

"Do you think that he will?"

"I don't know. I certainly hope so. If he doesn't, this project is dead before it even gets off the ground."

"Well, I wish you the best of luck in getting him to come," Dr. Norlin said. "I really do believe in your project. I think it would not only be good for the university, I think it would also be a good resource for historians who are studying the western expansion for many years to come."

Sugarloaf Ranch

Smoke was sitting in a swing on his front porch, peeling an apple, and throwing the peels to his dog. In front of the house was a Model T Ford, which

Smoke had modified. Behind the front seat and extending to beyond the rear axle was a truck bed, about the size of the bed of a buckboard. He called it his motorized buckboard, but some of the younger cowboys on his ranch called it a pickup truck.

Painted on the door of the truck, in arched letters, were the words SUGARLOAF RANCH. Beneath the arch was a picture of a horse's head, the markings on its face resembling the number seven. Under the horse's head was the name KIRBY "SMOKE" JENSEN.

Smoke was seventy-three years old, and still fast enough on the draw, and accurate enough with his shooting that he was often called upon to give demonstrations of his skills. The speed with which he could still extract his pistol and fire continued to amaze people.

He saw a cloud of dust billowing up from the road, and because this road ended right here, on Sugarloaf, he knew that whoever it was, was coming to the house. And, from the speed at which the vehicle was traveling, he also knew who it was, even before he could actually see the car.

"You know what I think, Dog?" he asked.

Dog cocked his head at an angle to study Smoke's face.

"It's not what I think, it's what I know. That's Sally, coming up the road like a scalded-ass cat. I think she only knows two speeds: stop and fast."

He watched until the car, a light blue Duesenberg phaeton, emerged from the cloud of dust. Thankfully she slowed down before she got too close, so that the dust dissipated before it rolled up onto the porch. Smoke stood, and rested his hand on one of the support posts for the porch roof as he watched her get out of the car.

"Indians after you, are they?" he teased.

"Indians?"

"The way you were barreling up the road there, I thought a pack of wild Indians might be chasing you."

"Oh, pooh. Automobiles are made to drive fast."

"Of course, why didn't I think of that?" Smoke replied with a chuckle. "You got 'nything you need carried in?" Smoke asked.

"Two bags of groceries in the backseat," Sally said, opening the door to get one bag. Smoke came out to carry the second.

"I picked up the mail down at the mailbox," Sally said. "You got a letter from the University of Colorado."

"Maybe they want me to come play on their football team," Smoke teased.

Not until the groceries were put away did Smoke read the letter.

Mr. Kirby Jensen
Sugarloaf Ranch
Big Rock, Colorado

Dear Mr. Jensen:

I am a professor of history at the University of Colorado, and I am currently doing research on some of the pioneers of the early days of our state. I wonder if I could persuade you to come to Boulder to be interviewed. I am particularly interested in direct information regarding two of our more colorful characters: a man named "Preacher" and another named John Jackson. I believe you knew both of them.

The University would be happy to offset any expenses you might incur in responding to this request.

> Yours Truly,
> Jacob Armbruster, Ph.D.

Smoke showed the letter to Sally.

"What do you think?" he asked. "Should I go?"

"Yes, of course you should go. How often have I heard you comment about something you've read about our past, that you know is wrong? This would give you the opportunity to make certain that the facts are correct."

"Yes, I guess you're right. Okay, I'll take the truck in to . . ."

"You most certainly will not take the truck," Sally said resolutely. "Didn't the *Rocky Mountain News* recently declare you to be one of Colorado's leading citizens? How would it look if you drove onto campus in that ugly old truck. We will take the car."

"*We* will take the car?"

"Yes, I'm going with you," Sally said with a smile. "I would dearly love to do some shopping in Boulder."

"I'd better tell Pearlie we're going to be gone for a few days, so he can keep an eye on things."

"I'll get us packed."

Boulder, Colorado—October 1923

Smoke and Sally checked into a hotel the night before he was to meet with Professor Armbruster. There were several college students in the lobby, the boys were wearing raccoon coats, and the girls had on cloche hats and dresses with short skirts. Some of the young girls were smoking, their cigarettes held in long cigarette holders.

Someone said something, and there was a loud burst of laughter. The hotel clerk apologized.

"These young people today," the clerk said. "They seem to have no respect or regard for ladies and gentlemen of riper age, like yourself. But you and Mrs. Jensen will be on the top floor, so you won't be able to hear them."

"Ehh? What did you say, sonny?" Smoke asked, cupping his right ear and leaning forward.

"Smoke, stop that!" Sally scolded. But she couldn't help but laugh at his antics.

"Smoke?" the hotel clerk said. "You are Smoke Jensen?"

"Yes."

"Oh, sir, what an honor it is to have you at our hotel. If there is anything you need, please, just let me know. The telephone in your room will connect you directly with the front desk."

The clerk banged on the little bell with the palm

of his hand. "Front!" he called, and a moment later a young man wearing the uniform of a bellhop arrived.

"Take Mr. and Mrs. Smoke Jensen to Room 406, please," he said. "Oh, and, sir, there is a radio in your room so that you may enjoy the broadcasts."

The bellhop escorted them to their room, carrying their luggage, and received a generous tip. Sally waited until he left before she turned to Smoke.

"That was awful, what you did to that poor clerk, pretending you couldn't hear." Her chastisement was ameliorated, however, by a broad smile.

"Don't you think he expected something like that? I mean, after all, we are of *riper* years," Smoke said.

"Oh, hush," Sally said, laughing. She turned on the radio, then began singing along with the song.

Smoke walked over to the window and looked out over the bright lights of the city. On the street below cars were moving steadily, forming a long streak of white lights in one direction and red lights in the other. Behind him, a little box was playing music, broadcast from some remote place. They had come here from Big Rock by automobile, traveling fast enough to cover in one hour a distance that took a full day when he first arrived in Colorado.

Tomorrow he was going to discuss Preacher and John Jackson. What in the world would they think if they could be here, right now, standing beside him looking through this same window?

"How on God's earth can anyone stand all this

noise and congestion? Who could live here more than a day?"

"What?" Sally asked.

Smoke chuckled. "I didn't realize I had said that aloud. I was just thinking about what Preacher would say if he were here to see and hear all this."

"Well, darling, you did say it aloud. And if you didn't know it, maybe you are of riper years," Sally teased.

"Hah. You're not that far behind me, woman," Smoke said. "Get your jacket. Let's go find us a nice restaurant somewhere."

"Oh, that sounds lovely."

"Think they might have raccoon on the menu?"

CHAPTER TWO

Campus of the University of Colorado

The next morning, Smoke parked the Duesenberg in front of the Old Main building on the campus. There was a young man waiting in front of the building, and when he saw the light blue phaeton glide to a stop, he smiled and hurried over to the car.

"Are you Mr. Jensen, sir?"

"I am," Smoke said.

The young man smiled. "I am Wes Pollard. Professor Armbruster asked me to watch for you so I could walk you to his office."

Smoke returned the smile. "Well, you did a good job," he said.

"I've read a lot of books about you," the young man said.

"About ninety percent of them are fanciful," Smoke said.

"But if only ten percent of them are true, you have still led a phenomenal life."

Smoke followed the young man up the concrete steps to the redbrick building. Inside the building, the hardwood floors smelled of oil and wax, and he walked by a glass case housing athletic trophies. At the end of the hall, the last door on the right had a frosted glass door. The sign on the frosted glass read: DEPARTMENT OF HISTORY.

The young man opened door, stepped aside to let Smoke enter first, then came in behind him.

"Mrs. Peabody, this is Smoke Jensen," the young man said, proudly.

"Did you say 'Smoke'?"

"Kirby Jensen," Smoke said.

"Oh, yes, Mr. Jensen," Mrs. Peabody said. "Professor Armbruster is expecting you. Just a moment."

Mrs. Peabody knocked lightly on the door, then went in, shutting the door behind her. A moment later the door opened again and a tall, bald-headed man came out. Smiling broadly, he extended his hand.

"Mr. Jensen," he said. "What an honor it is, sir, to meet you. Please, come in."

Smoke followed him into the room, where the professor led him not to his desk but to a seating area that had a leather sofa, and two leather chairs facing a low table. On the table Smoke saw a basket of bear signs, and a pot of coffee sitting on an electric hot plate.

"I have read of your penchant for bear signs,"

Professor Armbruster said. "I know these won't be as good as the ones your wife makes . . . after all, her bear signs are famous throughout the West. And the coffee, percolated on an electric hot plate, isn't quite like making it over an open flame. But maybe it will suffice, under the circumstances."

Smoke smiled. "I'm sure it will."

Smoke picked up one of the pastries and took a bite.

"As I stated in the letter I sent you, I am currently doing a study on some of the old mountain men of the Rockies. A man called Preacher, for example. I think you knew him."

"Yes, I knew him very well," Smoke said. "I was already sixteen when I saw him first, but I figure you could say that he partly raised me."

"Despite all the research I've done, I have never been able to ascertain his real name," Professor Armbruster said. "Some sources say it was Pierre, some say it was Clyde, but most reports say it was Art. It is the last name that I've had the most trouble with. Bode? Barnes? Garneau?"

"Preacher was pretty guarded about his name, that's for sure," Smoke said. "I think that's because he ran away from a slave owner, and until the day he died, he was worried about that."

"He ran away from a slave owner? See here, was Preacher black? None of my research has indicated that."

"No. But in those days, if a slave owner claimed you had a touch of the brush, and in that same claim said that he owned you, it was hard to prove otherwise if you were no more than a fourteen-year-old boy and had no kin anywhere about to vouch for you. That's what happened to Preacher."

"I never knew that."

"Bet you never knew that Preacher was in love once, either, did you? Her name was Jenny, and she was a slave. She was mostly Creole, but her grandma was black, and that was all that was needed then. He said she was the most beautiful woman he had ever seen."

"Why didn't he marry her?"

"She got killed. Preacher killed the ones who killed her."

"I imagine he would."

"Gregory," Smoke said.

"I beg your pardon?"

"Gregory. That was Preacher's last name. Or at least that was the name he used. But to be honest about it, he once confided to me that he had just taken that name. I never did learn his birth name, and I figure I knew him better than any other human being ever knew him. He seldom even shared his taken name with anyone. Art Gregory. I don't see any reason why the name has to be kept secret any longer. With Preacher dead, there's nothing anyone can do to him now."

Professor Armbruster chuckled. "No, I suppose not."

"Mind if I have another one?" Smoke asked, reaching toward the plate of glazed pastries.

"No, of course not," Professor Armbruster replied. "Speaking of names, let's consider John Jackson. He is often referred to, and I'm sure you know this, as Liver-Eating Jackson. Though the concept of him eating the livers of the Indians he killed has never been verified."

"Would you like me to verify it?" Smoke asked, as he bit into his second bear sign.

"You mean, you *can* verify it?" Professor Armbruster asked in surprise.

"Don't tell my wife, but these bear claws are very nearly as good as hers."

"You have actually seen John Jackson eat a liver. That's what you are telling me."

"The Crow had a belief that they couldn't get into the Happy Hunting Grounds if they didn't have the liver with them." Smoke licked some of the frosting off the end of his finger.

Professor Armbruster chuckled and shook his head. "You will forgive me, Mr. Jensen, but how can you sit there calmly eating a bear claw while talking about having watched John Jackson eat a liver."

"You are the one who brought it up, Professor. And there have been many times in my life when I've been in a position to where I had to eat things that would gag a maggot on the gut wagon."

Professor Armbruster looked a little pale. "Yes, I . . . can imagine so," he said.

"Now, Professor, what is it that you want with

me?" Smoke asked, wiping his hands and fingers with a damp cloth that was on the table.

"I want you to come to the recording room with me. I intend to make a voice recording of our discussion. That is, if you don't mind."

Smoke smiled. "Well, I've been speaking into telephones for a lot of years now, but I've never spoken into a recording machine. How long after I speak into it will it be before it is developed and I can hear my voice played back?"

"Oh, it isn't like photograph film," the professor said with a laugh. "We can have an instantaneous playback if you wish."

"I guess I would sort of like to hear my voice played back to me."

"Then come with me, if you would, please."

Smoke followed Professor Armbruster out of his office, down the hall, and into another room in the building. The walls of this room were lined with thick padding.

"This room is soundproofed, so that no outside sound will interfere. That way, the machine will only record our voices, and nothing else."

There was a table in the room and on the table were two microphones. Smoke looked up at a big glass window and saw the same young man who had met him when he arrived. He was standing by some sort of shelf putting a black disc into position. Behind him there was a panel with dials.

Professor Armbruster indicated that Smoke should sit behind one of the microphones, then the professor sat behind the other one.

"Should I?" Smoke started, but the professor held his finger vertically across his lips, then looked through the glass at the young man on the other side.

The professor moved a toggle switch, and spoke into a little box. "Wes, are we about ready?" the professor asked.

"One moment, Professor," Wes's voice came back through the box. A moment later Wes held one finger up for a second as it appeared he was doing something with his other hand, then he brought the finger down and pointed directly at Professor Armbruster. The professor began talking into the microphone that was before him.

"I am sitting here with Mr. Kirby 'Smoke' Jensen, a genuine pioneer of the West, and particularly our state . . . that is, the state of Colorado. During my research on another fascinating figure from the West, John 'Liver-Eating' Jackson, I learned that the paths of these two men had crossed, many years ago. John Jackson is no longer with us, having died on the twenty-first of December, 1900, in a hospital in Pennsylvania. But Smoke Jensen is still with us, and today I consider interviewing him about John Jackson to be as close to the actual source as it is possible to get.

"Mr. Jensen, would you state in your own voice, your name, please?"

"My name is Kirby Jensen, although I have been called Smoke for most of my life."

"I suppose we could start with how you came to get the name Smoke."

"Preacher gave me that name, on the first day we ever met. I had just been firing a Henry .44, and there was a little wisp of smoke curling up from the end of the rifle barrel. I don't know why Preacher made the connection, but he called me Smoke, and that's how I've been known ever since."

"You say you had just been firing your rifle. What were you shooting at?"

"Indians," Smoke said calmly.

"Were you actually engaged in battle?"

"I suppose you could call it that," Smoke said. "The Indians were trying to kill us, we were killing them. Yes, you could say that was battle."

"When and how did you meet John Jackson?"

"Preacher and I happened to come across him one day. It was in the middle of summer in 1869, and I was eighteen years old. But that's getting a little ahead of the story."

"Ahead of the story? What do you mean?"

"First, you need to know a little about John Jackson's background. I mean, before he came West."

"All right, please, go on," Professor Armbruster said. "I would love to hear about Mr. Jackson's background."

Smoke continued with the story, talking in a

deep, resonant voice that painted word pictures of the mountains, the streams, the cold of the winters, and the heat of the summers, the smell of smoke, drifting through the woods, the sound of wood-peckers and coyote and babbling brooks.

Armbruster asked no more questions; he didn't have to. He had been transported back in time to visit with the man John Jackson before he had become known to history as, John "Liver-Eating" Jackson.

[*This was the first time the actual discussion of "liver eating" was introduced in our discussion of John Jackson. Tales around the campfire say he'd cut out and eat the liver of every Crow he killed. He became known as "Liver-Eating" Jackson and "Dapiek Absaroka," meaning "Crow Killer." Throughout the Northern Rockies and the plains of Wyoming and Montana, Crow warriors who had come for him were found with their liver cut out, presumably eaten by Jackson.*

I was most anxious to find out if this was true, but rather than press the issue at this point, I decided to let Smoke Jensen continue with the story at his own pace. And indeed, had I rushed him at this point, the story might have lost some cohesion, and that would not be fair to the eventual readers of this tale.—ED.]

CHAPTER THREE

Gettysburg, Pennsylvania—July 3, 1863

There had been fierce fighting for the two previous days and if Captain John Jackson, of the 151st Pennsylvania, had to give an honest account of who was winning the battle he would be unable to do so. So far John had seen nearly one-half of his company killed, or so badly wounded as to be taken from the field.

"Captain, would you like to take your lunch with me?" Lieutenant Sanderson asked. "We've got a quiet moment; I don't know when we'll get a better opportunity."

"What are you offering for lunch, Bobby?" John asked his second in command. "Baked ham? Roast beef? Fried chicken, perhaps?"

"Ahh, you can have that anytime," Sanderson said. "How about some nice hardtack, fried in bacon grease?"

"Absolutely," John teased. "Who would want roast beef when we can have that?"

"I can also throw in a fresh peach that I took from a peach orchard," Sanderson added.

"I thought the orchard had been picked clean."

"It has," Sanderson said. He smiled. "It just so happens that I'm one of the ones who picked it clean."

"Cap'n, I believe them rebs is gettin' ready to come at us," one of his men said.

"I believe you are right, Sergeant Dunn," John replied.

"It's goin' to get pretty hot," Dunn suggested.

"Yes, but consider this. Would you rather be here, behind a stone fence, waiting for them? Or would you rather be one of those poor souls who are going to have to cross that field toward us?"

"Yes, sir, I see what you mean," Dunn said. "I'd rather be here."

"Here" was Cemetery Ridge.

At one o'clock two Confederate artillery pieces fired. John was sure that was a signal, because almost immediately afterward, a mile-long line of Confederate cannons began firing, keeping up a steady bombardment. John hunkered down against the stone fence as the missiles whistled and whizzed by overhead. Amazingly, the Confederates were, for the most part, overshooting their target, with the cannonballs bursting on the ridgeline behind the Union positions. The Federal artillery returned fire. The cannonading continued for one solid hour, with enough of the shells falling onto the waiting Union soldiers to do some physical damage, but causing considerably more fear and unease.

Then first the Confederate, then the Union artillery ceased fire and the loud thunder that had been washing across the field for nearly an hour grew silent.

As John listened, he could actually hear the sound of mockingbirds, and he marveled that nature could so turn off the folly of human warfare. Then he heard the faint notes of a bugle call as it rolled across the thousand yards that separated the two armies. That was followed by the long roll of drums.

"Here they come!" someone shouted.

"The rebs is attackin'!"

"They're a-fixin' to come at us!"

None of the proclamations were necessary, as every Union soldier in position could see the long gray line stretching out all the way across the field.

John stood up behind what was left of his company in order to be able to exercise command and control over his men. This also had the effect of inspiring his men, because while they could hunker down behind the stone wall, their commander was exposing himself to enemy fire.

For the moment all was quiet, save for chirping of the mockingbirds and the steady, rhythmic tat of the drums, urging the soldiers on. They were still too far away to separate the individual soldiers from the mass of gray. But he could see the flags . . . bits of red fluttering in the breeze, and the flag bearers who were taking the lead position of each of the committed units.

Slowly, steadily, inexorably, the Confederate soldiers, fifteen thousand in all, and under the command of General Pickett, moved across the field.

"Steady, men, hold your fire, hold your position," John ordered.

The drumbeat cadence grew louder, and as the advancing army moved closer, John could hear the clank and rattle of their equipment, and the fall of their footsteps on the open ground.

"Stay in line, men, stay in line!" a Confederate officer called to his men, his words drifting across the distance between them. He was in front, holding a saber upon which he had placed his hat, and John couldn't help but think of the courage it took to be exposed like this young Confederate officer was.

John did not believe he had ever seen a more magnificent sight, nor a more foolish one. What officer in his right mind would commit his men in such a way?

Suddenly one of the Confederate soldiers gave out a yell that John had heard before. It was what the others referred to as a rebel yell. The other Confederate soldiers joined in, and with that yell, the advancing soldiers stopped their measured march, and broke into a run. Thousands of throats roared their defiance, their shouts answered by many more thousand Union soldiers.

Union artillery opened up then, and John saw

the awful effect of the grape and canister as it tore into the Confederate lines.

"Fire!" John shouted, and not only his men, but Union men all up and down Cemetery Ridge began shooting.

For a moment John forgot that he was standing in the open, then he heard the angry buzz of minié balls flying by him, and he moved quickly to the stone fence. That was when he saw the dashing young saber-brandishing young Confederate officer go down.

The deadly musket fire, to say nothing of the sustained grape and canister artillery fire, so devastated the Confederate advance that within moments the fifteen-thousand-man massed front was broken into several smaller units. Finally the front row of the Confederate soldiers actually managed to cross the stone wall, where they engaged in hand-to-hand combat with the Federals as the two bodies of men slashed at each other with sabers, thrust with bayonets, clubbed with rifle butts, and shot from point-blank range with pistols. But quickly the Confederate ranks, which had been so decimated by cannon and rifle fire during their long approach toward Cemetery Ridge, began to be overwhelmed by the superior numbers of the Union troops. Realizing they could not sustain the attack, those who could manage it broke off the engagement and retreated back across the broad field, leaving the dead and dying behind them.

Gradually the constant bang and pop of gunfire

died out, and all that could be heard were the moans and cries of the wounded, and the shouts of soldiers in blue and gray, calling for assistance from hospital corpsmen.

John, who miraculously had not been wounded, walked over to sit on the stone fence and look back across the field, covered now with a low-lying fog of gun smoke. The smoke was so thick that the retreating Confederate soldiers were quickly enveloped by the cloud. What he could see, though, were the bodies of the dead, strewn across the field, many of which had been nearly cut in two.

The sounds on the battlefield which, but moments earlier had been the thunder of artillery fire, the rattle of musketry, and the challenging screams of men locked in deadly combat, had changed. Now the only sounds were the low moans and whimpers of the wounded. Many of the wounded were from John's company, and he stopped by to see each one.

One of the wounded was Lieutenant Sanderson.

"How badly are you wounded, Bobby?" John asked.

"I don't know," Sanderson replied. He chuckled. "It hurt like hell when I was first hit, but the truth is, I don't feel anything now."

"I'll get you to the aid station," John offered.

"No, sir. Not before the men," Sanderson replied.

John smiled, and put his hand on his friend's shoulder. "That was a collective 'you,' Lieutenant. I intend to get all of you to the aid station."

John mustered the rest of his company, and organized them to move the wounded, including Lieutenant Sanderson, to the aid station.

"Cap'n, do you reckon we're goin' to counterattack?" Sergeant Dunn asked.

"Do you want to leave as many blue-clad bodies out there as there are gray now?" John replied.

"No, sir."

"I'm pretty sure General Hancock doesn't want to either."

Old Main Building, University of Colorado—
October 1923

"John's prediction was correct," Smoke said as he continued to tell the story. "The next day, July Fourth, General Lee started back to Virginia, leading a twenty-seven-mile-long train of hospital wagons. He halted his army at the flooded Potomac River and had his men dig in to fight another battle, but General Meade's army was too battered and too exhausted to counterattack. Also his troops had used up almost all of their ammunition and would have to be resupplied before they could fight again."

"What happened to all the dead the dying?" Professor Armbruster asked.

"The citizens of Gettysburg, the civilians, were left to deal with the thousands of wounded. They turned private homes, businesses, schools, and public buildings into hospitals. For some time afterward, infection and unsanitary conditions caused

disease to spread through the town. But they didn't
have to handle it alone; volunteers came from the
North and the South. Northerner and Southerner
worked together to care for the wounded and bury
the dead, regardless the color of the soldier's uniform. They also piled up, and burned the carcasses
of horses and mules killed in the fighting."

[*It had been a grand plan with Lee proposing to take
the offensive, invade Pennsylvania, and defeat the
Union army in its own territory. Such a victory
would have moved the fighting out of Virginia,
bringing some relief to that beleaguered state, as well
as strengthen the hand of those politicians in the
North who wanted peace at any price. It was also
believed that it would undermine Lincoln's chances
for reelection. It would reopen the possibility for
European support that was closed at Antietam. The
result of this vision was the largest battle ever fought
on the North American continent. This was Gettysburg, where more than 170,000 fought and over
40,000 were casualties.*

*In the grand scheme of things, Lee's plans failed,
but this battle is now referred to as the high-water
mark of the Confederacy. From this point forward,
victory for the South was unachievable. How many
lives could have been saved, had the Confederacy realized then that further continuation of the war was
a terrible waste.*

*It is now believed that this battle had a profound
impact upon John Jackson, causing memories which*

remained with him for the rest of his life. Of course, John Jackson wasn't the only one damaged by the terrible consequences of the battle at Gettysburg. As of the publication date of this book, it is sixty-two years since that terrible battle was contested, and there are still many survivors who continue to bear the scars, as does, indeed, our entire nation.—ED.]

"Hold it up for a moment, will you, Professor?" Wes asked, his voice coming through the intercom box. "I have to set up a new disc."

"Very well, tell us when you are ready," Professor Armbruster replied. Then, taking his finger away from the toggle switch that activated the intercom, he spoke to Smoke.

"Jackson went all through the war without sustaining any wounds, didn't he?"

"It depends on what you call wounds," Smoke said. "He had the kind of wounds that you can't see."

"Traumatic shock."

"I beg your pardon?"

"Jackson, undoubtedly, suffered from a syndrome known as traumatic shock. Last year, Dr. Walter Bradford Cannon, a noted physiologist, published a book on this very subject. It refers to a severe anxiety disorder that can develop after exposure to any event that results in psychological trauma, such as being in a war."

"Yes. I've never heard of that term before, but it certainly had an effect on him."

"You know, one of the things that I found most

interesting in my research on John Jackson is that he did have a college degree," Professor Armbruster said. "But he never used that degree. Instead, he lived for many years in the wilds of Montana and Colorado."

Smoke chuckled. "I think the fact that John was an educated man did surprise a few people. But it wasn't something that ever got in the way."

"Got in the way?" Professor Armbruster replied. "What an odd thing to say, suggesting that, somehow, an education might get in the way."

"Professor, could you see any of your contemporaries in academia doing what John Jackson did? And I'm not talking about his vendetta with the Crow, I mean the many years he lived in the mountains, surviving off the land."

"No," Armbruster agreed. "No, to be honest with you, Mr. Jensen, I don't know that I, or any of my peers, could do that."

"It's because your education would get in the way," Smoke said. "You have learned to expect certain privileges as your due, because of your academic position. It is always hard for anyone to function in a milieu that is vastly different from the environment to which they have become accustomed. John Jackson was able to do this."

"I must confess, Mr. Jensen, that, given what I have read and heard about you, that I am—and please don't think this to be patronizing, because I don't mean it that way—but your language, your deportment, is considerably different from what I expected. Have I missed something in my research? Did you attend college?"

Smoke laughed. "Yes, the University of Sally."

"I beg your pardon?"

"My wife was a schoolteacher when I met her. She never quit learning, or teaching. And she shared it all with me."

"Well, I must congratulate her. She did a wonderful job with you."

CHAPTER FOUR

"I'm ready when you are, Professor," Wes said.

"Thank you, Wes. Give me a sign when you put down the stylus."

Wes held his finger up, then brought it down.

"As we finished with the last recording disc you were telling us about John Jackson's war experiences. Tell us, Smoke, did his war experiences have any effect on his personality?"

"Yes," Smoke answered. "And that was especially so after the war. It was as if he were having a more difficult time being a civilian during peacetime, than he had being a soldier at war."

Again, Smoke began telling the story, and again Professor Armbruster found himself transported beyond time and place so that he was an eyewitness, almost a participant, to the events as they transpired.

Media, Pennsylvania—September 1865

With a history that goes back to William Penn, Media is one of the oldest, continuously occupied settlements in Pennsylvania. Served by the West Chester and Philadelphia Railroad, it was only twelve miles from the city of Philadelphia. And, because of the railroad and its proximity to the city, it was a summer resort for well-to-do Philadelphians.

Father Nathaniel Jackson, rector of Christ Episcopal Church, drummed his fingers on the desk in his study as he stared at his son.

"Why would you do such a thing, John? Is it your intention to embarrass the church? Is it your intention to embarrass me?"

"No."

"Then why would you say such a thing in the men's Bible study?"

John didn't answer.

"Do you really think that the reason so many men were killed during the war was because God went fishing?"

John remained silent.

"God went fishing?" Father Jackson shouted at the top of his voice, slamming his hand down on the desk so hard that a bookend fell over and several books slid off onto the floor.

John started to pick up the books.

"Leave them!" his father said loudly.

John sat up again.

"Have you nothing to say to me, John?"

"Well, didn't Jesus tell Paul that He would make him a fisher of men?" John asked with a smile.

Father Jackson stretched out his arm and pointed

his finger at his son. "Don't you blaspheme! Don't you dare blaspheme!"

"I'm sorry," John said contritely.

"What were you thinking, John? When you disrupted the men's Bible study, what were you thinking?"

"You wouldn't understand."

"I am an Episcopal priest, John. And like all men of the cloth, I listen to the deepest fears, the most private sins, and the most earnest questions of my parishioners. Do you really think I can't listen to the problems of my own son? And you do have problems, John. You have manifested those problems ever since you returned from the war. You are not the same man who left."

"Pop, over three million men participated in that war, twenty percent of them were killed, and another twenty percent were wounded. How could anybody have gone through that hell, and returned as the same man who left?"

"You aren't the only member of this church who went to war, John. No one else seems to have the same degree of restlessness that you do."

"Are you talking about Frank Gilbert, who spent the war in Philadelphia recruiting other men to die? Are you talking about Mark Davidson, who spent his war in Washington? Or maybe Milt Goodpasture, who commanded a militia company that never left Delaware County?"

"They all did their part," Father Jackson said.

"Tell me one other member of this church who

killed a dozen men—sons, husbands, fathers—
good men—whose only sin was to be wearing a
different color uniform. Tell me one other man in
this church who had to wipe from his face the
blood and brain matter of his best friend who had
just had half his head blown off while standing right
beside him. Tell me one other man in this church
who shit in his pants because he was slitting the
throat of another human being, and he didn't have
the opportunity to go find someplace to relieve
himself."

"John, there is no need for you to be vulgar
about this. If you are going to discuss it, please be
Christian enough to use civil language," Father
Jackson scolded.

"Civil language? *Civil language?*" John shouted.
"I'm talking to you about hell! Do you understand
that? You preach about hell, you offer salvation to
keep your flock from hell, but have you ever seen
hell? Because I have seen it. I have not only seen it,
I have lived there! And you complain because I am
not using civil language? Well you tell me, Father
Jackson—and I'm asking you as my priest, and not
as my father—just how does a person describe hell,
in civil language?"

The small brick building sat alongside the railroad track, not a part of, but directly adjacent to
the passenger depot. The sign on the front of the
building read: PENNSYLVANIA FREIGHT BROKERAGE.

And though they handled railroad freight, they also handled freight that was moved by wagon, river-boat, and ship.

It was near the end of a busy day, and John was separating the bills of lading into the type of transportation required. Many of the shipments would use multiple means of transport before reaching their final destination.

John's place of employment was behind a counter that separated the entrance from the rest of the building. From this position he dealt with the public, assessing their shipment needs, suggesting the best solution for them, then, once the requirement was established, he would make all the necessary arrangements for them. He found the job boring, but for the time being it was the only job he could find. He had studied to be a teacher; the original idea was for him to start a school that was associated with Christ Episcopal Church. And, had there not been a war, he would no doubt now be the headmaster of the school, perhaps with one of his own children enrolled.

But when he returned to Media he was in no mood to teach school. By his own admission, at this point in his life, he would not be a good role model for children.

Eric Coopersmith, owner of the Pennsylvania Freight Brokerage company, stepped into the area behind the counter and looked over at John, who, by now, had four stacks of shipping documents.

"Mr. Jackson, did you tell Mr. Poindexter to go to hell?"

"Not exactly," John replied. "What I told him was that I was quite adept at processing shipping requirements as to carrier and destination, and I would be happy to arrange his transportation to hell."

"Did you think that was an appropriate response to a paying customer?"

"I thought it might be a little more appropriate than knocking him on his ass," John said.

"I see."

"Is this conversation going somewhere, Mr. Coopersmith? Or is it just your purpose to chastise me?"

"Oh, yes, it is going somewhere, Mr. Jackson. I'm sorry, but I'm afraid we just can't use you anymore. You don't fit in with the others."

"Fit in? What is there to fit in?"

"Were this the first incident, I would be inclined to overlook it. But this type of behavior has become far too common. In addition, our customers have told me they don't like to deal with you. There is a sense of melancholy about you that they find disturbing. Don't bother to come back tomorrow."

The oldest and most privileged of the city's old-guard clubs was located at 1301 Walnut Street. It was the club to which the most elite members of Philadelphia society belonged, and by education and social standing, John Jackson would have been considered a shoo-in for membership.

But on this day, shortly after he lost his job with the Pennsylvania Freight Brokerage, he was sitting in the outer sanctum of the club. He had been denied any deeper penetration into the building because that was reserved for members only, and he was not yet a member. He had every intention of rectifying that, however, and had applied for membership, having acquired all the necessary sponsors and recommendations. He was now waiting for the results.

He was reading a newspaper, but all the while keeping an eye on the door that led into the inner sanctum, looking for Morgan Phillips, who was his sponsor.

The expression on Phillips's face told John all he needed to know.

"I'm sorry, John," Phillips said by way of beginning. "But I have put your name in for membership three times. I'm afraid the rules of the Philadelphia Club are quite specific. You have been blackballed three times. You are not eligible to have your name submitted again."

There was no specific reason given for John's being blackballed. But John knew that it was not necessary for any reason to be given. It was sufficient reason for him to be denied entry in the club if even one person made the arbitrary decision that he didn't want John to be a member.

"I'm so sorry, John," Phillips said, apologizing again.

* * *

John went directly from the Philadelphia Club to Ye Olde Ale House, where, despite its name, one could also buy whiskey. And that's what John did, bought several whiskeys. It didn't take him too long to get drunk, and the drunker he got, the more generous a tipper he became. As a result he had at least three of the ladies at the bar hanging on his every word.

"Fired! I was fired from a job any moron could do, but I can't do it anymore because I was fired," John said.

"Honey, any man who would fire you is a fool," one of the young women said.

"Yeah, he musht be a fool," John said, slurring the words. "The very idea not lettin' me join their club. Well I din't want to be in their damn club in the firsht place. All it is, is a bunch of old stuffed shirts sittin' around a fireplace talkin' real quiet so's the devil doesn't find out where they are 'n come get 'em."

"Join their club? Honey, I thought we were talking about you gettin' fired," one of the girls said.

"My own father."

"Your own father fired you?" the first girl asked.

"Or wouldn't let you in the club?" a second girl asked.

"No. He's an Episcopal priest," John said, filling his glass and tossing it down, neat.

John was two days sober when he stepped up onto the wide, columned porch, and pulled the cord than hung alongside the door. He could hear the bell reverberating through the house. The home belonged to Swayne Manning, and it was one of the largest and most stately mansions in Chester Hill, one of Philadelphia's most elegant neighborhoods.

The butler answered the doorbell.

"Hello, Morris," John said as he started to step inside.

"I'm sorry, sir," Morris said, moving to block John. "But I have been asked to prevent you from entering."

"What? Morris, what are you talking about? What do you mean I can't come in? Is Lucinda here?"

"Miss Lucinda is not receiving, sir."

"Why not? Morris, is something wrong? Is she ill? Has she been in an accident? If so, I must see her."

"No, sir, nothing like that, I'm glad to say. She asks that I give you this letter."

Morris handed an envelope to John, who recognized at once the very small, but exceptionally neat penmanship of Lucinda Manning. He recognized it because she had sent many letters to him during the war.

"May I come in to read it?"

"No, sir, I'm afraid not."

"Morris, you know damn well that if I really wanted to come in that there is no way you can stop me."

"Yes, sir, I am well aware of that, Mr. Jackson. But it is my hope that you will be gentleman enough not to force your way in where you are not wanted."

"I'm not wanted? Is that what the letter says?"

"I have no way of knowing what the letter says, sir. But, as I say, I have been asked to deny you entrance."

"Yeah," John said. "All right." He turned away from the door, then drove off. He was at least a mile away when he stopped, then opened the letter.

Dear John,

This is a difficult letter for me to write, but I have been thinking of it for the entire year since you returned from the war. You have asked me many times when I would consent to marry you. Here is my answer.

I will never marry you. I know it is something that we had planned on, and though we were going to get married as soon as you graduated from college, it was you who suggested that we put it off until after the war. Of course at the time, neither of us realized how long the war would be.

I waited for you throughout the long war, I was faithful to you, and I maintained a correspondence. But I think now that you were right in suggesting that we wait, because the John Jackson who returned from the war is not the John Jackson I fell in love with.

I think it would be best, John, if we not see each other again. I wish you all the best.

Fondly,
Lucinda

Old Main Building

"Yes, the way you are describing John Jackson is certainly indicative of someone with traumatic shock," Professor Armbruster said. "I imagine that losing his job, and his fiancée, could well drive him to come west to lose himself in the mountains."

"Yes, but he didn't come west right away," Smoke said. "It was another four years before he showed up in the Rockies."

"What did he do during those years? Did he stay in Pennsylvania?"

"No," Smoke answered. He chuckled. "He joined the French Foreign Legion."

Chapter Five

It was a brisk day in mid-April and John stopped out front, and looked at the sign on the outside of the building.

Office de Recrutement Militaire
de la
Légion Étrangère Française

He was met just inside the door by someone in the uniform of a noncommissioned officer.

"*Bist du gekommen, um die Französisch Fremdenlegion?*"

"I beg your pardon?" John replied.

"Oh, you are English. I thought you were German."

"I am American."

"American, you say? And you have come to join the Foreign Legion?"

"Yes."

"Your name?"

John debated over whether or not to give him his right name, then decided that he may as well.

"John Jackson."

"Your name is Jean Jourdain," the noncommissioned officer said.

"John Jackson," John said, speaking his name a bit louder, thinking perhaps the sergeant hadn't heard him.

"*Non.* Here, we will give you a new name. Your new name is Jean Jourdain."

The noncommissioned officer pointed to a door. "Wait in that room with the others."

When John stepped into the other room he saw at least thirty more men, and he heard conversations being carried on in several languages.

"*Deutsch, Belge, Norsk, Español,* English?" someone asked.

"American."

"Oh, very good," the man answered in English. "I am Hans Frey. I am Swiss, but I speak English. We can talk as we wait."

"Is that your real name, or the name you were given?"

"It is the name that was given me by the noncommissioned officer when I reported, so now it is my real name."

"I was given a new name as well, but if we are to be friends, I prefer to use my real name. It is John Jackson."

"Yes, I think we will be friends," Hans said.

"It will be good to have someone to talk to."

"John, I have read of the terrible war in America," Hans said. "Were you in the war?"

"Yes."

"And yet you come to join the French Foreign Legion? You know, do you not, that the crazy French are in wars all over the world? They are in Mexico, and in Africa, and in Asia. And who do they send to fight their wars? They send the Foreign Legion."

"Yes, so I have heard."

"Have you a choice?" Hans asked.

"I beg your pardon?"

"I have no choice. I killed a man," Hans said. He held up his finger. "Mind you, I am not sorry that I killed this man, for if ever a man needed to be killed, it was Max Botta. He was a most despicable person, who by his fraud and deceit, ruined the life of a good man. My father took his own life because of Max Botta."

"Yes, I can see how you would want to avenge that."

"You can see that because you are my friend. But I fear that the law may not see things my way, so I left Switzerland, and where could I go but the Foreign Legion? Look around you," Hans invited. "What do you see, besides murderers, thieves, adulterers, men who have much reason to leave their homeland and no reason to stay?"

"I see."

For the next hour John and Hans, and an

Englishman, carried on but one of many conversations, the drone of voices filling the room.

The Englishman was Desmond Winthrop. Winthrop had been indiscreet enough to impregnate the daughter of the mayor of his town, and not wanting to get married, had left the country.

All during their conversation Sergeant Major Dubois, the noncommissioned officer who had welcomed them to the building in the first place, would periodically call out a name.

"Jean Jourdain?"

There was no answer.

"Jean Jourdain?" Sergeant Major Dubois said again, and this time he stared directly at John. That was when John remembered that he was Jean Jourdain.

"I'm here," John replied, holding up his hand.

"Come, you must speak with the capitaine," he said.

Capitaine Pierre Beajou had a very large moustache, but no beard. He was wearing a dark blue uniform with brass buttons, and he was looking a piece of paper as John came in. Automatically, John saluted.

"Have a seat, Monsieur Jourdain," Capitaine Beajou said. "I see by the papers you filled out that you are a capitaine in the American army."

"Yes."

"For the North, or the South?"

"For the North."

"That is most unusual, monsieur. We have many

men who were officers for the South, leaving because their army is no more, their country is no more. We do not have so many from the army of the North. You will, no doubt, be serving with many of these men. Will you be disturbed by that?"

"No."

"That is good. You do understand, do you not, Monsieur Jourdain, that even though you were an officer in the American army, that you cannot be an officer here? Only Frenchmen who have gone to school at Saint-Cyr—that is like your West Point— can be officers."

"Yes, I know."

"You were in the war, but in your war, gentlemen were fighting gentlemen. Here, the ones you fight are not gentlemen. You are likely to get your throat cut by some Arab or Tonkin. Or, maybe you'll just be wounded. In that case, the women will make sausage out of you.

"And if that doesn't happen you'll have to deal with fever, sunstroke, bad water, and bad food. All in all, it is a bad business.

"And who will you be serving with? Deserters, thieves, murderers, scallywags who have run out on their families, or who have squandered their wealth.

"Why are you here? A petticoat, is it? Were you deceived by a faithless sweetheart?"

John thought of Lucy Manning.

"I have my reasons," he replied.

"Yes, don't you all," Capitaine Beajou said. He made a dismissive motion with his hand.

"Go away, Monsieur Jourdain. Leave while you still can. Have a good dinner tonight at the Moulin Rouge. Watch the pretty girls, enjoy some wine, and think about this.

"Tomorrow, we will swear in the new recruits. If you come tomorrow, you will be sworn in with the others. If you do not come tomorrow, you are still free to go, and that, my friend, would be the wisest thing for you to do."

When the recruiting office opened for business the next morning, John was there. Hans and Desmond were there was well, as were all the others he had seen the day before.

The oath of enlistment was issued in French, German, Spanish, Norwegian, Italian, and English. Then, when all were sworn in, all the new recruits shouted: *"Vive la France. Vive la Liberté. Vive la Légion Étrangère!"*

And after shouting it in French, each new recruit repeated it in his own language. "Long live France. Long live Liberty. Long live the Foreign Legion!"

[*Part of the defining characteristic of the legion is its rule of anonymity, which says that all legionnaires must give up their civil identity upon enlisting. With their old identities set aside, recruits join the legion under a declared identity—a new name that they use during their first year of service. At the end of the first year a legionnaire may reclaim his old name through a process known as "military regularization of the situation," in which fresh identity papers are obtained from the person's home country. Alternatively, a legionnaire can choose to spend his entire career under his declared identity, and many do.—ED.]*

French Indochina—October 1867

On the 30th of October, at 1:00 A.M., John was with the 3rd Company of the Foreign Legion, consisting of sixty-two soldiers plus three officers, en route to Bien Hoa. At 7:00 A.M., after a fifteen-mile march, they stopped for a breakfast of bread and coffee. Soon after, the Black Flag force of Liu Yongfu was sighted. He was leading a cavalry battalion of over six hundred men, which meant that the 3rd Company was outnumbered by a ratio of ten to one.

Capitaine Beajou ordered the company to take up a square formation, and, though retreating, he rebuffed several cavalry charges, inflicting heavy losses on the Annamese army by use of accurate long-range fire.

Looking for a place that would provide a better defensive position, Capitaine Beajou moved his troops to a nearby *ngôi nhà trang trại*, a farmhouse protected by a stone wall that was three feet high. His plan was to keep the Black Flag forces occupied until relieved by Capitaine Ernest Doudart de Lagrée. While his legionnaires prepared to defend the farm, Liu Yongfu demanded that Beajou and his soldiers surrender, noting the numeric superiority of the Black Flag Army.

Beajou replied: "We have munitions. We will not surrender." He then swore a fight to the death, an oath which was seconded by the men who were with him.

John could not help but think back to Pickett's Charge at Gettysburg. There too, he had the protection of a stone fence. But there, he had at least ten thousand men deployed along Cemetery Ridge. Here, there were but sixty-five of them, against six hundred.

The legionnaires put up a spirited defense, but the situation was growing critical. They had lost their pack mules during the retreat, so they were without food or water, and quickly their supply of ammunition reached the critical point as they had only such rounds as they were carrying on their person.

The two lieutenants were killed early in the fight, then at midday, Capitaine Beajou was shot in the chest and died. Now under the command of Sergeant Major Dubois, the legionnaires continued to keep up a spirited fight, despite the overwhelming odds against them.

By five o'clock that afternoon, only twelve of the legionnaires remained, with not an officer or a noncommissioned officer among them. John assumed command and the others readily followed him. They continued to fight until their ammunition was nearly exhausted.

After repulsing the last charge, only three men remained: John, Hans Frey, the Swiss, and Desmond Winthrop, the Englishman.

The Vietnamese had pulled back after the last assault and were now approximately one hundred yards away, on the other side of a rice paddy.

"You both know that when they come the next time, it will be the end, don't you?" John asked.

"Yes, I know, and I have already made my peace with God," Desmond said. "But I do hope to kill at least three more of the buggers before they get me."

"I figured I would die at the hands of some jealous husband, never thought I would die in some stinking rice paddy," Hans said. "What about you, Jean? Are you ready to die?"

"I'm already dead," John replied. "I was killed at Gettysburg, and I've been on borrowed time ever since. So, what the hell?"

"I think our little yellow friends are getting ready to come again," Desmond said.

"Yeah, it looks like it," John said. "All right let's . . . wait! Listen! Do you hear that?"

The three men could hear the sound of a bugle, coming from behind them.

"Quickly," John said. "Let's get a few of these bodies up against the wall, put their rifles out, maybe they'll think relief has already come."

* * *

The soldiers of the Black Flag attacked again, but this time John, Hans, and Desmond had pulled back to the other side of the house. Each of the three had found a place to hide, and they picked off Liu Yongfu's attackers from concealment. The positions of Hans and Desmond were found, and both were killed. John fired his last round, then fitted his bayonet to his rifle and waited for the final attack.

It was at that moment that the relief element of the legionnaires arrived on the scene, twelve hundred strong. They swept through the compound, and over the walls, shooting down the Vietnamese where they could, capturing five, and chasing the rest from the field.

When General de Lattre arrived he saw John sitting on the stone fence, surrounded by the dead officers and men of his company. John stood, and saluted the general.

"Were you with Capitaine Beajou?" General de Lattre asked.

"I was, sir," John replied.

"How many of you remain?" the general asked.

"I believe I am the only survivor," John replied.

General de Lattre put his hand on John's shoulder. "I am sorry that I did not arrive in time to save your comrades."

Chapter Six

Cholon—November 1867

The five captured Black Flag soldiers were tried and condemned. They walked to their death without tremor or hesitation. They were chatting together, and chuckling, as if they were going to some sort of social event, instead of their own execution. They threw curious glances at those who were gathered to watch them die, the witnesses not there by choice, but by command.

They were ordered to stand five meters apart, and they did so, spitting out the red juice of the narcotic betel leaves they were chewing. Behind them, and not seen by the condemned men, the five executioners, all wearing black hoods and carrying wide-bladed swords, approached them. A French officer stood in front of the five men for a moment, then shouted, *"Vive la France!"*

That was the signal, and at the shout all five executioners swung their blades at the same time. The severed heads of the prisoners bounced off the cobblestone square, as the headless bodies tumbled forward.

.

Later that same afternoon, John was standing at a window in the headquarters building in Cholon, looking down at the Saigon River. A large boat was docked at a pier, an eye painted on the bow in order to allow the boat to see, and avoid, demons. A young man wearing a conical straw hat was squatted on the bow, working with fishing net.

"Bun mae! Bun mae!" The haunting calls came from an old woman who was walking the cobblestone road alongside the river, calling out for customers to buy the hot, small baguettes of bread she was selling. A man, pushing a cart that contained a steaming cauldron of soup, was using a young boy to advertise his product, the young boy walking in front, beating sticks together in a precise rhythm that was the specific signature of this man's soup.

[*This was probably very similar to the Annam soup now known as pho, though in fact pho did not become an Annam staple until 1907. It is very likely that the soup peddler Jackson refers to here was Chinese, as Cholon had already become a center for Chinese immigrants into Annam.—ED.*]

John watched as customers bought both the bread and the soup. It was nearly time for lunch and he wished he could be down there on the riverfront, buying the soup and bread, rather than standing here, awaiting his appointment with General de Lattre.

What did de Lattre want? He had asked that question of Capitaine Ernest Doudart de Lagrée, his new commanding officer, but de Lagrée told him that he didn't know.

"I am but a capitaine. Generals do not consult with me."

"Private Jourdain," a sergeant said. "General de Lattre will see you now."

John nodded, then stepped into the general's office. De Lattre had piercing dark eyes, and a vandyke beard.

"Private Jourdain reporting as ordered," John said, saluting the general. The general made a casual return of the salute.

"Private Jourdain, I am pleased to report that I am sending you back to Paris, where you will receive the *Légion d'Honneur*, the highest award that can be given to a member of the Foreign Legion."

"Why?" John asked.

John's response was totally unexpected, and the general looked up in surprise.

"Why? You ask why? It is because of your heroic stance in the battle so recently fought."

"General, I wasn't a hero, I was a survivor," John said. "If anyone is to get the medal, it should be Capitaine Beajou, Sergeant Major Dubois, and the sixty-one others who died in the battle."

"Your hesitancy to accept the medal is commendable, Sergeant Jourdain."

"I'm a private, sir."

"You were a private. I have promoted you to sergeant. And, as I was saying, your hesitancy to accept the medal is commendable, but it is being awarded to you precisely because you are still alive. You will go back to Paris, be awarded the medal, be given two weeks of leave, then assigned as a recruiter to bring other young men into the legion."

"To come to Algeria, or Indochina to die gloriously?" John asked.

"Yes, yes! You do understand!" General de Lattre said.

What was obvious to John at that moment was that General de Lattre didn't understand that John was being sarcastic.

"You are happy to go to Paris, are you not?"

"Yes, General. I am happy to go to Paris."

Old Main Building

"And did John go to Paris?"

"Oh, yes."

"All of this happened before you and John Jackson ever met, didn't it?"

"Yes."

"I must confess that in my own research, this is new to me. I never knew that he had been a member of the French Foreign Legion. Also, I am curious. How is it that you can speak in great detail and with such authority about events that transpired before the two of you met?"

Smoke chuckled. "Professor Armbruster, this is just a guess, mind you, but I would be willing to bet that you have never wintered in the mountains with just one other person."

Armbruster laughed. "You would win that bet," he said.

"Well, when there are just two of you, in a small twelve-by-twelve cabin, and you spend an entire winter together—sometimes snowed in for days at a time—all you can do is talk. There is very little about John's life that I don't know. And, though at the time I had very little history of my own to share, there was little of my life that John didn't know."

"I wonder why John never told anyone else about his experience with the French Foreign Legion. There is, after all, a certain élan about that. You would think it would be something he would speak of with a degree of pride."

"It wasn't a part of his life that he was particularly proud of," Smoke said. "For one thing, he didn't feel all that good about being part of a military establishment that was depriving a people of their freedom. And for another thing, he wasn't proud of being a deserter."

"A deserter?"

"Yes, the enlistment period for serving in the legion was five years. John served less than one year. When he returned to Paris to accept the *Légion d'Honneur* he was given a two-week leave. During that leave, he boarded a ship at Le Havre, bound for Southampton, England, and from there, took a ship back to the United States."

"All this you are telling me about John Jackson, the difficulty he was having in adjusting from the war, and his time with the Foreign Legion, was before you met him, wasn't it?"

"Yes, it was."

"I'm curious, Smoke. You say you had very little history of your own at the time, but hadn't you already located, and, uh, dealt with, the men who killed your father and brother?"

"Yes." Smoke's answer was nonspecific.

"I've read about that. The man's name was Casey, wasn't it?"

"It was. Ted Casey."

"You found him," Professor Armbruster said. It wasn't a question, it was a statement of fact."

"Oh, yes, I found him, all right."

"Since your story is so inextricably related to John's story, I wonder if you would share with me, for the purposes of my research, just what happened when you found Casey. I think that, for future historians, having the story in your own words would be invaluable."

"All right," Smoke said. "It started with Prosperity."

"Prosperity? You mean when you became a wealthy man?" Professor Armbruster asked.

Smoke laughed. "No, I'm not talking about prosperity with regard to wealth. I'm talking about a town that was named Prosperity. On the banks of the Cuchara River, it was a ranching and farming community, with a rather grandiose sign posted just outside the town limits with the proud boast:

COME WATCH US GROW
WITH PROGRESS
AND **PROSPERITY**
IN *Colorado*

[*The town of Prosperity no longer exists. It was one of many such towns in the emerging western United States of the nineteenth century. Some grew and died within a matter of a few months, towns that boomed with gold fever, then went bust when the gold played out . . . or more often, when the promise of gold never bore fruit.*

Prosperity was not a gold town, but rather a town that had been born on the promise of a railroad. At its peak, Prosperity had a population of 1,325. It lasted for three years, then when it became obvious that there would be no railroad, it disappeared quickly. The 1890 census listed its population as 25. By 1900 it was listed only as a "populated place" and by 1910, even that mention was gone.—ED.]

Prosperity, Colorado

The city marshal, having seen Smoke approaching from some distance away, met him just outside of town.

"Welcome to Prosperity, stranger," the marshal said. "The name is Crowell, Marshal Crowell." He put his hand to his badge, even though Smoke had already seen it.

"Marshal," Smoke said, touching the brim of his hat.

"I didn't catch your name," Marshal Crowell said.

"Folks call me Smoke."

"Smoke?" The Marshal chuckled, more in dismissal than in humor. "That's it? Smoke? Smoke what?"

"I've been spending some time in the mountains," Smoke said. "One name is all anybody needs up there."

"Well, Smoke, if you're just makin' a friendly visit to my town, then you're welcome," Crowell said. "But if you're comin' here for any other reason, well, I'm goin' to have to ask you to just keep ridin'."

"I'm looking for a man named Casey," Smoke said. "Ted Casey."

"What do you want with him?"

"That's my business."

"I'm the law here'bouts," Crowell said. "I reckon that makes it my business."

"Is that a fact?"

"You know what, mister, I don't much like your attitude," Crowell said. "Why don't I just . . . ?"

That was as far as Crowell got. He was reaching for his gun, but stopped in mid-draw and mid-sentence when he saw the pistol in Smoke's hand.

"What the hell?" Crowell gasped. "I didn't even see you draw!"

"Like I said, where is Casey?" Smoke asked. He neither raised his voice, nor made it more menacing. Ironically, that made his question all the more frightening.

Crowell hesitated for a few seconds. "His ranch is southeast of here, on the flats. You'll cross a little creek before you see the house. I ought to warn you, though, he's got several men workin' for him, and they're all good with a gun. Maybe not as fast as you, but there's only one of you."

"You got an undertaker in this town?" Smoke asked.

"Of course we do. Why would you ask?"

"I'm about to give him some business," Smoke said.

Ten miles out of town, Smoke encountered two rough-looking riders.

"You're on private land," one of the men said. "Turn your horse around and git."

"You're not being very hospitable," Smoke said.

"Don't intend to be. Strangers ain't welcome here."

"I'm looking for Ted Casey."

"You deef or somethin'? I told you to git."

"I'm looking for Ted Casey," Smoke repeated.

"What do you want with Casey?"

"Just to renew an old friendship from the war," Smoke said.

"From the war?" one of the men said with a laugh. "Boy, you're still wet behind the ears. You ain't old enough to have been in the war."

"I'm sorry, I wasn't very clear. I'm actually looking him up for my pa."

"What was your pa's name?"

"Jensen," Smoke said. "Emmett Jensen."

"Jensen?"

"Yeah. You remember him, don't you?" Smoke said. His words were calm and cold.

"Kill 'im!" one of the riders shouted, and both grabbed for their guns.

They were too slow; Smoke had his pistol in his hand and he fired twice, the shots coming so close together that there was no separation between them.

The two riders were dumped from their saddles, one dead, the other dying. The dying rider pulled himself up on one elbow. Blood poured through his chest wound, pink and frothy, indicating that the ball had passed through a lung.

"Figured when we killed your pa that would be the end of it," he said. He forced a laugh, and blood spattered from his lips. "You're good, a hell of a lot better 'n your brother. Casey shot him low and in the back. It took him a long time to die too. I enjoyed watchin' him. He was a coward, squealed like a pig and cried like a little girl."

Smoke made no reply.

"So was your pa a coward."

Smoke was quiet.

"What's the matter with you?" the rider asked. "You just goin' to let me talk about your folks like that? You're yellow."

Smoke turned his horse and rode around the two men, following the road in the same direction from which the two riders had come.

"Shoot me!" the rider shouted. "You yellow-bellied coward, don't leave me here to die like this! Shoot me!"

Smoke continued to ride away. Thirty seconds later he heard a gunshot, the sound muffled by the fact that the shooter had put the barrel in his own mouth.

Smoke didn't bother to look around.

CHAPTER SEVEN

Stopping in a copse of trees a short distance from the ranch house, Smoke studied it for a moment or two. The house was built of logs and had a sod roof. If it came to it, it would burn easily.

"Casey!" Smoke called. "Casey, come out!"

"Who's callin'?" a voice shouted from within the house.

"Jensen."

"Jensen? I thought we killed you."

"That was my pa. And my brother," Smoke said.

"What do you want?"

"I'm here to settle up."

There was a rifle shot from the house, and though it missed, the bullet came close enough for Smoke to hear it whine.

Smoke took his horse into a ravine that circled the house. Fifty yards behind the house he dismounted, snaked his rifle from the saddle sheath, then lay against the bank of the arroyo. Inside, he saw an arm on the windowsill. He shattered the arm with one shot from his new Henry. A moment later he saw someone's outline through one of the other windows and he shot him, hearing a scream of pain.

"You boys in there," Smoke called. "You want to die for Casey, do you? I've already killed two of you back on the road."

"Your Daddy ride with Mosby?" someone called from inside.

"That's right."

"You had a brother named Luke?"

"I did."

"Yeah, well, he was shot in the back and the gold he was guardin' was stole. Casey done it, not me! You got no call to come after me."

Smoke fired several more rounds into the house.

"Jensen! The name is Barry! I come from Nevada. Din't have nothin' to do with no war, never been east. They's another fella in here just like me. We herd cattle for wages; we ain't got no stake in this fight."

"Come on out and ride away then," Smoke called. "I won't shoot you."

The cabin door opened and two men came out with their hands up.

"We're just goin' to get our horses," one of them shouted.

"Go ahead."

The two men were moving toward the barn when a couple of shots rang out. Both were shot in the back by someone from within the house.

"What'd you do that for, Casey?" Smoke shouted. "They weren't part of this."

"When I pay men to work for me, I expect loyalty," Casey called back.

Smoke didn't answer. He was quiet for several moments, trying to decide what he should do.

"Jensen? Jensen, you still out there?" Casey called.

Casey's voice was getting nervous.

"Jensen? Come on down. Come out in the open so I can see you and we can talk."

Smoke still didn't answer.

"Jensen, you there?"

"I think he's gone," another voice said.

"That's what he wants us to think, you fool," Casey's voice replied.

Smoke followed the arroyo on around to the bunkhouse. In a pile behind the bunkhouse he found a bunch of rags, and in the bunkhouse, a jar of coal oil. He stuck the rags down into the mouth of the coal-oil jar, lit it, then threw it at the ranch house. The jar broke and the fire erupted almost immediately. As the logs burned they began filling the house with smoke and fumes.

From inside the house Smoke heard coughing. Then one man broke from the cabin and started running. Smoke cut him down with his rifle. A second began running and Smoke pulled the trigger on the rifle, only to hear the hammer fall on an empty chamber. He pulled his pistol and shot the man once, watching him double over with a slug in his gut.

Casey waited until the last minute before he stumbled out into the yard, his eyes blinded from the smoke and fumes. He fired wildly as he stumbled around, finally pulling the trigger repeatedly on an empty gun.

Smoke walked calmly up to him, even as Casey was trying to reload, and knocked him out.

Just outside the little town of Prosperity, Smoke dumped a bound and gagged Casey onto the ground. Curious about what was going on, several townspeople came forth to watch as Smoke took a rope from the saddle of Casey's horse and began making a noose.

"What do you think you are going to do here?" Marshal Crowell asked.

"Obvious, isn't it?" Smoke replied. "I'm going to hang the son of a bitch who killed my brother and my pa."

"I am an officer of the law. What if I ordered you to stop?" Crowell asked.

"Then I'd just kill you and hang him," Smoke answered.

"But you can't do this," Crowell insisted. "He hasn't been found guilty."

"Yeah, he has. He's already admitted it to me," Smoke said. "I also watched him kill two of his own men. He shot them in the back."

"That doesn't make what you are doing right," Crowell said.

"It's right in my book," Smoke said. He put the noose around Casey's neck, then threw the other end of the rope over a tree limb. "Get up on your horse," he ordered.

"You go to hell," Casey said, spitting at him.

"Have it your way," Smoke said. He tied the end of the rope to the saddle horn, and started to slap the horse on the rump.

"No, wait!" Casey shouted. "Not that way." Casey's hands were tied in front of him, but he put them on the pommel, then swung himself into the saddle.

"You got anything to say before I send you to hell?" Smoke asked.

"Yeah. I already sent your brother and your pa there, and when I get there I'm going to kick them both in the ass. Now, do your damndest, you son of a bitch."

Smoke slapped Casey's horse on the rump. With a protesting whinny it leaped forward and Casey, dying quickly from a broken neck, swung back and forth, the only sound being the creaking of the rope and the cawing of a distant crow.

"I'll be notifying the governor about this," Crowell said.

"You do what you think you need to do," Smoke said. Without looking back, Smoke walked over to his horse, swung into the saddle, and rode way.

"Son of a bitch," someone said, almost reverently. "That's the damndest thing I done ever seen."

[*This was but the first of what would become Smoke Jensen's legacy, one of "making things right." Smoke Jensen was uncommonly fast with a gun, and could shoot with unerring accuracy.*

Because much of the law, in Smoke's time, was ineffective, Smoke often took the law into his own hands. For many, this power could have been abused for personal enrichment.

This wasn't the case for Smoke, though, because he considered himself a knight, bound by rules of right and chivalry.

The number of men who fell before Smoke Jensen's gun has never been made known, but what is known, and has been recognized by every local, county, state, and federal law enforcement agency is that Smoke never misused his power. He was an invaluable asset as an unpaid deputy to Sheriff Monte Carson of Big Rock. Carson's autobiographical book, Both Sides of the Badge, *states, clearly, that Smoke Jensen had some sort of internal compass that always pointed to what was right. Therefore, according to Sheriff Carson, every killing was justifiable.—ED.*]

Old Main Building

"How much longer after you avenged your father and brother, before you met John Jackson for the first time? Did he come to Colorado right away after he got back to the United States?" Professor Armbruster asked.

"Pretty soon after he got back," Smoke said. "The

first thing he did when he returned was go to Philadelphia to see Lucinda Manning. He was going to tell her that he had changed, and he was ready to settle down and become a useful citizen."

"But she didn't believe him?"

"It wouldn't have made any difference whether she believed him or not," Smoke said easily. "Lucinda had gotten married to a member of the Pennsylvania state legislature. He was just the kind of man her father wanted her to marry."

"I see," Professor Armbruster said. "What did John do next?"

"He went to a high-priced Philadelphia lawyer. He wanted to know if he was in trouble for deserting the French Foreign Legion."

Philadelphia—February 1869

"I have done some research," the lawyer, Robert Dempster, said. "It seems that desertion is higher in the French Foreign Legion than it is in any other military unit in the entire world. And, because desertion is so high, and because they have few records of the actual identity of the men who serve with them, they rarely make any attempt to look for those who have deserted. Apparently, they never do so for Americans. So I would say that you are safe."

"Good, thank you."

"But tell me, Mr. Jackson, is the training and service really as difficult as they say?"

"Yes, especially the training to be hungry," John replied.

"I beg your pardon? Training to be hungry?"

"The legion embraces the philosophy that if you want soldiers to fight hungry, you train them hungry. Breakfast might be watery coffee and a baguette, lunch a few pieces of ravioli and a pear."

"I see. But somehow I get the idea that it wasn't the rigorous training that caused you to desert. It couldn't have been. They don't award medals to those who aren't up to the rigors of training," Dempster said.

"No, it wasn't the training that drove me away. It was the killing."

"The killing? But, Mr. Jackson, you recently came through the Civil War. Surely there wasn't killing on such a scale among the Foreign Legion?"

"It isn't the number of people killed," John replied. "It is the reason they are killed. In the Civil War both of the competing armies had honor on their side. The men of the North and the men of the South thought they were fighting for the survival of their nation.

"France has no such honorable motive. France is fighting wars, not of liberation, or of survival. France is fighting wars of aggression . . . killing innocents so that the country may add to its empire. I saw that when I was in Indochina, and I have neither desire, nor intention to kill those who are defending their own homes and their own culture, merely to add to the glory of France."

"I understand."

"I'm not sure you do," John said. "Had I not been there, to see for myself what was going on, I wouldn't understand."

"What are you going to do now?" the lawyer asked.

"I'm going west."

"Texas? California?"

"No. To the mountains."

"You have to have more in mind than simply going to the mountains, Mr. Jackson. You have to have some idea of how you are going to support yourself."

"I'm going to become a fur trapper."

"Surely, sir, you jest. Have you ever read about such men?"

"I have."

"And that appeals to you?"

"It does."

Dempster shook his head. "Mr. Jackson, I wish you luck. Because I am absolutely certain that you are going to need it."

[*The Rocky Mountain fur trade is the catalyst for one of the most interesting and influential periods of America's movement west. The fur trade as well as the mountaineers who conducted it have caught the American fancy. This subject has probably received more attention, scholarly and popular, than any other phenomenon of the history of the previous century, with the obvious exception of the Civil War. The literature dealing with the mountain men is voluminous and detailed. They are unique in our history: pathfinders and trailblazers, not by design, but simply because they had a need to go from one place to another. They were men who were possessed of common sense, bravery, and coolness under trying conditions. They were noted for the ability to shoot straight, ride hard, fight ferociously, to withstand numbing cold and blistering heat. They were blissfully unaware of their unique qualities, considering them simply a matter of survival.—ED.]*

CHAPTER EIGHT

Old Main Building

"I wonder if, before you speak of your first meeting with John Jackson, you might tell us a little about Matt Jensen? I have read some reports that he is your son, other reports that he is your younger brother, and still other reports that he is of no kin at all. Yet, he does share your last name."

"His birth name was Cavanaugh," Smoke said. "He honored me by taking my last name, shortly after he left."

"This was before you met John Jackson?"

"Yes. Matt was a fourteen-year-old boy when he ran away from an orphanage. I found him half frozen to death in the mountains and took him back with me. Once he recovered he stayed with me quite a while until he left to be on his own. He was with Preacher and me when we first ran across John."

The Colorado Rockies—1869

Smoke and young Matt were with Smoke's friend and mentor, a man who had never given anyone— and very few at that—anything more than his Christian name, Art. To his contemporaries and to history, he would always be known as Preacher.

"You two fellas hold it up there for a moment," Preacher said, lifting his hand. He pointed to the top of some trees. "See them birds up there? The way they're actin'?"

"Yes."

"What does that tell you, boy?" Preacher asked Matt.

"They're studying something that's holding their attention pretty good," Matt said.

"You think it's a critter?" Preacher asked.

"No, I don't think it is. The way they're acting, I think it might be a man. Or men."

Preacher chuckled. "Smoke, I'd say you're learnin' this boy pretty good," he said.

"I had a pretty good teacher myself," Smoke said.

"Yeah, I reckon you did," Preacher replied. It wasn't a boast; it was a statement of fact.

"I would tell you to loosen up that hog leg of yourn, but no need to. You can get it out fast enough, I reckon. Let's the three of us ride on up there, but let's do it real quiet."

Smoke reached down to stroke his horse's neck, then, with a slight pressure of the knees, urged him on.

Preacher, Smoke, and young Matt were approaching a break in the trees without making a sound. It was as if their mounts knew to be quiet, because their hoofbeats were but soft plops in the dirt, no breaking twigs, no rattle of crushing leaves.

Then, just before they reached the opening in the woods, the three heard a long string of curses from just ahead, and Smoke reached down to put his hand on his pistol, though he didn't pull it. They rode a bit farther, then Preacher held his hand up. What they saw ahead of them was a man, probably fifteen years older than Smoke, trying to hold on to a wild turkey that had been caught in a snare. The turkey, with flapping wings and pecking beak, was fighting hard to get free.

"Grab him by the neck," Preacher called to the man.

"I'm trying to grab him by the neck, but the bird apparently has his own ideas. He just won't cooperate," the man replied.

Smoke slid down from his saddle, hurried up to the man and the flapping bird, then reached up with his left hand to grab the turkey just under his head, while with the knife in his right hand, he cut the head off. The man who had been holding on to the bird dropped him, and the four of them watched the turkey flop around until, finally, it grew still.

"Well, it would be quite ungentlemanly of me not to invite you three gentlemen to help me eat this bird," the man said.

"We appreciate the invitation," Preacher said. "But who will we be eating with?"

"The name is Jackson. John Jackson. And who would you three be?"

"I'm called Preacher. This is Smoke. The boy is Matt."

"You're a man of the cloth, are you?" Jackson asked.

"Nope."

"But you're called Preacher?"

"Yep."

Preacher's monosyllabic responses were indications that he had no intention of explaining his moniker, and Jackson didn't pursue it.

Without being asked, Matt picked up the turkey and began plucking it. Once the feathers were removed, he gutted it, then cleaned it in the nearby creek.

"You seem to be quite a capable young man," John said.

"Smoke is bringing me along," Matt replied.

All the while Matt had been cleaning the turkey, Smoke had been gathering wood, and now had a good fire going. He had made a pile of rocks in the middle of the fire, and the turkey, now quartered, was laid out on those rocks to cook.

"Are you three out hunting?" John asked.

"Sort of," Preacher replied.

"What are you hunting for?"

"Whatever we find," Preacher said.

"Were you watching me?"

"Some."

"Does this one talk?" John asked, nodding toward Smoke.

"I talk," Smoke said. "When there's something to talk about."

"Smoke," Matt said. "Look over there. Isn't that sage?"

Smoke chuckled. "It is indeed, boy. You have good eyes."

"Mr. Jackson, it's your bird. Do you mind if I rub in some sage?"

"Do I mind? No, not a bit," John replied. "Show me what it looks like. That might be something good for me to know."

Matt led John over to the growth of sage, then he picked it and began rubbing it between his hands, breaking the leaves down so he could put it on the turkey.

The four were quiet for a long moment as the four quarters of the turkey cooked, and, as it cooked, the air was perfumed with its aroma.

"Damn, that smells good," John said. "I have to confess, I would never have thought of piling up rocks like that to cook it."

"How did you plan to cook it?" Smoke asked.

"I'm not sure what I planned to do. I guess I was just going to throw it in the fire."

"It would've burned half of it away, maybe all of it," Smoke said.

"Yeah, well, when it was just me, there would

probably have been enough left. With four of us, I can see how this is the best way to cook it."

Finally, Smoke went over and pulled on a wing. It came off easily.

"Turkey's ready to eat," he said.

"I'll get some salt out of my pouch," John offered.

"No need for you to waste your salt. You furnished the turkey, the least we can do is furnish the salt," Preacher said.

"Well, that's mighty kind of you."

"You're new to the mountains, aren't you?" Preacher asked.

"Is it that obvious?"

"No, it's just that I've been in these mountains for some thirty years now, and I ain't never run across you before."

"Well, sir, you're right, I just got here a few days ago. I'm from Pennsylvania, and I read about the Rocky Mountains, and how there's land here that no man has ever seen before. So I bought a book that told me everything a man might need in order to live in the mountains. It also had a list of everything I needed to buy, so I went out and bought everything it suggested.

"Now I have supplies for about six months." He laughed. "But it has left me just about dead broke."

"What do you figure on doin' after your six months is up, and you don't have any money to resupply?" Smoke asked.

Jackson chuckled. "To tell you the truth, Smoke,

I don't know as I've given it too much thought," he said. "I guess I just sort of figured that something would come along. It's my plan to trap beaver, but if that doesn't work out, I've got enough to get by until I can find employment somewhere and just give up the notion."

"Pilgrim, looks to me like you are a fella in the need of a lot of education."

"Well, if it is education I need, I do have a degree from the University of Pennsylvania," he said.

"It ain't book learnin' I'm talkin' about," Preacher said. "The kind of learnin' you need out here don't come from no college or no books. It don't even come from them books you was talkin' about."

"Then where does one acquire such an education?" John asked.

"It most comes from just bein' out here, and doin'," Preacher said. "After you make the same mistake over a few times, why it just sort of sets in your mind not to do them same things again.

"But it also helps to have someone with you, to help learn you."

"You mean to 'bring me on,' like Smoke is doing with the young man?" John asked.

"Yeah, something like that."

"Well, I can't argue with that. Matt seems to be a most capable young man, despite his youthful age." John laughed, a grunting, rather self-deprecating laugh. "I must confess that my degree in fine arts does little to prepare me for the adventure I'm about to undertake."

"What do you think, Smoke?" Preacher asked. "Would you be willin' to take this pilgrim under your wing for a while?"

"What about Matt?" Smoke asked.

"What about him?" Preacher asked. "You've got a cabin, the boy can hunt and fish, I've no doubt he can take of his ownself. Besides which, I'll look in on him from time to time."

"What do you think, Matt? You think you're up to livin' on your own for a while?"

"I reckon I can," Matt said with a broad smile.

"Damn, you're looking forward to it, aren't you?" Smoke said.

"Why not? It'll be good to get away from your bossin' me around," Matt said with a teasing laugh.

"All right, I'll take him under my wing," Smoke said.

"Whoa, not so fast here," John said. "I agree that my education may be somewhat remiss, but I wouldn't feel right about burdening someone with the task of undertaking my education."

"Pilgrim, I come out here as a boy, no more 'n fourteen years old, I was, when I got here," Preacher said. "I'd done freed a slave girl that was mostly white, fought river pirates on the Mississippi, took a raft down the river, and fought the Battle of New Orleans with ole Andy Jackson hisself. I thought I was ready to take care of myself, but I run into a couple of mountain men by the name of

Pierre Garneau and Clyde Barnes. They took me in, and ever'thing I know I learned from them two mountain men. Then, when Smoke come along, well, I sort of took him in, like them mountain men did me, and I taught him as much as I could.

"I reckon it would only be fittin' to give you the same kind of learnin'. And there wouldn't be nobody any better at it than Smoke Jensen. So what do you say? Are you wantin' to actual learn somethin'? Or do you plan on stayin' out here makin' a fool of yourself and maybe even windin' up gettin' yourself kilt?"

John looked over at Smoke, studying him for a long time before he nodded.

"All right," he said. "I'm not too proud to admit that I need help. It's fine by me, if it's fine by you."

Smoke grinned. "I think we'll get along just fine, Mr. Jackson."

Jackson held his hand out. "No, sir. Now we have to start this off right between us. I'm not Mr. Jackson. If we're to be friends, you'll call me John."

"All right, John it will be," Smoke said.

"Say, you ain't no kin to Andy Jackson, are you? I mean, what with your name 'n all," Preacher asked.

"He and my grandfather were first cousins," Jackson said.

"Is that a fact? Well, he was a good man, General Jackson was. Seems to me like I heard he was the president of the United States once. Is that true?"

"Yes, he was the seventh president."

"I thought so. I'll be damn. To think that I once

knowed a president of these here United States is some kind of an awesome thing."

One of the first things Smoke did was tell John that if he was serious about trapping, they were going to have to move.

"The Colorado Rockies have been mostly trapped out," he said. "I think we're goin' to have to go north."

"How far north? All the way into Canada?"

"No, there is no need to go that far. But I reckon we'd better head on up to Wyoming, or more 'n likely, all the way up to Montana."

"Montana," John said. "Yes, that sounds quite interesting. I'll bet there are more places up there that no one has ever seen, than there are down here."

"I'm sure there are," Smoke said. "It's a lot bigger area, and there are a lot fewer people."

"I'll be ridin' on then," Matt said.

"Matt, you know where the money is," Smoke said. "If you start running short of the possibles—flour, coffee, sugar, beans, bacon, that sort of thing—well, just ride on down to Schemerhorn's Trading Post and pick up what you need there. You might go there once a month or so anyway, 'cause if I decide to send you a letter, I'll send it to you care of Schemerhorn."

"All right," Matt said. "Smoke, is it all right if

I practice drawing and shooting my pistol while you're gone?"

"Yeah, you've come far enough, I don't reckon you'll be shootin' yourself," Smoke said. "You might need to buy some more cartridges while you're getting your possibles."

"All right," Matt said. "I reckon I'll see you early next summer."

"Take care," Smoke said to the boy as he rode off.

"You sure he'll be all right alone?" John asked. "He seems awfully young."

"Don't let the boy's age fool you," Smoke said. "He's already a better man than three-fourths of the men I know."

They watched Matt until he was out of sight, then Preacher spoke.

"You'll be needin' a pack mule, John," he said. "And to get one of them you're goin' to have to go some way from here, maybe a hunnert miles or more. That'll be a town called Big Rock. It's sort of a new town, just growin' up, but me 'n Smoke has been there three, maybe four times, already, an' they's some pretty good folks there, don't you think, Smoke?"

"So far, the few times we've been there, the folks we've run across have been friendly," Smoke said.

"They got 'em a new sheriff there," Preacher said. "Fella by the name of Monte Carson. Folks say he's honest, and I figure if a town has an honest sheriff, then it's more 'n likely an honest town."

"Any proper town has to have a saloon," John

said. "It's been a month of Sundays since I had a beer, and I would be more than willing to dip into my meager resources to remedy that situation."

"They got a saloon there," Preacher said. "It's a good one too, and it's run by a man that ain't always tryin' to cheat you. Besides, it's been a while since either one of us been in town. Might be good . . . I'd like to have a beer my ownself, 'n maybe a meal I didn't have to kill, or cook."

CHAPTER NINE

Old Main Building

"I know that you ultimately settled near Big Rock," Professor Armbruster said. "Sugarloaf Ranch is only a few miles away, isn't it?"

"Yes, my ranch is just under five miles from Big Rock."

"But the time of your story is, I believe you said, 1869?"

"Yes."

"Big Rock was still quite new then, wasn't it? I believe it was founded in 1860."

"Yes, Big Rock is proud of its position in Colorado history," Smoke said. He continued with his story and, as before, Professor Armbruster was able to lose himself in the narrative, so that he was actually there as an eyewitness to the events Smoke was describing.

Big Rock

The star on the man's vest was still new because he had only been the sheriff for a short time. Before he moved to Big Rock to become their sheriff, Monte Carson had ridden the outlaw trail. It was mostly down in Texas, and most of the money he stole was from the carpetbaggers and reconstructionists who were taxing the ranchers and farmers to the point that more and more were having to sell out.

He was good with a gun too, and had demonstrated that skill many times, though almost always with someone who was also on the outlaw trail. The only exceptions had been when he killed Marcus Shardeen, a bounty hunter who was looking to take a dead Carson in for the reward, and Lou Bona, who, six months later, tried to do the same thing.

Carson looked again at the telegram he had received just this morning.

DREW CULPEPPER AND MARTIN DINGLE BELIEVED TO
BE HEADED FOR BIG ROCK STOP BOTH MEN WANTED
FOR MURDER STOP

Carson knew Culpepper; he had had a run-in with him two months earlier. Then it had been for getting drunk and throwing a rock through the front window of Murchison's Leather Goods store, a dispute over a pair of saddlebags. Carson had forced Culpepper to pay for the damages, and

Culpepper, before he left town, had uttered some threat about "getting even." Carson didn't know Martin Dingle, and had never even heard of him.

Laying the telegram aside, the sheriff walked over to the stove and, using a rag to protect against the heat, picked up the blue-steel pot to pour himself a cup of coffee. He drank it black, simply because it was easier that way, and holding the cup in his hand, he walked over to look through the front window, out onto Front Street. He blew into the coffee to cool it a bit before taking his first swallow.

Big Rock was a bustling town, primarily because of the gold mines in the area. When Smoke, Preacher, and Jackson rode into town they were treated to the sight of new buildings being erected, and the air was rent with the sounds of saws and hammers. There was a sawmill on the outer edge of town, and the ear-splitting screech of its steam-powered circular saw could be heard all over town. There were freight wagons moving up and down the streets, and the boardwalks on each side of the street filled with people conducting commerce.

"Coach comin' in! Coach comin' in!" someone shouted, and looking around Smoke saw a team of six horses coming into town at a gallop. The stagecoach behind the team was rocking left and right as it was pulled at a rapid pace north, up Tanner Street.

"Surely he didn't run that team like that out on the road?" John asked.

Preacher chuckled. "No, they just like to make a point of arrivin' and leavin' at a gallop," he said. "It calls attention to 'em, and makes some people think that maybe the whole trip is fast like that."

They passed the Delmonico Café. "Now, that's where we'll eat after we have us a few beers," Preacher said. "Ain't no finer café in all of Colorado. 'Course, I ain't et in ever' café in Colorado."

The three men stopped in front of Longmont's Saloon. Preacher and Smoke dismounted, but John remained in his saddle.

"I appreciate what you men are doing," John said. "And while I can buy my own beer, I'm not so sure I should be wasting money by eating in a restaurant. Especially if I'm going to have to buy a pack mule."

"Don't you be worryin' none about that," Preacher said. "When we take a feller in, he becomes our pardner. We ain't goin' to let you go thirsty, or hungry, or without a mule."

"We'll be buying all that we need," Smoke said. "And you won't be beholden to anyone. This is just the way we are out here."

"I shall be in your debt then, and I fully intend to discharge that debt at my earliest opportunity," John insisted.

"I have no doubt but that you will," Smoke replied with a friendly smile. He held his hand up in invitation. "Now come on in before the beer goes stale."

What only Preacher and Smoke knew was that Smoke's father, Emmett, lay buried in a place called Brown's Hole, up in the northwest corner of Colorado, near the Idaho line. And buried right beside him was several thousand dollars in gold. Though he didn't show it in the way he lived, because he was always moving around, and staying in the mountains mostly, and avoiding towns and civilization, Smoke was a very wealthy man.

They tied up their animals in front of the saloon. A sign on the front of the saloon featured a beer mug containing a golden brew with a white foamy head. Beneath the sign were the words: COLD BEER HERE.

That was all the invitation they needed, and they pushed their way through the batwing doors to step inside. It was so dark that they had to stand there for a moment or two until their eyes adjusted. The bar was made of burnished mahogany with a highly polished brass footrail. Crisp, clean white towels hung from hooks on the customers' side of the bar, spaced every four feet. A mirror was behind the bar, flanked on each side by a small statue of a nude woman set back in a special niche. A row of whiskey bottles sat in front of the mirror, reflected in the glass so that the row of bottles seemed to be two deep. A bartender with pomaded black hair and a waxed handlebar mustache stood behind the bar, where he was industriously polishing glasses.

"Is the beer really cold, like the sign says?" Smoke asked.

The bartender looked up at him, but he didn't stop polishing the glasses.

"Any colder and the glass would freeze to your lip," he said in a matter-of-fact voice.

"Good. Two beers," Smoke said.

"Just two? There are three of you. What does the other one want?"

"I reckon they'll be orderin' for themselves," Smoke said. "The two beers are for me."

"I'll have two," Preacher said. "How about you, John?"

"As I said earlier, it has been a month of Sundays since I had a beer, so I think two beers would go a long way toward alleviating that situation," John said.

The bartender chuckled, filled six mugs of beer, and set them in front of the three men.

"If all my customers were like you boys, I could get rich real quick, close this place down, and go on to California," a tall, well-dressed man said, from his table near the piano.

"The sign out front says Longmont's Saloon. You would be Mr. Longmont, would you?" Smoke asked.

"I am, sir, Louis Longmont, proprietor of the finest wines, beers, and whiskeys, at your service. And you gentlemen would be?"

"I'm Smoke Jensen. This is John Jackson. And the old gentleman is Preacher."

"Preacher?" Longmont smiled. "I do believe I've heard of you, Preacher. Folks say you were here as soon as Jedediah Smith, Jim Bridger, and Kit Carson."

"Jedediah Smith welcomed me to these mountains. I welcomed Bridger and Carson," Preacher said.

"What's in California?" John asked.

"Beg your pardon?"

"You said if you got rich you would close this place and go to California. What's out there?"

"I'm afraid I can't actually tell you that," Longmont said. "I started out for California, but I never quite made it. I stopped here for a while and I haven't left. But I expect I'll get there someday."

"Why would anyone ever want to leave?" Preacher asked. "I've been to a lot of places, never found a place I like better 'n these mountains."

"*Oui,*" Longmont said. "I will confess that there's something about the mountains that gets in a man's blood."

Smoke picked up the first beer and took a long drink before he turned to look around the place. A card game was going on in the corner and he watched it for a few minutes, drinking his beer while Preacher and John were carrying on a conversation behind him.

"Pilgrim, you'll be in good hands with Smoke," Preacher said. "I never knew anyone that learned as fast as he did."

"I appreciate it," John said.

"And here's another thing. You make this boy your friend, and you'll have a loyal friend for the rest of your life. And out here, one of the first things you learn is that the most valuable thing a man can have, is a loyal friend."

The back door opened and a tall, broad-shouldered man wearing a badge, stepped through the door. Smoke recognized Sheriff Monte Carson, and he started to speak to him, but saw that the sheriff's attention was directed to a table in the corner of the room.

"Culpepper," Sheriff Carson said. "I heard you were in town. I didn't think you'd be dumb enough to come to my town. Not after killin' those two men down in Pueblo."

The man Carson was talking to, one of the card-players, stood up slowly, then turned to face the sheriff.

"What gives you the idea this is your town? And anyway, am I supposed to be afraid of some small-town sheriff like you?"

Because the situation had the look of an impending gunfight, the remaining cardplayers jumped up from the table and moved out of the way.

"You had to know that if you were going to come back to Big Rock, I was going to find out about it, and put you in jail."

"You ain't puttin' me in no jail, Sheriff."

"You're either goin' to jail, or you're goin' to die, right here, and right now," Sheriff Carson said.

Culpepper smiled. "Sheriff, have you considered the possibility that you might be the one dyin'?"

Smoke was watching the drama play out before him, when he heard something, a soft squeaking sound as if weight were being put down on a loose board. Looking up toward the top of the stairs, he saw a man aiming a shotgun at Sheriff Carson. Carson didn't see him, because the man was behind the sheriff.

"Sheriff, look out!" Smoke shouted. When he shouted the warning, Sheriff Carson turned quickly, drew, and fired. The man at the top of the stairs fired the shotgun wildly, and the heavy charge of buckshot tore a large hole in one of the tables. Sheriff Carson's shot had been right on target, and the man with the shotgun dropped his weapon and slapped his hand over the wound in his chest. He stood there just for a second as blood spilled between his fingers. Then his eyes rolled up in his head and he fell, belly down, headfirst, sliding down the stairs, following his clattering shotgun to the ground floor.

The sound of the two gunshots had riveted everyone's attention to that exchange, including Sheriff Carson, and while his attention was diverted from him, Culpepper took the opportunity to go for his own gun.

"Don't do it, Culpepper!" Smoke yelled, and Culpepper turned his gun toward Smoke. The saloon was filled with the roar of another gunshot as Smoke drew and fired at Culpepper, even though Culpepper already had his gun in his hand.

Smoke's shot hit Culpepper between the eyes, and he fell back on the table that was still covered with cards and poker chips. He lay there, belly up with his head hanging down on the far side while blood dripped from the hole in his forehead to form a puddle below him. His gun fell from his lifeless hand and clattered to the floor.

"What's goin' on in here?" a new voice asked. "What's all the shootin'?"

When Smoke turned toward the sound of the voice he saw a man standing just inside the open door. Because of the brightness of the light behind him, Smoke couldn't see him clearly enough to identify him.

"Get out of the light," Smoke ordered.

"You don't tell me what to do, I . . ."

Smoke pulled the hammer back and his pistol made a deadly metallic click as the gear engaged the cylinder.

"I said get out of the light, or I'll kill you where you stand."

The figure moved out of the light. When he did, Smoke saw that he was wearing a badge. He put his pistol away.

"It's all right, Emile," Sheriff Carson said to his deputy. "Put your gun away. This man just saved my life."

Emile Harris put the gun away, then advanced

farther into the saloon. He looked first at the man lying at the foot of the stairs, then at the other man, spread out on the card table with his head dangling over the edge.

"Damn, what happened here?" he asked.

"What happened here is that these two men made the mistake of thinking they could run roughshod in our town," Sheriff Carson said.

"And you killed both of 'em?"

"No, just that one," Carson replied, pointing to the man at the bottom of the stairs. "That one, I presume, is a man named Dingle. This is Culpepper. Carson pointed toward Smoke. This man killed Culpepper."

"Would you really have shot me if I hadn't moved out of the light?"

Smoke picked up his beer and took a drink before he responded.

"Yeah," he said.

CHAPTER TEN

Old Main Building

"The event in Longmont's saloon would be termed a shoot-out, I believe. At least, that's what the western novelists call it, people like Owen Wister, Zane Grey, and Max Brand," Professor Armbruster said.

"A shoot-out, yes. They use the term accurately. I have met all of them, by the way," Smoke said. "And Ned Buntline. I've met him as well."

"Surely you don't equate someone like Ned Buntline with the more legitimate figures of western literature, men like Wister, Grey, and Brand," Professor Armbruster said.

"Why not? He was a storyteller, just as the three men you have mentioned were. In fact, all three of those men told me they had read Buntline, and it was because of his stories that they developed an interest in writing about the West."

"I . . . I must apologize," Professor Armbruster

said. "I didn't mean to be pedantic, nor to give offense."

"No offense taken."

"Was that the first time you met Monte Carson?" Professor Armbruster asked.

"Yes. It was the first time I met Louis Longmont, as well."

"But you and Carson, and you and Longmont, became very good friends after that, didn't you?"

"Yes, eventually. Not right away, not until I moved there, some years later."

"How old were you when this shoot-out happened, Mr. Jensen?" Professor Armbruster asked.

"Nineteen, twenty, maybe, I don't remember exactly."

"But, it was before you established Sugarloaf Ranch."

"Oh, yes, long before Sugarloaf, even before Nicole. But I thought I was here to discuss John Jackson, not Preacher and me. You are sort of getting off the track, aren't you?"

"I am indeed. Though many times during the course of research one finds that divergent paths can lead to other fascinating subjects. And quite often, those subjects don't detract from, but rather enhance your original research, as has happened here, with you. But, you are right, we should get back to our discussion of John Jackson.

"Earlier you said that the man, Preacher, suggested you should educate him. Did you undertake that responsibility?"

Smoke chuckled. "Oh, yes, I spent the next year with John. It turns out that he required a lot of education."

"Please, continue with your story," Professor Armbruster said.

"After we left Big Rock, Preacher went one way, John and I went another."

Smoke resumed telling his story, and as it had before, his low, well-modulated voice began to paint word pictures, so that, again, Armbruster wasn't merely listening to a story, he was reliving it, traveling through time and space with Smoke and John Jackson.

Colorado Rockies

"How'd you meet up with Preacher?" John asked Smoke.

Following Smoke's instructions, John was building an oven from stones. They had shot a possum, and Smoke was cleaning it as John worked on the oven.

"My pa and me come west right after the war," Smoke said. "Then one day this old man just sort of appeared. He was the dirtiest, most stinkingest human being I had ever laid my eyes on. I tell you the truth, John, I just about threw up smelling him."

"That bad?"

"Whoowee, you don't have any idea how bad he was. He told us he'd been watching us for about an hour, and that we were crazy for keeping out in the open the way we were. He said we were prime targets for Indians."

"And what did you think?"

"All I could think about was how bad he stunk and how much I wanted him to go away, or at least get downwind from us."

"What happened?"

"I'll tell you what happened," Smoke said with a grunting chuckle. "It wasn't fifteen minutes later we were jumped by a bunch of Kiowa. We had to fight them off. And that stinking old man? He killed as many as my pa and I did combined."

"I guess you didn't mind having him around so much then, huh?"

"I didn't mind at all. Here, let's put this meat in there and let it start cooking."

They roasted the possum, along with some wild onions and sun roots that Smoke gathered. On top of the oven he set a pan of water to boil, and cooked some cattails.

"Always be on the lookout for cattails," Smoke explained. "They have more uses than you can shake a stick at. In the summer you can harvest the tender stems. The lower part of it will be white and ready to eat, just as it is. If you eat them raw, they taste a little like cucumber. If you cook them, they taste like asparagus. Later, the green flower heads can be cooked and eaten like corn on the cob. And when the yellow pollen starts up, you can gather it up, mix it with flour. That will not only make your flour last longer, it makes a real tasty bread.

"Then, in the fall you can dig up the roots, mash them in water, and let the mix set for a few hours. What you'll get when you pour off the water is a gooey mass of starch at the bottom of the container. That will provide you with a thickening base for soups, whether it be squirrel, rabbit, bird, or, if no meat is available, it's not a bad soup all by itself. Especially if you are in a position where you're near about to starve. Of course, if you pay attention to what's around you, you won't ever actually starve."

"You talk as if a true mountain man never needs to come into the store for supplies," John said.

"Well, the truth is, you just about don't. As long as you've a good supply of salt handy, you'll find that you can make a meal out of almost anything," Smoke said.

"We'll see about that," John replied.

Later, as John chewed the last bit of meat from a bone, then finished up with the boiled cattails, he nodded. "You know, you may be right," he said. "This is about as tasty as anything I've ever eaten. And these things, what did you call them?"

"Sun roots."

"Damn if they don't taste just like potatoes."

"I thought you might like that."

Over the next three days the rain was hard and cold, and Smoke showed John how to build a shelter under an overhanging rock by draping canvas across the front to keep the rain out. Such meat as they could find they cooked over a fire they made just in front of their shelter, and Smoke continued with his lessons.

"There will come a time when you will want to build yourself a cabin against the weather. One with a fireplace and chimney so you can keep warm on the coldest days. I'll help you build it."

"Do you build a new cabin every winter?"

"No, Preacher's been in his same cabin for more than twenty years now. I reckon we can build one that you'll be proud to come back to, every winter. But there's no need in building you one down here. We'll wait until we get to Montana. That way you can be where you can still trap."

"What is the value placed on a beaver skin? How much can you get for one?"

"They are called plews," Smoke said. "And they aren't worth as much as they once were. It used to be one beaver plew was worth three martens. Now martens are worth more than beaver, so it's martens you want to go after. You'll get about three dollars apiece for martens, two dollars for beaver. In a good year, you can trap maybe two hundred marten, and three hundred beaver; you could make as much as twelve hundred dollars."

"Well, now," John said with a broad smile. "That certainly makes the endeavor worthwhile."

"It does, indeed, my friend, it does indeed. I tell you what. If we survive the winter, we'll go to Rendezvous come spring," Smoke said.

"If we survive the winter?" John replied with a bit of a start in his voice.

Smoke laughed. "Most likely, we will," he said.

"What is Rendezvous?"

"They aren't quite as big now as they were back when Preacher was younger, but they are still fun to go to. They are almost like a county fair. Merchants come from the east to sell supplies, whiskey, books, candy, and such. There's music, and generally some women around for dancing. There's shooting contests and knife- and ax-throwing contests. And it's a place where you can sell all the skins you've managed to trap in the past year."

"Where is it held?"

"A different place every year. I guess we'll find out from some of the other trappers."

It was one week later when the two saw their first Indians. There were six of them, all mounted, and painted up.

"I was afraid of that," Smoke said.

"What?"

"Pawnee. They've been following us for the better part of an hour. I thought, or maybe I was just hoping, that they would go on their way. But now they've showed themselves to us, I don't think they have any intention of leaving."

"Are the Pawnee friendly?"

"Not friendly enough so's you can count on it," Smoke said.

"You think they're going to attack us?"

"Yeah, I think maybe they are. You were in the war, so I reckon you can use that long gun."

"Yes, I can use it," John said.

"Problem is, you've got a lot of range and hitting power with that Sharps, but you've got to reload it after every shot."

"Then I shall just have to make every shot count, won't I?" John replied.

The six mounted Indians let out loud war whoops, then, slapping their legs against the sides of their horses, they started galloping toward Smoke and John. Smoke and John stood their ground.

"Now would be a good time to make one of those shots count," Smoke said, and he no sooner spoke the words, than the big, large-bore Sharps boomed loudly beside him. John rolled back from the recoil of the big rifle, but one Indian was knocked down from his horse, and, even from here, Smoke could see the fountain of blood that gushed forth from the strike of the heavy, .50 caliber bullet.

Smoke had a lever-action Henry and he fired once, jacked a new shell into the chamber, and fired a second time. Within less than five seconds the attacking Indians had seen their number cut from six to three. Now, only three, they realized that they no longer had a substantial numerical advantage. The remaining Indians hauled back on the reins so hard that the horses nearly squatted down on their hindquarters. They turned and started galloping away.

Because the Sharps was a breech-loading weapon, and not a muzzle-loader, John had managed to reload more quickly than Smoke had anticipated. John raised his rifle to his shoulder to take aim.

"No, John, don't shoot!" Smoke said, reaching out to push the barrel of John's rifle down before he was able to pull the trigger.

John looked at him in surprise.

"We've got them on the run. By not shooting, we are shaming them as they are running from us; we are showing them that we don't fear them."

"What if they come back?"

"They won't come back today."

Boulderado Hotel, Boulder, Colorado

The university had put Smoke and Sally up in the finest suite in the hotel, or, as the hotel advertised it: "seven hundred square feet of pure luxury." The suite, consisting of a living room, dining room, and bedroom, was on the corner so that there was an excellent view of the city.

Sally was sitting on a leather sofa in the living room, her legs folded up to her side, reading a *Saturday Evening Post* magazine when Smoke came in.

"Finished already?" she asked.

"Just for the day," Smoke said.

"How is it going?"

"It's going well, I think. He has me talking into a microphone, and my words are being recorded on a record, just like the ones you play on the Victrola, only I'm not singing," Smoke said with a smile.

"Too bad. I've heard you crooning. You have a good voice," Sally said.

"They played it back for me today, and I heard my voice. You should hear it."

Sally laughed. "Smoke, I've been hearing your voice for a long, long time now."

"Oh, yes, I guess you have. But I have to tell you that it did sound strange to me. It didn't sound like me. The professor said it did, and he said the reason it sounded different to me is that we never really hear our own voice as others hear it. We hear by the waves caused by sounds in the air, but at the same time we also pick up the vibration of the bones in our skull.

"That's why, when I hear myself recorded and played back, it sounds completely different, because all I hear back from the recording is sound coming through the air, minus the skull vibration and bone conduction."

Sally laughed. "And you understood all that, did you?"

"Yeah," Smoke said with a crooked grin. "It might sound strange, but it makes perfect sense to me."

Sally got up from the sofa and kissed Smoke. "I'm proud of you," she said.

"What are you looking at in the magazine?"

"An ad for a new car."

"A new car? You don't like the Duesenberg?"

"No, I love the Duesenberg," Sally said. "I mean, for your truck."

"I'm not getting rid of my truck."

"Listen to this," Sally said. She cleared her throat, then began reading the ad, as if reciting on stage.

"'Somewhere west of Laramie there's a bronco-busting, steer-roping girl who knows what I'm talking about. She can tell what a sassy pony, that's a cross between greased lightning and the place where it hits, can do with eleven hundred pounds of steel and action when he's going high, wide, and handsome. It's a hint of old loves, and saddle and quirt. The truth is, the Jordan Playboy is built for her.'"

"What is that?" Smoke said with a puzzled expression on his face. "'High, wide, and handsome, hint of old loves, saddle and quirt'? That says nothing about the car."

"I think the idea is to create a feeling," Sally said. "I think the words are beautiful. And so is the car. Look at the picture."

Sally showed Smoke the ad.

"Doesn't look very practical," Smoke said. "It only has one seat, and you can't haul anything in it. I can't see trading the truck for it."

"You're right. Okay, keep the truck. Just buy the car."

"What if we wanted to go somewhere and take some folks with us? There's no room in this car."

"Well, then we would just go in the Duesenberg," Sally said.

Smoke laughed. "So what you're saying is we'll have two cars and a truck?"

"Smoke, don't tell me we can't afford it."

"I'll tell you what we can afford. We can afford to have something good to eat. How about we order up room service for supper, and use this fancy dining room table?"

"Oh, no," Sally said. "We don't get to come to a city that often. You're taking me out, Kirby Jensen. And not for supper, for dinner."

CHAPTER ELEVEN

Old Main Building

"Are you ready to resume, Mr. Jensen?" Professor Armbruster asked the next morning when Smoke returned to the Old Main building on campus.

"Yes, sir, I am," Smoke said. "Where did I leave off yesterday?"

"You and Jackson had just been attacked by six Pawnee," Professor Armbruster said, "but you drove them off."

"So we did."

"Did you have any more Indian encounters?"

"Not immediately. We kept moving north until we left Colorado, then we wound up at Fort Laramie, in Wyoming."

"Laramie?"

Smoke thought of the car ad Sally had read to him yesterday—"Somewhere west of Laramie"— and he smiled. "No, sir, we were at Fort Laramie," he said.

Fort Laramie

When Smoke and John reached Fort Laramie, they were stopped by the guard at the front gate of the post.

"What is your business here?" the guard at the gate asked.

"We have no particular business, private," John said. "We are just passing through and thought we would take shelter here for a couple of days."

"You're both civilians, I can't let you through."

"I realize that you can't authorize our entry. But your post commandant can. So I'm asking you to call the corporal of the guard so that he may escort us to the post headquarters where we will secure permission from your commanding officer."

"The corporal won't take you there."

"Oh, I think he will," John said. "Army regulations twenty-two-dash-five specifically state that civilian personnel may be billeted on a military reservation under certain conditions where safety is concerned, and permission for such visits may be granted at any time by authority of the post commandant."

The guard looked at John with a shocked expression on his face, but he was no more shocked than Smoke.

"Go ahead, Private, call him," John said. There was an air of authority in John's voice that Smoke had not heard before.

"Corporal of the guard, front gate!" the private called.

The other sentries repeated the gate guard's call until, after a few moments a corporal came strolling up to the gate.

"What is it?" the corporal asked.

"Corporal, under the provisions of army regulations twenty-two-dash-five, my friend and I wish to petition the post commandant for permission to spend a few nights inside the fort," John said.

"I ain't never heard of no regulation like that," the private said. "Have you ever heard of it, Corporal?"

"Of course I have," the corporal replied. He stared at John and Smoke for a moment, then nodded. "All right, come with me."

"John, is there such a regulation?" Smoke asked, quietly, as they followed the sergeant across the open area toward the headquarters building.

John chuckled. "I don't have the slightest idea," he said. "But it has gotten us this far."

Smoke laughed. "Yeah, it has."

"Wait here," the corporal of the guard said when he led them into the orderly room. The first sergeant and the company clerk were both sitting at their desks.

"Top, these men want to see the commandant," the corporal of the guard said.

The first sergeant gave Smoke and John a cursory glance, then nodded and stepped into the CO's office. A moment later a major stepped out of his office. At first there was a rather irritated look on his face, but when he saw John, he broke into a wide grin.

"Captain Jackson!" he said.

"Lieutenant Sanderson," John replied. "I haven't seen you since Gettysburg. What happened to you? Other than the fact that you made major?"

"I went to the hospital in Washington, D.C., and when I recovered, I was assigned to General Grant's staff."

"Ha. I can see why you made major then. Oh, this is my friend, Smoke Jensen."

"Mr. Jensen," Sanderson said.

"Smoke, during the war Bobby Sanderson and I served together."

"Served together? Don't you mean you were my commanding officer?" Sanderson replied.

"Congratulations on making major, though I'm sure the congratulations are late," John said.

"What brings you to Fort Laramie?" Sanderson asked.

"I'm in a new business now," John said. "I'm a fur trapper, and my friend, who knows about these things, tells me that the best place to trap now is in Montana. So we're headed up that way, and I thought you might be generous enough to put us up here for a couple of nights."

"Of course I will," Sanderson said. "And you are here just in time to help us celebrate Independence Day."

"Independence Day? What day is this, anyway?"

"July third," Sanderson said.

"Yes, we would love to celebrate the Fourth with you and the troops."

"First Sergeant, get these gentlemen billeted in the officers' quarters," Sanderson said.

"Yes, sir. If you gentlemen will come with me?" the first sergeant invited.

The first thing Smoke did after being assigned a room in the bachelor officers' quarters, was to take a bath, and get into clean clothes. Although he had bathed in streams, this was his first real tub bath in over a year, and he sat in the tub for a long time, just luxuriating in the water. He heard a knock on the door.

"Smoke? Smoke, are you in there?"

"Yeah, John, if you don't mind seeing me in the bathtub, come on in," Smoke said.

When John came in, Smoke was surprised to see that he was wearing the uniform of an army captain.

"I'll bet you didn't even know I had this uniform with me, did you?"

Smoke chuckled. "Hell, John, I didn't even know you had ever been in the army. Let alone an officer. And a captain, no less. That's pretty damn impressive."

"Not all that impressive. The army was huge during the war, and it required a lot of officers. Those of us who had college educations sort of had a leg up on the rest of the troops."

"Well, it impresses me," Smoke said.

"Bobby has invited us to his quarters for supper tonight," John said. "I took the liberty of accepting the invitation for both of us. I hope you don't mind."

"No, why should I mind? I never turn down a free meal. But I'm afraid the best I can do for clothes would be a buckskin outfit that's clean, instead of the dirty one I've been wearing. Hand me that towel, would you?"

"Your buckskins will be fine," John said, handing Smoke the towel as he stepped from the tub.

"I have to tell you, I'm a little out of place here, on an army post," Smoke said. "I wanted to go to the war, but my pa and my brother went, and my sister ran off, so that left me to take care of ma."

"You would have been too young anyway, wouldn't you?" John asked.

"I could have lied about it."

"Well, for the time being, you and I will be trading places," John said. "You have the lead when we are in the mountains; I'll take the lead while we are here, on the army post."

"Sounds like the best way to handle it," Smoke said.

Major Sanderson lived in the commandant's house, which was a rather large, two-story home with Corinthian columns supporting the porch roof. Smoke and John were met at the front door by an enlisted man who was Sanderson's striker.

"Come in, sirs, the major is expecting you."

"Thank you, Private," John said.

Major Sanderson and his wife were waiting in the parlor.

"Hello, John. I would like you to meet my wife, Cindy."

John smiled. "You have done well, Bobby, both in your military career and your choice of a wife. What a lovely lady you have married. I'm most pleased to meet you, Mrs. Sanderson."

"Mrs. Sanderson," Smoke said with a slight nod of his head.

"I have heard much about you, Captain Jackson," Cindy said. "It is good to finally meet you."

For the next half hour, and even after they were called to dinner, Smoke listened, with interest, to the stories John and Major Sanderson exchanged.

"Were you in the war, Mr. Jensen?" Major Sanderson asked.

"No, I missed it. My father and my older brother were." Smoke smiled. "But I'm afraid they fought on the opposite side from you gentlemen."

"Men of good conscience fought on both sides," Sanderson said. "Who was your father with?"

"He was with Mosby's Raiders."

"Mosby? Wait a minute," Major Sanderson said. "Jensen? Your father wouldn't be Emmett Jensen, would he?"

"Yes."

"My, what a warrior he was," Sanderson said. "John, it was before I came to your company. I was on General Stoughton's staff when Mosby's Rangers showed up. Two men went into the general's quarters and awakened him, most rudely I must say, by a slap on his rear. General Stoughton was incensed and, pulling himself up in righteous indignation, said, 'Do you know who I am?'

"One of the two men replied by saying, 'Do you know who John Mosby is?'

"'Yes! Have you got the rascal?' General Stoughton asked.

"'No, but he has got you!' The two men in the room with the general that night were John Mosby"—Major Sanderson looked over at Smoke—"and your father."

John laughed out loud. "How did the men take it?" he asked.

"I have to tell you, John, that General Stoughton was a pompous ass. The truth is, I think at least half the men applauded Mosby, and Emmett Jensen. Myself included," he added.

"Good," Smoke said. "I wouldn't want to make enemies from new friends."

John and Major Sanderson continued to discuss the war. The incident where General Stoughton was captured happened in March 1863. In May, Lieutenant Sanderson joined Captain Jackson's company and fought under him in the greatest battle of the war, the Battle of Gettysburg.

In Smoke's young life he had already faced death many times, and smelled the acrid smell of gunpowder, so he was not unfamiliar with violent death. But the scale of Gettysburg, with thousands of men on either side facing shot and shell, advancing and withdrawing across battlefields strewn with the dead and dying, was enough to hold even his attention.

John and Major Sanderson continued to share such stories.

"What made you decide to go into the fur-trapping business?" Sanderson asked. "I thought you had some girl you were anxious to marry back in, where was it? Boston? Philadelphia?"

"Philadelphia, and it didn't work out," John said.

"That happened to a number of people, I think," Sanderson said.

"Yes. But not everyone did something as foolish as I did."

Sanderson chuckled. "What did you do that was so foolish?"

"I joined the French Foreign Legion."

"What? You did? But wait . . . I've read about the Foreign Legion. The term of enlistment is five years, isn't it? If you joined the Foreign Legion, how is it that you are no longer a member?"

"Let's just say that I altered my contract with them."

"You altered your contract? What do you mean?"

"I deserted."

"Oh," Sanderson said. "Are you afraid that . . . what I mean is, do you think they'll come looking for you?"

"No. They would have to come, not only to America, but to the Rocky Mountains to find me. They won't waste their time, they'll just recruit someone to take my place."

"Bobby, can't we find a more pleasant subject to discuss?"

"Yes, forgive me, my dear," Major Sanderson said. He smiled. "Because tomorrow is Independence Day, it will be a day of no work for the men. We plan to have a day-long celebration, and a barbeque. You'll probably smell the meat cooking tonight."

Smoke did smell the meat cooking all night long, two beef halves on spits that were suspended over glowing coals. By the next morning morale on the post was high, not only because of the barbeque, but because the day was given over to celebrations and games. One of the games was baseball, the first time Smoke had ever seen the game played.

That night there was a dance. Held at the sutler's store, it was for everyone on the post, enlisted and officers alike, though it was somewhat limited, due to the lack of women. The wives of the post did their part by allowing their dance cards to be filled by the bachelor officers and men, and it wasn't all that unusual to see Major Sanderson's wife, Cindy, dancing with a young private.

There were very few single women at the post, mostly laundresses who lived on "Soapsuds Row" washing and ironing the post laundry. As a rule, the laundresses did not stay single very long. They were prime candidates for marriage to the noncommissioned officers of the post.

Both John and Smoke danced once with the

major's wife, but generally stayed out of the dance in order to give the men of the post more opportunities. There were a few of the women, though, who made it known by looks and gestures that they would welcome a dance with the two handsome strangers.

The next morning, the two men left immediately after breakfast.

CHAPTER TWELVE

Two weeks later Smoke and John reached the town of Theresa, Montana. Theresa was a one-street town that had grown up at this location in order to take advantage of the only water in the area. They surveyed the town as they rode in, and realized it could be any out-of-the-way town, anywhere in the West. There was almost an ethereal quality to them.

The Cattleman's Saloon wasn't hard to find. It was the biggest and grandest building in the entire town. Inside, the saloon was out of the sun, but the air was still and stuffy, and the dozen or so customers who were drinking had to use their bandanas to continually wipe the sweat from their faces. Behind the bar was a sign that read: PLEASE USE THE SPITTOONS. Despite that admonition, the floor was stained with tobacco juice.

There was no gilt-edged mirror, but there was a real bar and an ample supply of beer and decent whiskey. The saloon had an upstairs section at the back, with a stairway going up to a second-floor landing. When Smoke glanced up, he could see rooms opening off the landing. A heavily painted saloon girl was taking a cowboy up the stairs with her. Smoke had never been upstairs with a bar girl, but he had a pretty good idea of what went on there.

The upstairs area didn't extend all the way to the front of the building. The main room of the saloon was big, with exposed rafters below the high, peaked ceiling. There were three tables with drinking customers, and a fourth table that had a card game going on.

Smoke and John bellied up to the bar.

"What'll it be?" the barkeep asked as he moved down to the two men. He wiped up a spill with a wet, smelly rag.

"Beer," Smoke said.

"I'll have the same."

Smoke slid a dime across the bar and the bartender drew two mugs of beer from the barrel behind the bar.

Smoke turned his back to the bar and looked out over the room. A bar girl sidled up to him then. She was heavily painted and showed the dissipation of her profession. There was no humor or life left to her eyes, and when she saw that Smoke wasn't interested, she turned and walked back to sit by the piano player.

The piano player wore a small, round derby hat and kept his sleeves up with garter belts. He was pounding away, though whatever music he was playing was practically lost amidst the noise of the many conversations.

A girl came down the stairs and went up to the bar. Glancing over at her, Smoke saw that one eye was red and swollen nearly shut. It still had the glowing look of a very fresh injury.

"Millie, what happened?" the bartender asked.

"Nothing happened," the girl said, putting her hand up to cover the eye. "Don't worry about it."

"What do you mean, don't worry about it? It's clear to see that someone just hit you."

"Please, don't say nothin' about it," Millie said. "He wants a bottle of whiskey." Millie put some money on the table.

"The hell he does. Did Colby hit you?" The bartender tried to touch her eye, but Millie pulled away from him.

"Please, Don, just drop it," Millie said. "It's no big thing and I don't want to . . ."

"You don't want to what?"

"I don't want to make him mad at me."

"Honey, looks to me like he's already mad at you. And if he isn't already mad, looks like it makes no difference to him one way or the other."

"It's all right, please, don't make any trouble."

"No trouble. I'll just go up there and tell him his time is up." Don started from around behind the bar.

"No, don't, please!" Millie said. "I told you, nothing is going on." She reached out to grab him.

"Don, I'm afraid he'll kill you. You know how good he is with that gun, and how he's always lookin' to use it. He'll use it on you."

Don hesitated. "All right," he said. "I won't go up 'n say anything to him, but you don't go back up there neither."

"We ain't . . . done nothin' yet," Millie said. "He'll just say he ain't got what he's paid for."

"Then I'll give him his money back. But you don't have to go back up there. Not if he's beating you."

As the two were talking, Colby, bare-chested, and wearing only his trousers and gun belt, appeared at the railing on the upper balcony.

"Hey, you! Bitch!" he shouted down at the girl. "What the hell's keeping you? You've been down there long enough. Get back up here!"

"Colby, she's not coming back up there," Don said. "You've had her long enough."

"What do you mean, I've had her long enough? I'll by damn have her as long as I want her. Do you understand? How long I have her ain't none of your business."

"No, now, your time is up. There's another gent wantin' her."

"Yeah? Just who would that be?" Colby looked down over the floor of the saloon. "Who else is wantin' her?" he asked. "Who wants her bad enough to come through me to get her?"

Millie looked out over the rest of the saloon patrons, the expression in her eyes showing her fear of Colby, and her desperate bid for someone to help her.

There was absolute silence as all the other men in the saloon found something on the floor, or the back wall, or the front window to examine. Not one man would meet Millie's eyes.

"Well, now, turns out you was lyin', doesn't it?" Colby said. The smile that spread across his face was totally devoid of all humor.

"Why don't you leave her alone, Colby?" The other bar girl said. This was the same one who had made a tentative advance toward Smoke and John when they first came into the saloon.

"There ain't nobody asked for your opinion," Colby replied with a snarl. "Besides, if she don't come with me, who would she go with? You done seen that nobody else wants her. Hell, she's nothin' but a whore, same as you. Now, you, Millie, if you know what's good for you, you'll get your ass back up here, now!"

Millie clinched her hands into fists and shook her head resolutely. "No," she said, her voice so quiet that Smoke could barely hear it. "No, I'm not coming back up."

"What do you mean you ain't comin' back up? I paid for you. You hear me, girl? I paid for you! You belong to me."

"Your time is up," Millie said.

"My time is up when I say my time is up."

Millie put her hand down in a dress pocket, then pulled out two pieces of silver.

"Here is your money," she said. "I'll give it back to you."

Colby pulled his pistol and pointed it toward Millie.

"I don't want my money, bitch. I want you. Now you get back up here or I'll shoot you dead where you stand."

"Like the lady said, your time is up," Smoke said. "I believe I'm next, miss, if you don't mind." If the girl had actually gone back upstairs, then he wasn't going to try and stop her. But she was showing courage enough to refuse, and Smoke felt that her courage should be rewarded. He intended to see to it that she didn't have to go up if she didn't want to.

Millie looked at Smoke with an expression of hope, but when she saw how young he was, the expression of hope died.

"No," she said quietly. She held her hand out and shook her head. "No, honey, I appreciate it, but you don't need to get involved."

"Ha!" Colby said. "I say let him get involved. You want to take me on, do you, sonny?"

"If I have to," Smoke said.

Colby chuckled. "Oh, you don't have to, sonny. You can just tell me you're sorry, then tell the bitch there to get on back up here where she belongs."

"Well, I don't plan to apologize, and I don't plan to tell her to go back up there. It seems pretty obvious to everyone here that she doesn't want to."

"Now, do you want to tell me why the hell I should care what she wants? She's got no choice,"

Colby said. "Neither do you, mister. Or haven't you noticed that I happen to be holding a gun in my hand."

"Oh, yeah, I see the gun," Smoke said. "And I'm asking you, nicely, to put it away."

Colby laughed out loud. "Do you people hear this young punk? He's asking me, nicely, to put the gun away."

"Or drop it," Smoke said.

"And if I don't do either?"

"I'll kill you," Smoke said easily.

"You," Colby said to John. "You're a dumb son of a bitch to be standin' there next to him like that. When I start shootin', I ain't goin' to be all that particular about where I'm shootin'."

John leaned back against the bar and took a swallow of his beer before he replied.

"I'm in no danger," John said.

"You're in no danger, huh? And what gives you that idea?"

"I'm in no danger because you won't be shooting," he said.

"What do you mean, I won't be shooting?"

"I mean if you don't do what my friend says, if you don't put your pistol away, or drop it, he'll kill you before you can even get a shot off."

It was the calm and very understated way John made his comment that made everyone's hair stand on end.

With a shout of rage, Colby swung his gun toward Smoke, but in one smooth and incredibly fast motion,

Smoke drew and fired. Colby dropped his gun over the rail and it fell with a clatter to the bar floor, twelve feet below. He grabbed his chest, then turned his hand out and looked down in surprise and disbelief as his palm began filling with his own blood. His eyes rolled back in his head and he pitched forward, crashing through the railing, then turning over once in midair before he landed heavily on his back alongside his dropped gun.

Colby lay motionless on the floor with open, but sightless eyes staring toward the ceiling. It had all happened so fast that no one else in the saloon had made so much as one move . . . it was as if they had all been frozen in position, an eerie tableau, watching the action take place around them.

The gun smoke from the single shot formed a cloud which drifted slowly toward the door. Beams of sunlight became visible as they stabbed through the cloud. There were rapid and heavy footfalls on the wooden sidewalk outside as more people began coming in through the swinging doors. One of them was wearing a badge.

"What happened here?"

Everybody began talking at once.

"Hold, hold it!" the lawman said, holding up his hands. He walked over and looked down at Colby's body.

"The world is a better place without this son of a bitch," he said. "All I need to know is, was it a fair fight?"

"Fair fight? Marshal, Colby had his gun out and

was fixin' to shoot before the young feller there even drawed his gun!" the bartender said.

"Then I see no reason to get the judge to come here and hold a hearing," the marshal said. "You the one that did it?" the marshal asked.

"Yes."

"You're a stranger here, ain't you?"

"Yes, my friend and I are going up to Montana to trap beaver and marten."

"Tell you what. I got no quarrel with you. Seein' as ever'one in here says you was in the right. And, seein' as Colby was one worthless son of a bitch. But it might be better if you moved on tonight."

"Do you mind if we stay long enough to have our supper?" Smoke asked.

"Yeah, you can. Go on over to the café and order anything you want. I'll even pay for it. For the both of you."

"That's very nice of you, Marshal."

Finishing their beer, Smoke and John followed the marshal over to Waggy's Café. They were met by a small, gray-haired man.

"Gentlemen, this is William Wagner, owner of Waggy's Café. And you'll not find a better café in town."

"Well, now, James, I'd just feel real complimented, if I wasn't the only café in town," Wagner said.

"Waggy, I want you to give these two men anything they want, and bill the city."

"All right, Marshal," Waggy replied. "Have a seat, gentlemen."

John started to sit at a table in the middle of the room, but Smoke shook his head no.

"We'll sit back there in the corner," he said. "That way we'll both have our backs against the wall."

"You really think that's necessary?"

"Yeah, I do," Smoke said. "It's hard to imagine someone like Colby with friends, but if he does have any, I wouldn't want them coming toward us without our seeing them."

"Yeah, I see what you mean," John said. John smiled. "I have to tell you, I'm really looking forward to this meal."

"Now I'm hurt," Smoke teased. "Why, that sounds like you aren't all that pleased with my cooking."

"Oh, don't get me wrong, I'm pleased, all right. But it's been a month of Sundays since I've had fried chicken, and I see that they have that here. I intend to enjoy myself."

"Yeah, me too," Smoke admitted.

The men ordered, and the waiter began bringing food to the table. Between them they ate an entire chicken, a dozen biscuits, mashed potatoes, gravy, and green beans. They finished the meal off with two slices each of black and blue pie, made with a combination of black- and blueberries. Their eating was of such a prodigious nature that it drew the attention of everyone else in the café.

"I'll tell you two boys the truth," Waggy said. "If

the city wasn't payin' for your meals, I'd just about let you eat for free. Seein' you boys enjoyin' your food that much is about as good a job of advertisin' as I could hope for."

"It's not hard to appreciate good food, and we thank you," John said.

Old Main Building

"I've read about that shooting in the Cattleman's Saloon," Professor Armbruster said. "The town of Theresa doesn't even exist anymore, and when you look it up, turns out that the shooting you just described is one of the highlights of its entire history. The man you killed was Braxton Colby. He is said to have killed more than twenty men, and, after he was killed, turned out that he had murdered at least three women."

"I gave him a chance to back out of it," Smoke said.

"Yes, the way you just told the story squares with everything I've read about it. Did you have any repercussions from killing Colby?"

"Do you mean did anyone come after us for revenge?"

"Well, did they?"

"Yes, that very night," Smoke said.

"I thought that might be the case, though I must confess that in the reports I have read the stories vary so that I've never been able to ascertain which one was true or even if it actually happened."

"It happened," Smoke said.

CHAPTER THIRTEEN

Theresa

Smoke opened his eyes. Something had awakened him and he lay very still. The doorknob turned and he was up, reaching for the gun that lay on a table by his bed. He moved as quietly as a cat, stepping to the side of the door and cocking his Colt .44. His senses were alert, his body alive with readiness. Smoke could hear someone breathing on the other side of the door. A thin shaft of hall light shone underneath. Outside the hotel he heard a tinkling piano and a burst of laughter.

Smoke heard a rattling of the doorknob. He had locked the door but whoever was on the other side either had a key, or was very good at picking locks, because in less than a minute, the door opened, and an increasing wedge of light spilled into the room.

Was it John?

He didn't think so. John wouldn't have let himself into the room that way. He would have knocked.

Smoke watched as a hand stuck in through the opening. The hand was clutching a pistol, and the pistol was aimed toward the bed, exactly where Smoke had been but several seconds earlier.

Smoke watched the thumb pull the hammer back, but just before the intruder pulled the trigger, Smoke stuck a pencil just in front of the hammer so that when it fell, it made only a slight clicking sound.

"What the hell?" the intruder asked in surprise.

Smoke grabbed the gun arm and pulled the intruder on into the room. The intruder called out in surprise, and Smoke jerked his arm around behind his back, then twisted the arm up behind the intruder's back.

"Who are you?" Smoke hissed.

"Emile Colby," the intruder replied.

"What are you doing here, Colby?"

"I come to avenge my brother."

"Yeah? Well, it isn't goin' to work out like that, is it?"

Smoke grabbed Emile Colby by the scruff of his neck and the seat of his pants, then rushed him out into the hallway.

"Hey! Leggo of me! Leggo of me!" Colby started shouting. His shouts and the loud disturbance caused half a dozen other doors to open onto the hall.

"Here, what's goin' on here?" someone shouted.

"Nothing much," Smoke replied. "I'm just taking out the trash."

"You've got no right to . . ."

"To what?" Smoke said.

By now everyone was laughing at Colby.

When they reached the head of the stairs, Colby had pretty much quit his shouting, and was now quiet, the silence brought on by fear.

"What are you going to do?" Colby asked. "Where are you taking me?"

"You don't understand," Smoke replied. "I'm not taking you anywhere. This is as far as you go."

Smoke bent Colby over, then gave him a kick in the rear. Colby tumbled down the stairs, screaming all the way.

[*In presenting to the public this story of Kirby Jensen and John "Liver-Eating" Jackson's life and adventures, I was cautioned against embellishing any particular incident too highly, and to leave out of the book any element of fiction.*

"I have observed," Smoke Jensen said, "in reading much of work written about me and my contemporaries, that the tendency has been to exaggerate nearly everything. The effect of this has been to give the public a wrong idea of the character of the men who found their way into the young West in search of wealth and adventure. Please tell the story so that those who read it may draw from it correct conclusions as to the kind of lives we really lived, and avoid such coloring of the truth as might lead them to think

I am boasting of my own prowess, or exaggerating my own importance."

There have been many books written about Smoke Jensen, and as he is generally considered to be a true treasure of Colorado, there will be many more. And, no doubt, many of these books, especially those that make no pretense of being anything more than a novel, will attempt to build upon a basis of truth, a degree of fact and fiction ingeniously combined.

I am attempting in this endeavor to present the stories of Smoke Jensen and John Jackson's life as truthfully as I can. But the plain fact, perhaps not understood by those of us in the twentieth century, is that men like Jensen and Jackson lived the kind of lives that are written about by such men as Owen Wister and Zane Grey, or portrayed by Tom Mix and William S. Hart. Such men are passing from the scene, but they will never pass from our history.—ED.]

Montana—late September 1869

The trapping didn't really start until the cold came because, as Smoke explained, it wasn't until then that the beaver and marten would have their full coats.

"All right, this looks like a good place," Smoke said.

"The old man, Preacher, has he been out here long?" John asked, as the two men started unloading their traps.

"He came out here soon after the War of 1812," Smoke said. "And he was taken in by a couple of old-timers who had been here since the late seventeen hundreds."

"Late seventeen hundreds? That was before Lewis and Clark."

"Which Preacher's friends described as nice young men, who were wet behind the ears."

"Ha! It would have been interesting to meet them. But then, Preacher is an interesting man too."

"More than interesting. He is one of the finest, if not the finest man I have ever met. Let's get some traps out. *La langue n'attrape pas le castor.*"

"What did you just say? I know that it is French, but I must confess that I learned very little while I was in the Foreign Legion."

Smoke laughed. "It's a saying that Preacher learned from his friend, Pierre Garneau. It means 'the tongue does not catch the beaver.'"

John laughed as well. "*La langue n'attrape pas le castor.* Very good, I shall have to remember that."

After trapping for several weeks, and skinning and cleaning the beaver pelts, several buffalo came by.

"John, have you ever eaten buffalo?" Smoke asked.

"I can't say as I have."

"Your Sharps fires a heavy enough bullet to take one down. I'll give you the honor. Come with me."

The two men approached the buffalo . . . not part of a large herd, there were no more than six in the group.

"Do you think you can hit one from here?"

"Yes."

"That one," Smoke said, pointing one of them out.

John slipped a .50 caliber bullet into the chamber, closed the block, and took aim, and fired.

A puff of dust flew up from the buffalo's coat, its front legs buckled, then straightened as the animal fought to stay on its feet, then it went down. The sound of the gunshot rolled back in repeating echoes.

"Great shot, John!" Smoke said.

"They didn't run," John said, puzzled.

"That's because you shot the leader. Since he didn't run, none of the others did either. Now, shoot that one, and we'll both have a robe for the winter."

John shot the second buffalo, and this time the remaining four did run. Smoke and John hurried out to the downed buffalo and discovered that both were dead by the time they got there.

[*Less than twenty years after the experience described above, the buffalo were very nearly extinct. Dr. William T. Hornaday of the National Museum directed public attention to the impending extinction of the buffalo. In 1889, he conducted a census which disclosed only 1,091 living buffaloes in the entire world. Another census taken in 1903 turned up only 969, in forty-one herds in the United States, and an additional 675 in Canada, for a world total of 1,644.*

It is easy to point to the cause. Some might say that they were hunted out during the westward expansion of the railroad, and to a degree that is true. But it is also true that the survival of the buffalo did not have a very high degree of importance among the western settlers, whose economy was incompatible with the continued existence of the buffalo. Today the cattle on a thousand hills provide a far greater economic resource than the buffalo, if left to thrive in their primitive paradise, could possibly supply.—ED.]

"We've got some work to do," Smoke said, pointing to the two dead animals.

After skinning the two buffalo, their hides had to be fleshed and thinned. Smoke started at the edges, and began removing the meat and the fat, using a very sharp knife, and working his way toward the center.

The buffalo had already been butchered into chunks of meat that weren't too heavy to carry, and those chunks were hanging from the limbs of a tree to keep the wolves away.

"We'll have meat all winter," Smoke said. "The cold will keep the meat fresh."

"I have got to get me a better knife than this," John said as he tried to emulate Smoke's work on the hides. "This damn thing is as worthless as tits on a boar hog."

"You need a Bowie knife," Smoke said, showing his.

"Well, since I'm not helping much with the cleaning of the skin, suppose I get a fire started and we carve off some of that buffalo for supper."

"Sounds like a good idea to me," Smoke said, without looking up.

Smoke continued to work on the buffalo skin while John began gathering wood for the fire.

"Smoke?" John said a moment later. There was quiet urgency in his voice.

"What?"

"We've got company coming."

"Trouble?" Smoke asked.

John shook his head. "I don't know. I don't think so, though, because there are women with them."

Smoke dipped his hands in the icy cold water to wash off the blood and tissue that had been collected from the inside of the buffalo skin. When his hands were clean, he stood up to watch the Indians approach. There were seven of them, three men and four women. One of the men and one of the women were very old.

Smoke held his hand up, palm out as the Indians approached.

"I am Ketano," the oldest of the men said.

"I am Smoke."

The Indian looked confused, and he made the symbol of smoke with his hand twirling around and lifting.

"Smoke?" he asked, not sure he understood the name.

"Yes, Smoke," Smoke said, repeating the hand sign, then pointing to himself.

The old Indian smiled. "It is a good name," he said, then he repeated to the others, saying the name both in English and his own language.

"What kind of Indians are these?" John asked.

"Mandan, I expect," Smoke said. "More than likely if they were Crow, they would be after our scalps."

"Trade?" Ketano asked, again backing up his English with sign language.

"Yes, we will trade," Smoke said. "What do we have that you want?"

"Buffalo meat," Ketano said, pointing to the hanging chunks.

Smoke walked over to the meat and put his hand on one of the two humps. "This you cannot have," he said. He pointed to the rest of the meat. "You may take some of the remaining meat."

Again Ketano spoke to the others. They laughed, and one of them said something.

"He says you know what part of buffalo is good," Ketano said.

"What have you got to trade?" Smoke asked.

The Indians had honey, corn, dried berries, and wild greens. They also had a beaded knife sheath that John wanted.

Before they left, Ketano gave Smoke and John a warning.

"The Crow do not like the white men trapping here," he said. "I think if they can, they will kill you."

"But we aren't on Crow land. This is public land," Smoke said.

"The Crow believe that any land they want is their land," Ketano said.

With other signs of friendship, the Indians left, carrying bundles of buffalo meat with them.

On the Missouri River—December 1869

A bright sun, reflected back by the mantle of snow, made it necessary for both John and Smoke to keep their eyes at a squint. The river whispered slowly on its never-ending journey to St. Louis where, joining the Mississippi, it would flow all the way down to the Gulf of Mexico.

"Smoke, you do know we're being trailed, don't you?" John asked.

"Good for you, John, you're picking it up fast," Smoke said. "Yes, I know. I just wanted to give you the chance to mention it first. How many do you make?"

"Four, I think. Crow?"

"More than likely," Smoke said. "You remember,

Ketano told us they were trying to keep white trappers out."

"Do we confront them? Or try and elude them?" John asked.

"We may as well face them down," Smoke said. "We won't have any peace, otherwise."

"Look, just ahead," John said. "See how that rock juts out toward the edge of the water? It will give us cover and concealment. And it's big enough for both of us."

"Yeah," Smoke said. "Let's get up there quickly enough to get our horses out of the way."

Smoke and John urged their horses into a gallop, and the pack mules came along without much urging. They rode around behind the big rock John had pointed out, secured their animals, then climbed up onto the rock.

The rock was absolutely perfect for their purposes. It was in two steps, one step that allowed them to get into a kneeling position behind the second step, which was high enough to conceal them.

The four Indians were very skillful in their approach. Not one word was spoken, and they were handling their animals so adroitly that their unshod hooves could not be heard.

"When they get to about fifty yards from us, we'll challenge them," Smoke said. "Use my Henry. You can get your shots off faster that way."

"What will you use?"

"If we wait until they are within fifty yards, I'll use my pistol," Smoke said.

The two men waited until the four Indians came around the bend. Then, suddenly, Smoke stood up. And seeing him stand, John did so as well.

"Stop there!" Smoke cautioned.

"Ayiee!" one of the Indians shouted. He was armed with a bow and arrow, and he raised the bow and loosed an arrow.

The arrow flashed by so close that Smoke could hear the wind of the arrow passing.

"You take the two on the right, now!" Smoke said, firing even as he said the word "now."

John didn't need a second invitation; he fired almost as quickly as Smoke, and jacking another round into the chamber he fired a second time as Smoke was also firing. In less than the time it took to tell about it, all four Indians had been knocked from their horses.

"Looks like at least two of them had repeating rifles," Smoke said. "I see no sense in letting them go to waste, do you?"

John chuckled. "I see no sense at all," he said.

Keeping wary, because Smoke knew that sometimes an Indian would fake death to get an advantage over his adversary, the two men approached the four Indians.

Extreme caution wasn't necessary. All four were dead.

John picked up the two Henry repeating rifles, and examined them very carefully.

"Well now," John said with a broad smile spreading across his face. "These are superb weapons. Absolutely superb. I'll be quite happy to keep these."

"Good," Smoke said. "Let's go find a place to get our traps in the water."

Although there had been periodic snowstorms beginning in late fall, they were hit by a blizzard in the middle of December. They had no wagons to use in the construction of a shelter, but Smoke showed John a time-proven trick of survival he had learned from Preacher. They each carried a buffalo robe with them, and they wrapped the robes around themselves and dug in under a protecting bank. With the rifle set up, and the breech open, the barrel acted as an air vent. That way, they could let the snow drift and pile over them. The snow helped insulate them from the cold and, under the buffalo robes, their natural body heat, trapped by the insulated shelters, managed to keep them warm. They had a third rifle running between them, the barrel pointed toward John, and the open breech under Smoke's robe. That way they could talk to each other, the rifle barrel carrying the sound between them.

"Can you hear me, John?" Smoke asked, speaking into the open breech.

"Yes, I can hear you," John's voice replied.

"Good, that means we can talk to each other while we're waiting out the storm. But if you notice, the breech is on my side. So I would advise you not to say anything to piss me off."

John laughed, then he stopped. "Uh . . . I assume you are joking."

Smoke laughed. "All I'm saying is, watch your p's and q's."

"Oh, I will. Believe me, I will."

Old Main Building

"I take it you got through the blizzard with no difficulty."

"Yes. We came through it fine."

"How did the trapping go that winter?" Professor Armbruster asked.

"It went exceptionally well. I was used to trapping down in Colorado, and as I had told John, the rivers and streams there had been just about trapped out. But when we got to Montana, it was all virgin territory. First of all, you have to understand that the population of the entire state . . ." Smoke paused, then corrected himself. "Well, it wasn't a state then. But the population of the entire territory of Montana at that time, wasn't much over five thousand people. Not counting Indians, that is."

Smoke chuckled. "Just for the fun of it, John and

I figured out what the population density was then. It worked out to about one person for every thirty square miles."

"Yes, I can see how that would have given you a lot of elbow room," Professor Armbruster said. "Shall we walk over to the cafeteria for lunch?"

"Sounds like a good idea," Smoke said.

Outside the Old Main building, several students had gathered, and they were singing:

> *"Glory, Glory, Colorado*
> *Glory, Glory, Colorado*
> *Glory, Glory, Colorado*
> *Hurrah for the Silver and Gold!"*

After the song, a cheer went up.

> *"Co lo ra dah*
> *Sis boom bah*
> *Rah rah rah!*
> *Co lo ra dah"*

"We are playing a football game against Denver tomorrow," Professor Armbruster said. "It's our fourth game, and the aggregate score of the first three games has been 152 to zero. So you can perhaps understand the excitement."

"I guess I can," Smoke said.

All during lunch the students were abuzz about the undefeated football team, and they were talking about the shellacking they were going to give Denver the next day.

After lunch Smoke and Professor Armbruster returned to the recording room.

"I'd like you to talk about Rendezvous, if you would," Professor Armbruster said.

"All right."

CHAPTER FOURTEEN

[*Rendezvous was an annual gathering held at various locations by fur-trading companies. The purpose of the rendezvous was to allow the fur trappers and mountain men to sell their furs and hides, and to make purchases of supplies and other goods from those vendors who accompanied the representatives of the fur-trading companies. The large fur companies put together teamster-driven mule trains which packed in whiskey and supplies into a preannounced location each spring-summer and set up a trading fair—the rendezvous—and at the season's end, hauled the furs out.*

The trappers, most of whom had lived in total isolation for many months previous, very much looked forward to the rendezvous. It was here that the trappers and mountain men could mingle with other human beings, renew old friendships, and make new friends. The gatherings were known to be lively, joyous places, where all were allowed: trappers,

Indians, Native trapper wives and children, travelers, and later on, even tourists who would venture from as far as Europe to observe the festivities. As Smoke Jensen described, there was "mirth, songs, dancing, shouting, trading, running, jumping, singing, racing, target shooting, yarns, frolic, that entertained and delighted white men and Indian alike."—ED.]

Rendezvous, Montana Territory—Spring 1870

The smoke of scores of campfires could be seen from some distance away. Then, as John and Smoke got closer, they were also aware of smells, and sounds of Rendezvous, aromas of roasting meat from the many cooking fires, but also odors that were considerably less pleasant, being the stench of scores of mountain men who had neither bathed, nor changed clothes for the entire winter.

In addition to the mountain men, there were also merchants, photographers, painters, writers, and more than a hundred Indians. The air was alive with the sound of drums, Indian flutes, Indian chants, as well as guitars, and even a bagpiper.

And of course, there was the fur trader. Only one fur trader.

There was a time, in the early days of trapping, back before the war and the western migration, when Rendezvous would be the biggest city between the Pacific Ocean and St. Louis. And though those days were over now, and Rendezvous was no longer the mountain men's only contact with civilization, Rendezvous were still big and important events, still attended by everyone who called himself a trapper.

This rendezvous in 1870 would be Smoke's third but it was John Jackson's first and he was very much looking forward to it. The two men rode in to the rendezvous leading mules that were laden with both beaver and marten skins. They were greeted by a representative of only one fur-trading company, which meant there was no haggling for the best price. You took what the fur company offered, or you would have to take your furs to someplace like St. Louis and try and sell them there.

"*Ahch*," one old mountain man said in disgust. "In the old days there were many dealers who came, and we could find the best price."

"Well, there you go, old-timer. This isn't the old days. Now the price we're paying this year is seventy-five cents for a beaver plew and a dollar and a half for marten fur. Beavers aren't that much in demand anymore. The beaver hats have gone out of style, and the womenfolk think the marten fur is prettier. Are you going to take my offer, or not?"

"What choice do I have?" the trapper complained. "Yes, I will take your unfair offer."

"Hell, Seth, what does it matter to you, anyway?" one of the trappers said. "You'll be spendin' it all on whores and trinkets and such while you are here, anyway. By the time you leave, you won't have two coins to jangle in your pocket."

The others laughed.

"I might want one or two extra whores, and an extra trinket or two," Seth replied, and again, there was laughter.

After John sold his plews, he had money in hand for the first time in almost a year.

"Look at this," he said, displaying his new wealth. "I've got twelve hundred and thirty-five dollars. Why, I'm practically rich."

"I didn't do bad myself," Smoke said. "I've got a little over a thousand dollars."

"You've actually got more than that. I feel like at least half of my money is rightly yours for coming along with me, and teaching me the ropes. To say nothing of the liquor and food and pack mule you bought me whenever we were able to get into town."

"Nonsense. I learned everything from Preacher. It's only right I should pass along what I know to you. The liquor and food is nothing, you were my and Preacher's guest. You can pay for the mule, but it only cost forty dollars."

"I don't know, it doesn't seem right to me." John smiled as he counted out forty dollars. "But who am I to argue? If you say this money is rightly mine, I have no compunctions about keeping it."

"What are you going to do with all your money?" Smoke asked.

"First off, I've got to buy a few of the necessaries," he said. "Some more ammunition, maybe a rubber slicker, never knew how much one would come in handy. And a knife, boy, do I need a good knife. I want you to help me pick one out."

"Nothing to it," Smoke said. "We'll find you a Bowie knife with a good handle. That's all you'll need."

"You stay right there until I come get you. Do you understand that, you ignorant bitch? You don't move, you don't say nothin' to nobody, you don't do nothin' till I come back."

The speaker was a wiry-looking man with a hawk-like nose and pockmarked skin. His hair was long and stringy. The person he was talking to was a young Indian woman, probably in her early twenties. She was pretty, but there was a cowed look about her, obviously the result of being browbeaten by the man who was yelling at her. John looked at her and smiled in an attempt to cheer her up, but she looked down at the ground, as if frightened to be caught returning his smile, or even his glance.

"Who is that most unpleasant gentleman?" John asked.

"I don't know who he is, but I know who he isn't. He isn't a gentleman."

"You certainly have that right."

"Let's pick you out a knife," Smoke suggested.

"All right. I need some ammo too, some more .50 calibers, some .44s for the carbine and pistol."

"Sounds like a good idea."

"Are you going to stock up for the next season?" John asked.

Smoke shook his head. "No, this is it for me. After Rendezvous, I'll be going my own way. I've taught you about as much as can be taught. The rest of it you're going to have to learn on your own. But I expect that you have acquired enough skills that you can move around without getting yourself killed."

"I would certainly hope so," John said.

"Mister, if you ain't plannin' on a-buyin' one of them blankets, move on out of the way so the others can have a look at them," a harsh voice said, and looking around toward the speaker, John and Smoke saw that it was the same man who had been yelling at the young Indian girl a few minutes earlier.

"I'm sorry about that," John said. "I didn't know I was blocking your merchandise."

"You dumb-assed mountain men are so damn stupid that it's a wonder you can even find your way here ever' year."

John said nothing but he did move away. He was smiling as he did so. "Did you hear that, Smoke? He called me a mountain man. All right, it was a dumb-assed mountain man but a mountain man nevertheless."

Smoke chuckled. "You are a mountain man, John, and there is absolutely nothing dumb assed about it. Like I said, you have acquired all the skills you need."

John reached out to take Smoke's hand, and he covered it with his other hand.

"Skills aren't the only thing I've acquired, Smoke. I've acquired a friend, a good friend. And I'm telling you now that if there is ever anything I can do for you, all you have to do is let me know. If I have to, I'll soak my britches in kerosene and walk into hell to kick the devil in the ass for you."

Smoke laughed. "Well, I haven't been that much into churchgoing since I came out here. But I sort of have a hope that I won't ever be needing someone to go into hell on my part. I'd just as soon not be there, if it's all the same to you."

"Friend, if I had followed my father's avocation, I would grant you absolution right here on the spot." He made the sign of the cross. "Have mercy upon you; pardon and deliver you from all your sins."

"You do that well," Smoke said.

"I should, my father is a priest. I was raised listening to him grant absolution every Sunday."

"A priest?" Smoke asked, curious at the pronouncement. "How can that be? I didn't think priests could be married."

John laughed. "He is an Episcopal priest. Oh, what about this knife?" he asked, picking up a Bowie with a beautifully polished, wide blade, sharp on one side, as it was also on the arch that led away from the point on the other side. The handle was a stag's horn.

"Great-looking knife," Smoke agreed.

John bought the knife, then slipped it into the

beaded knife sheath the Mandan Indian had given him.

"Yeah, that looks good on you," Smoke said.

"It feels good on me," John agreed.

After all the purchases were made, Smoke and John went into one of the tents where there was a sign that read: DEER AND BEER. It referred to a meal of deer meat, and a mug of beer.

"Well, the deer isn't all that inviting, seeing as we had plenty of it over these last eight months," Smoke said. "But the beer sure is."

The men bought their meals—the deer served with fried potatoes and freshly baked bread, the beer in large mugs—and took them over to a table.

"Here's to a good winter," John said. He lifted his beer mug, and held it out over the table.

"A good winter indeed," Smoke replied, and lifting his mug, he clicked it against John's.

They took a drink and were just setting their mugs back down when, once again, they heard a familiar voice.

"Here, you worthless bitch!" someone shouted. "Pick that up! There ain't nobody goin' to pay no five dollars for a blanket that you have dragged through the dirt."

Both Smoke and John looked toward the loud voice and saw that it was the same man they had seen earlier, again yelling at the same young Indian girl.

The man went over to the young woman and jerked the blanket away from her.

"Look at this!" he said loudly. "Do you see the dirt on this blanket? Look at it."

The woman looked away.

"Don't look away, you bitch! I told you to look at it!" The merchant shoved the blanket into the young woman's face, and when he did so, she dropped the rest of the blankets she was holding.

"Now look what you have done, you ignorant slut! One blanket isn't enough? You have to ruin them all!" the trapper shouted. He slapped her, hard.

Smoke started to say something but before he said anything John got up and walked over to pick up the things the woman had dropped.

"Here, let me help you," he said.

"Who gave you permission to talk to my woman?" the merchant asked, angrily. "This is none of your business. You just stay the hell out of it."

"A little courtesy is everyone's business," John said. "Apparently, you are too dumb to comprehend that."

"What did you say? Did you just call me dumb?"

"Yes, as a matter of fact, I did," John said. "And if you would like me to be more specific about it, I will say that you are a low-assed, piss-complexioned, terminally ignorant, inconsequential, dumb son of a bitch! Do you need me to repeat any of that?"

"Did you just call me a inconse . . . uh, a termin . . . uh, a son of a bitch?"

"I did, indeed, sir."

"Look here, you! Just who the hell do you think you are talking to?"

"I thought we had already covered who I thought I was talking to," John said. "Do you really want me to repeat it?"

Suddenly the man drew a knife, then he crouched in a fighting stance. "I told you, you got no business bein' around my woman," he said. "And you got no business talkin' to me like that, neither. So unless you get away from her and apologize to me right now, I reckon I'm just goin' to have to carve your heart out."

John smiled and pulled out his knife. "Well now, it appears that I am going to have the opportunity to try out this brand-new knife I just bought. And here, I thought the first use for it would be to skin a bear. But I believe I would just as soon skin your hide."

"Mister," one of the bystanders called out to John. "I ain't never seen you before, so I reckon you be new. But iffen I was you, I'd be apologizin' to Dan Cooper. He's done kilt hisself three men with a knife."

"And about to make it four," Cooper said. Cat-like, he lunged toward John, but John, even though he was much larger, managed to pivot around the lunge as adroitly as a ballet dancer. Cooper's knife found only thin air.

As Cooper leaped back, John struck him in the

face with the butt of his knife. He felt Cooper's nose go flat under the blow.

"Arrgh!" Cooper shouted in pain and anger. His beard and teeth were covered with the blood that was streaming from his nose. He made a swipe at John, and though John jumped back again, this time he wasn't quite quick enough and Cooper's knife opened up a slice on his arm. Instinctively, John covered the cut with his hand and that gave Cooper the opening he was looking for.

"I've got you now, you son of a bitch!" Cooper said, putting his hand behind John's neck as he stepped up to him to make the killing thrust.

Smoke watched, as did all the others, as the two men closed to within inches of each other, so close that for a moment no one could see the knives, or what was going on. A knife fell to the floor, but was kicked away in the scuffle before Smoke could see it.

Then Cooper gasped and stepped back. It wasn't until then that Smoke saw John's arm extended, the Bowie knife in his hand now embedded in Cooper's side, all the way up to the knife hilt. John had slipped the blade in, sideways, between the ribs, and now he twisted it so that the blade turned up. As Cooper fell, the weight of his body against the very sharp, and upturned blade opened up his stomach, causing his intestines to spill through the wound.

John pulled the bloody knife out as Cooper, with

his hands over the wound and an expression of surprise on his face, collapsed to the floor. He lay there with his guts spilling out of the wound, dead within two more gasps.

John leaned down and used Cooper's pant leg to wipe off the blood from the wide blade of his knife. He put the knife back in the beaded scabbard he had traded for with the Mandan Indians, and looked up at the fifteen or so people who gathered to watch the fight.

"What do I do now?" he asked. "Is there a sheriff or someone I need to see?"

"Ain't no law within two hunnert miles of here," one of the onlookers, a trapper by the name of Emerson, said. "Hell, mister, as far as I'm concerned, there ain't no need for you to do nothin' at all."

"Yeah," another added. "Ever'body here seen what happened. Cooper's the one that started it. I figure the son of a bitch got what he deserved."

"Me too," another man said. "And truth to tell, there ain't nobody what liked that low-life bastard anyway, so there ain't goin' to be nobody pissed off about it. Good riddance, I say."

That seemed to be the general consensus, which eased John's mind. Then he looked over at the young Indian woman who had been the catalyst behind the fight.

"What about the girl?" John asked.

"What about her? She's a hell of a lot better off without Cooper, I can tell you that for sure."

"Was she his wife?"

"No, I don't think you'd call her that. I think he bought her."

"Bought her? What do you mean, he bought her? I just fought four years of war so people couldn't be bought and sold no more."

"This here's a Injun girl," one of the men said. "Far as I know, the war was fought so's black folks wouldn't be slaves no more. It didn't have nothin' to do with Injuns."

"It most indubitably did," John said. "Nobody can be bought or sold as slaves anymore."

"Don't matter now, nohow. Cooper's dead; that means the girl is free."

"Yeah, she's free, but where does she go?"

"That's her problem."

"Do you speak English?" John asked the girl.

Je ne parle pas anglais, mais je peux parler français, the girl said.

"I'm sorry, I don't speak French well enough to understand what you said."

"She said she doesn't speak English, but she can speak French," a man said. The man who spoke was speaking with a French accent.

"What is your name, sir?" John asked.

"Mouchette. Jean Mouchette," the man replied.

"Monsieur Mouchette, will you translate for me?"

"*Oui.* What do you want to say?"

"Tell her she is free. She can go wherever she wants to go now."

Mouchette translated John's words.

"*Quel est le nom de cet homme?*" the Indian girl asked.

"She wants to know your name."

"It's Jackson. John Jackson." John said the words very slowly and very distinctly.

"*Je veux aller avec John Jackson,*" the girl said.

Mouchette laughed. "I don't know how you're going to take this," he said.

"What did she say?"

"She says she wants to go with you."

"Go with me? Go where with me?"

Mouchette asked the question.

"*Je veux être sa femme, que j'étais la femme de Cooper.*"

Mouchette shook his head as he looked at John. "She says she wants to be your wife, as she was the wife of Cooper."

"I, no, that's impossible," John said. "Tell her no."

"Wait a minute, Mouchette," Smoke said. "Let me talk to my friend here for a moment before you say anything else."

"All right," Mouchette said. "Talk away."

"John, you might want to think about this before you just dismiss it out of hand."

"Smoke, do you expect me to marry this girl?" John asked.

"No, and I don't think she expects it either. In the first place, when she said 'wife,' I don't think she actually meant it in that way. You know damn well she wasn't Cooper's wife. I think she just wants to come with you, that's all."

"That's all? If you ask me, that's asking quite a bit."

"Look at it this way. If she was sold by her father, or her tribe, she can't go back to them. She can't go into some town and live with white people, and she can't survive on her own. It's easy to see why she wants to come with you. If she is left on her own, she'll more than likely be dead within a month. And in a way, you are responsible for her."

"How am I responsible for her?"

"You killed Cooper. And regardless of how he treated her, she is still alive because of him. And now she will live, or die, because of you."

John let out a big sigh of frustration.

"What am I going to do with her?" he asked.

Smoke smiled. "Whatever you want to do with her, I'm thinking."

John looked at the woman who had been following the conversation with great intensity.

"Damnit," John said, though he spoke the word quietly. "Damnit," he said again. Then, "Mouchette?"

"*Oui, monsieur?*"

"Ask the girl her name."

"*Quel est votre nom?*"

"*Hanhepiwi. Cela signifie 'clair de lune.'*"

"Her name is *Hanhepiwi*."

"I heard her say 'Claire.'"

"*Hanhepiwi* means *clair de lune*, or, in English, the clear moon."

John looked her and smiled. "Tell her, her name is Claire. And, yes, she can come with me."

Mouchette translated, and Claire smiled, then looked down at the floor.

CHAPTER FIFTEEN

Old Main Building

"That is a most amazing story," Professor Armbruster said. "And did he take her with him?"

"Oh, yes," Smoke said.

"Professor, it's four o'clock," the young man who had been handling the recording said.

"Very well, Wes, we'll call it quits for today," Professor Armbruster said. He smiled at Smoke. "You've spoken about all the saloons you have visited; how would you like to visit one of ours?"

"One of your saloons?" Smoke replied with a puzzled look on his face. "Professor, have you forgotten prohibition?"

"Oh, my, indeed, there is that pesky little problem, isn't there?" Professor Armbruster answered with a conspiratorial smile on his face.

"But, if you will come with me, I believe I know a place where people wink at prohibition. In fact, you might say they ignore it altogether."

"Would this be one of those speakeasies I've heard about?" Smoke asked.

"Indeed, it might be," Professor Armbruster replied. "As you know, Colorado went dry January of 1916, but thanks to Clyde Smaldone and dozens of others like him, we have never been totally dry. In fact, we got a four-year head start on the rest of the country in learning how to beat the system. I know that Louis Longmont is a long-time friend of yours. How is he dealing with it?"

"Louis is a wealthy man," Smoke said. "He closed his business down and is totally retired." Smoke smiled. "He does, however, have a private reserve of, as he likes to call it, fine liquors, which he shares with his friends from time to time."

"I tell you what. If you would like to drive me to the establishment, I'll show you where it is. I'll get a ride home."

"Are you sure? I can bring you back."

"No need."

Professor Armbruster followed Smoke out to his car.

"Duesenberg, nice car," he said.

"Thanks. What do you think of the Jordan Playboy?"

"I beg your pardon?"

"The Jordan Playboy. Apparently it is a sports car, and my wife would like one. I believe she's going through a second childhood."

Professor Armbruster laughed. "Wouldn't you

rather have her young and vibrant, than an old fuddy-duddy?"

"I suppose you have a point there," Smoke said.

Smoke parked in an empty lot on High Street in what looked like an industrial section of the town. He followed Professor Armbruster across the road to a two-story brick building which had all its windows boarded over. There was nothing outside the unmarked building to indicate that it was anything other than a deserted building. There was a wooden door with a small window which, like the large ones, was boarded over.

Professor Armbruster knocked on the door, and when the little window opened, he passed a dollar bill and a card through the door. A moment later, the door opened.

"Good evening, Professor," the doorman said.

"Hello, Marty. Good crowd tonight?"

"If you ask me, the whole student body is here," Marty said. He looked, suspiciously, at Smoke.

"It's all right, Marty, this gentleman is my guest," Professor Armbruster said.

Marty stepped aside to let them in.

Inside was a large room, tall and majestic with beautifully molded ceilings. The bar itself was worn, and could have been taken directly from any of several hundred saloons Smoke had visited over his lifetime. Conflicting with the bar were booths that looked brand new, running around the outer edge of a large, open space. The open space was a dance floor, the dancers being painted by hundreds of glowing dots reflecting from a rotating mirrored ball that was hanging down from the ceiling.

Professor Armbruster led Smoke to the bar. "The whiskey is good and safe here," he said. "It's not moonshine; it's brought down from Canada."

Smoke ordered a whiskey.

"Hey, old man," someone said from the bar. "Ain't you a little old to be out with the young people? What are you, some old pervert looking to pick up some young girl?"

"I'm afraid I'm beyond that," Smoke said. He picked up the whiskey and held it out toward the man, who didn't appear to be a student. "Here's to you."

"Hey, old man, aren't you afraid that whiskey will make your false teeth fall out?" He laughed, and the three people with him, another man and two women, laughed as well.

"They aren't students, are they?" Smoke asked Professor Armbruster.

"Not on your life," Professor Armbruster replied.

"Hey, old man, look here. Don't you wish you could do this?" He had his hand stuck down inside the top of the dress of the young woman he was with. His hand was, clearly, gripping her breast. "I'll bet you don't even remember what a young woman's titty feels like."

"Hell, Vinnie, women didn't even have titties when he was young," the other man said.

"Come on over, old man," Vinnie said. "I'll let you feel Linda's titty."

"Vinnie, no you won't," Linda said, pulling his hand away from her. "You act like that, I'm not even goin' to let you feel it."

"Ah, ha, Vinnie, you've stepped in it now," the other man said, laughing at him.

"Hey, old man, this is all your fault," Vinnie said, continuing his harassment of Smoke. "Now, you come here and apologize to my girl. You hear me? You come over here and apolo—"

That was as far as Vinnie got before Smoke, in a lightning, and totally unexpected move, brought a roundhouse right, connecting with Vinnie's jaw and dropping him to the floor. It was doubly effective as the first half of the swing had been hidden from Vinnie's view because of Smoke's position at the bar.

"Hey, you old son of a bitch! That was my friend you just hit!" the other man shouted and he picked up a barstool, lifting it over his head.

"Huh, uh, not a smart move," Smoke said, and to the surprise of the man holding the barstool, as well as everyone else in the speakeasy, Smoke was holding a .44 pistol in his hand, the hammer back.

"You . . . you have a gun," the man said, surprised.

"Yes, I do, don't I?"

The man started to put the barstool back down.

"No," Smoke said. "If you move that barstool so much as one inch, I'll kill you where you stand."

"I'm not going to hit you with it, I'm just going to put it down."

"No, you aren't. You're going to hold it until I tell you, you can put it down."

"What? Are you crazy?"

Smoke shook his head. "I might be. Or maybe I'm just senile. I am an old man, as you and Vinnie have been pointing out to me."

The man continued to hold the stool over his head, and by now the dancers had stopped dancing, and the band had stopped playing. Everyone was watching the drama play out before them.

"Please, mister, this stool is getting heavy."

"Is it, now? And that's what you were going to bring crashing down on my head? A barstool? Aren't you ashamed of yourself? You were going to hit an old man in the head with a heavy barstool? Something like that could have killed me. You know, I believe I could shoot you right now, and claim that it was self-defense. I don't believe any jury in the state would convict me."

"No, mister, please, no! Don't kill me!"

"It's your own fault, Eddie," the other woman said. "Vinnie was being a fool. You had no business getting involved."

Eddie's arms started shaking.

"My God, mister, I can't hold it any longer! I'm going to drop this stool and you're going to shoot me!"

"That's right," Smoke said calmly. "If you so much as move that stool by one inch, I'm going to shoot you."

A wet stain appeared on the front of Eddie's pants.

"Miss, would you take the stool from him, please?" Smoke said. "Eddie seems to have had an accident."

"Look at that, he peed in his pants!" one of the college students said, pointing to Eddie.

The young woman took the stool down, and Eddie doubled over in pain and embarrassment.

Vinnie sat up, groaning, and rubbing his jaw. "What happened?" he asked.

"Apparently, you tripped over the footrail," Smoke said.

By this time nearly everyone else in the speakeasy had gathered around, and confident now that there wasn't going to be a shooting, they all laughed.

"What the hell is everyone laughing at?" Vinnie asked. Then seeing the front of Eddie's pants, he laughed as well. "Damn, Eddie, you pissed in your pants!"

"Let's go," Eddie said.

"I'm not ready to go anywhere," Vinnie complained.

"Stay if you want to. Remember, I drove."

Eddie started toward the door, and both of the women went with him.

"Wait a minute, what's goin' on here?" Vinnie shouted. He turned toward Smoke. "I've got a feeling you're behind . . . you're holding a gun in your hand. Are you crazy? I'm going to call the cops."

"Right, you are going to call the police and bring

them to a speakeasy," Smoke said. "Where everyone in here would be subject to arrest. And by the way, I'm a deputy United States marshal. I not only have the right to have a pistol, I also have the authority to arrest you right now, for consuming alcohol."

"What are you talking about, arresting me? Everyone in here is drinking."

"Really? It looked to me like they were all dancing. You are the only one I actually saw drinking."

Very pointedly, Smoke picked up his glass and took a drink of whiskey.

"Get out of here, mister," one of the college kids said to Vinnie. "Or we'll throw you out."

With a final look of hate and anger toward Smoke, Vinnie turned and hurried toward the door, chased by the laughter of the others.

When Smoke turned back to the bar, Professor Armbruster was laughing. "Last night I told Edna I would like to have seen you in your prime. By damn, I think I just did."

When Smoke returned to the Boulderado Hotel, he saw that china and silver had been laid out on the table in the suite's dining room. Two unlit candles were in the middle of the table, and Sally was standing by the table, dressed in an evening gown.

Smoke smiled at her. "I don't know who you are, you young hussy, but you can just get out of this room now. I'm happily married to a sixty-eight-year-old woman, and I don't need some floozy here, trying to make me go astray."

Sally laughed. "How you do carry on. You are so full of blarney. Your tuxedo is laid out on the bed. Please change into it."

"My tuxedo? What are you talking about? I didn't bring a tux."

"Yes, you did. I packed it. And tonight, I want you to wear it."

Reluctantly, Smoke went into the bedroom, where he saw his tux laid out on the bed. The last time he had worn the tux was at the world premiere of the movie *Guns of the West*, in which the actor Tom Mix portrayed Smoke. In fact, that was the only time he had ever worn the tux.

When he came out of the bedroom, Sally flashed a big smile. "My, my, it's true what they say, you know."

"What is true?"

"Men, at least, some men, never age. They just get more distinguished looking, and more handsome. I'm glad we are dining in tonight. I would hate to have to fight off all the young ladies who would be throwing themselves at you."

"Now who is full of blarney?" Smoke teased. He kissed her, and was still kissing her when there was a knock on the door.

"Room service," a voice called from the other side of the door.

Sally tried to pull away, but Smoke continued to hold her.

"Uhmm, that's our dinner," she said. "It'll get cold."

"Let it," Smoke teased. "Don't forget, you are the one who started this."

"Smoke," Sally said, laughing.

Smoke opened his arms and stepped back from her, but he continued to smile.

The white-jacketed bellhop brought their dinner in on a cart, the various dishes protected by domed silver covers. He lit the two candles, then served the meal.

"Thank you, Reginald," Sally said,

Dinner was a lobster bisque, followed by a filet mignon with asparagus and baked potato.

CHAPTER SIXTEEN

Old Main Building

There were several young people out in front of the Old Main building when Smoke parked his car the next morning. Many of the young men were wearing gold sweaters, with the block letter C.

"Hello, Mr. Jensen."

"Hi, Mr. Jensen."

"Good morning, Mr. Jensen."

The greetings were friendly and numerous, and Smoke returned them all as he went into the building.

"What's going on out front?" he asked Professor Armbruster.

Armbruster chuckled. "Don't you know? It is all over campus what you did last night, putting Vinnie Sarducci and Eddie DeSchamp in their place. Those two have made themselves very unpopular around here, and I think what you did was much appreciated. You have become a campus hero."

"There must be a scarcity of heroes," Smoke said.

"Not at all. It's just that they have put you up there with them, and given your history, rightly so."

"So you say."

"Well, shall we go on? What happened with John and the Indian girl?"

"John and I separated after Rendezvous. He and Claire went back into the mountains of Montana, I went back to Colorado."

Upper Missouri River, Montana—1870

John Jackson and Claire rode west along the upper reaches of the Missouri. Because of his experience with Smoke the year before, John was well aware of the potential danger that threatened from behind every stand of trees and every butte or rock. They were just crossing a tributary when Claire called out to him.

"John Jackson," she said. She pointed up the tributary. "We go that way."

"What? You speak English?" John asked, surprised to hear the words.

"Yes."

"But you said you only speak French."

"I did not want Cooper to know I can speak English. He was not a good man."

John chuckled. "That is as true a statement as I've ever heard. Why do you think we should go up this tributary?"

"When the cold returns, the trapping there will be good. There would be a good place to build a house, because there is water and shelter from the cold winds in the winter, and shade from the hot sun in the summer. Also, the only Indians are friendly Indians."

"And you say that is where I should build the house, huh?"

"Yes."

"All right, if you say so, that's where we'll go."

The tributary took them into a wide ravine that, as Claire had pointed out, kept them shaded from the hot sun. It also tended to shield them from observation.

"We'll camp here, tonight," John said. He led his horse and pack mule to the stream so they could drink. Claire, by agreement of everyone at Rendezvous, had inherited Cooper's saddle horse and pack mule, and she led them to the stream to drink alongside John's animals.

"I'll gather up some firewood," John said. "Can you make us a fire pit from stone?" He picked up a couple of rocks and put them on the ground, then made a circle with his hand. "We'll make the fire here."

"Yes," Claire said, nodding her head.

John wandered off into the trees, where he started gathering old, downed limbs, branches, and even a piece of rotted-out log. When he came back he saw that Claire had laid the fire pit, but he didn't see her. Concerned, he put the wood down and started looking around. When he found her, he stopped in his tracks.

Claire was standing knee-deep in the water, and she was totally nude. Her back was to him, and he couldn't help but enjoy the gentle curves, and the smooth golden skin. She was taking a bath, and though he felt that he should turn away, he couldn't make himself do so. He leaned against a tree and watched as she splashed water on herself. Then, unexpectedly, she turned and started out of the water, affording a total view as she did so.

When Claire glanced up, she saw that John was looking at her, but she showed no alarm, nor did she display any modesty. She smiled at him, then reached down and picked up a clean dress and pulled it down over her still-wet body.

"Did you start the fire?" she asked.

"Uh, no," John replied.

"We cannot cook if we have no fire."

John chuckled. "I guess you have a point there. I'll get a fire started, then carve off a piece of ham for us."

"Not ham," Claire said. "Fish."

"Fish? Might be good but we'll have to catch . . ." John stopped in mid-sentence when, with a broad smile, Claire walked over to the edge of the stream and picked up two good-sized salmon that he hadn't seen earlier.

"How did you catch those? Where is your hook and line?"

"I use my hands," Claire said, making a swooping motion with her hands to demonstrate.

John started the fire as Claire cleaned the fish,

then she ran a green stick down through each of them and leaned them out over the fire to cook.

That night, John lay in his bedroll by the fire, watching the red sparks ride the rising columns of heat into the sky, there to blend with the stars. He thought back over the last few years of his life . . . the fiancée who promised to wait, but who spurned him after he returned from the war . . . the friends he had met, and who were killed during the war . . . and the difficult time he had adjusting to peace-time civilian life, then his experience with the French Foreign Legion in Annam.

He recalled his last conversation with his father, just before he left Pennsylvania to come west.

"I don't know what is wrong with you, son," his father told him when he returned from Europe. "When you came back from the war you said you just needed a little time to readjust, so you went to Europe and joined the French Foreign Legion. I told you then that you were making a mistake, but you didn't listen to me.

"So, what happened to you in Europe? You were just as disturbed when you came back from there as you were when you came back from the war. You've told me nothing of your experiences with the Foreign Legion. Was it an unpleasant experience?"

"There is nothing to talk about," John replied.

"You've said nothing about going into battle with the Foreign Legion, but you have returned with a medal that you can only get by being in battle. Was it bad?"

John didn't answer.

"John, you have been much in my prayers for these last

several years. While you were in the war, I prayed for your physical survival. But since the war, I have prayed for the survival of your soul. You just aren't the same sweet boy, or even good man, you once were. You are too quick to anger, you have too little patience, you don't enjoy the things you once did, you haven't reconnected with your old friends, and you can't sleep at night. I know the stress you went through during the war, and maybe even when you were with the Foreign Legion, is causing that. Maybe someday there will be a name for it . . . but nothing I have ever read addresses it."

"You don't understand," John had told his father. "I can't sleep at night, because when I do, I hear the gunfire . . . I hear the moans of the wounded and the dying."

"I know you were upset when you returned from Europe, and found that Lucy had married another. But you've made no effort to meet any other young women. You shouldn't let what she did keep you from seeing other women."

"To tell you the truth, Pop, I'm actually glad she found someone else. I just don't feel like being around any women now."

"I know you said you wanted to go west, into the mountains where you would be away from everyone. Maybe that's not such a bad idea. Maybe if you are alone long enough, you'll get back to normal."

And so here he was, the sum total of his entire life had brought him to this time and this place, in the mountains, alone. No, he wasn't really alone, nor had he been alone. There had been Preacher and Smoke. But he was thankful to Smoke. What he had learned from Smoke in the last year was worth a four-year college degree. It was certainly more valuable than the degree he had earned at the University of Pennsylvania.

Claire was lying in her blankets, not five feet away from him. She had certainly not been a part of his plans. There was no room in the life he wanted now for any kind of a companion, let alone a female companion, and especially not an Indian woman. He had been forced into taking her, convinced that the circumstances were such that she would not survive had he not done so. He had tried, to the degree that it was possible, to maintain a separation between them. He had thought that the difference in language would help in that regard.

Then he learned that she could speak English.

All right, it was probably a good thing that she could speak English. If they were going to be together, there would be times when it would be necessary for them to communicate. He would just put her out of his mind as much as he could.

But tonight, he saw her naked, and he saw, for the first time, what an exceptionally beautiful woman she was. And now she was lying beside him, totally dependent upon him for her survival, and for all intents and purposes, his to do with as he pleased.

If he went to her now, what would she do? Would she acquiesce to his advances? Or would she fight him off?

What about her time with Cooper? Had she been with Cooper?

Of course she had, there was no way she could have avoided it. And she did say that she had been Cooper's wife.

For a moment the thought of Claire having been with Cooper disgusted him, and he thought the less of her for it.

Why? Why did he think that? She was absolutely helpless. How could she have possibly controlled her own fate?

Now John felt guilty for having such negative thoughts about her. The truth was, in the few days they had been together, he had grown comfortable with her. Yes, she was dependent upon him for her survival, but to a degree he was dependent upon her as well.

She knew the country and had offered suggestions from time to time, such as following this tributary from the river. She was helpful around the camp, she could make a fire, she could cook, she was able to point out what plants were edible, she could find wild, sweet berries, as well as honey. And tonight she had shown him that she could fish.

Yes, having her with him was not the burden he thought it would be.

A gas bubble, trapped in one of the burning logs, popped loudly, and sent up a shower of sparks. A couple of them landed on Claire's blanket, and John, afraid that the blanket would catch on fire, moved over quickly to brush the sparks off.

Claire opened her eyes and looked up at him. Her eyes reflected bright orange points of light, and her face gleamed in the glow of the fire. She stared up at him for a long time with those big, brown, trusting eyes, and when John put his hand on her cheek, she reached for it, not to push it away, but to hold it in her own hand.

With Claire's other hand she opened the blanket in invitation and he saw that she was as nude as she had been when he saw her in the water. Quickly taking off his own clothes, John got under the blanket with her.

John was awakened the next morning by the loud, rapid hammering of a woodpecker. The first thing he realized was that Claire wasn't in bed with him. Raising up on his elbow, he saw her by the fire, cooking something in the skillet. He could smell it, and it smelled very good.

"What are you cooking?" he asked.

"Breakfast."

"Yes, but what?"

"You eat first, then I will tell you," she said.

John chuckled, then he started to get up from the blankets. That was when he realized that he was naked and, inexplicably, he felt a sense of embarrassment. He reached for his clothes and dressed, all the while keeping himself covered with the blanket.

The breakfast meal consisted of Indian fry bread,

which John had eaten for the first time at Rendezvous, bacon, and something else, something that resembled scrambled eggs, though it was more orange than yellow.

Claire spooned it out of the frying pan and onto two tin plates. She gave one plate, and a fork, to John.

"Eat," she said.

John knew that he liked bacon, and he knew that he liked the fry bread. He didn't know what the orange stuff was, but he took a bite.

Claire studied his reaction, intensely.

It wasn't at all an unpleasant taste, but John had never tasted anything quite like it. It had sort of a salty taste, but not overly so. He took two or three bites, hesitantly, then with a little more confidence, and by the time he finished he discovered that he was actually enjoying it.

"What was that I just ate?" he asked.

"Come, I will show you."

Claire led John to the water's edge, then she pointed to some leaves that were growing in the water. Clinging to the leaves were hundreds of little, round, almost translucent balls.

"What is that?" he asked.

"Fish eggs," Claire replied with a broad smile.

John chuckled. "I'll be damned," he said. "I know that some rich folks back in Philadelphia serve fish eggs. They call it caviar. If I ever get back there, I'll have to tell them how good it can be when it's fried in bacon grease."

"You like?"

"Yes, I do. Claire, what do you say we build our cabin here?"

"I think here is a good place," Claire replied.

CHAPTER SEVENTEEN

Old Main Building

"Let's see," Professor Armbruster said. "Just to make certain that I have the time line straight, we are now up to 1870, is that correct?"

"Yes."

"And where is Matt at this time?"

"Matt had left by then. Our paths continued to cross after he left and of course we remained friends. Actually we are still friends; he spent last Christmas with us at Sugarloaf. But, for the most part by then, Matt was on his own."

"And, I believe, if I remember correctly, 1870 is when you met your wife."

"It is when I met my first wife, Nicole."

"As I intend to blend yours and John Jackson's stories together, I wonder if you might share that with us now."

Uncompahgre Plateau—Spring 1870

Shortly after Smoke returned from his almost year-long stay with John, he joined Preacher in pushing a herd of mustangs south. They had been on the drive for three days when Preacher stopped and held up his hand.

"What do you smell, boy?" he asked.

Smoke sniffed the wind. "I'm not sure," he said. "It's not new growth, I know that. It's more like . . . well, I want to say smoke, but it isn't exactly smoke. It's something else."

"It's burnt hair," Preacher said.

"Yes," Smoke said, realizing that burnt hair is exactly what he was smelling. "That's not good."

"No, it ain't," Preacher said. "It ain't good at all. It's comin' from that way."

"You want me to ride over there and check it out?" Smoke asked.

"Not by yourself, I don't. Ain't no tellin' what we'll find over there. It might take the two of us to handle it."

"What about the horses?"

"I've been here before, they's a box canyon just ahead. We can put the critters in there, then block off the entrance. They's water and grass in there too, so they ain't likely to be tryin' to get out."

"All right," Smoke agreed.

Putting the horses into the box canyon that Preacher spoke of, they blocked off the entrance, then rode over to investigate the smell. As they got closer, the smell became more cloying.

"What is that?" Smoke asked.

"It ain't only the hair what was burnt, Smoke. It's the flesh too."

They followed their noses until they found a wagon that had been burned, but not entirely consumed. They also found the source of the burnt flesh odor, a man, suspended by his ankles from a tree, was hanging head down over a fire. His head, face, and shoulders were burned black. They found another man lying on the ground, his body mutilated, and a third man tied to the wheel of the wagon, also dead. All three men had been tortured.

"They died hard," Preacher said.

Tied to the side of the wagon, and undamaged by the fire, was a shovel.

"I'll get them buried," Smoke said.

"No need in diggin' more 'n one grave," Preacher said. "They was either friends or family. They all died together, so they may as well lie together."

Smoke dug only one grave, but he dug it large enough to bury all three men. Then he and Preacher covered the grave with rocks, to prevent wolves and coyotes from digging them up.

After they buried the dead, they took a closer look at the burned-out wagon, and that was when Smoke found a dress.

"Preacher, there were women with them. Or at least a woman."

"Most likely the Injuns took 'er with 'em."

"No, I don't think so. Look." Smoke pointed to a set of small footprints, shoes, not moccasins, leading away from the wagon.

"Praise be, maybe she got away. Let's find her," Preacher said.

It didn't take long to find her; the tracks led right to some brush.

"Girl, come on out from there," Preacher called. "You're among friends now. You ain't goin' to be hurt."

The young woman came out. She was an exceptionally pretty woman and Smoke was so struck with how beautiful she was that for a moment, he just stared at her.

"What's your name?" Smoke asked.

"Nicole."

"Pretty name."

"Who are you?"

"My name is Smoke. This is Preacher."

"Smoke? Preacher? Are those real names?"

Smoke smiled. "My real name is Kirby Jensen. His real name is Art, but he doesn't like to be called that. He only wants to be called Preacher."

"Did you see my father, my two uncles?"

"Yes," Smoke said, grimly.

"They are all dead, aren't they?"

Smoke nodded, but said nothing.

"What about my aunt? Did you see her?"

"Looks like the savages took her," Preacher said.

"What will they do to her?"

"Depends a lot on her. Was she a looker?"

"I beg your pardon?"

"Was she a handsome woman?"

"She was beautiful," Nicole answered.

Preacher shrugged. "Then they'll probably keep her."

He didn't tell the young woman her aunt may have been, by now, raped repeatedly and then tortured to death.

"They'll work her hard, beat her some, but she'll most probably be all right. Some buck with no squaw will bed her down. Then again, they might trade her off for a horse or rifle."

"Or they might kill her?" she asked.

"Yep."

"You don't believe I'll ever see her again, do you?"

"No, darlin', it just ain't likely," Preacher said.

Nicole put her face in her hands and began to weep. "I don't know what to do. I have a brother somewhere, but I don't know where he is. I don't have anyone else."

Smoke put his arms around her. "Yes, you do, Nicole. You have us," he said.*

Smoke, Preacher, and Nicole built a cabin and shortly after the cabin was built, Preacher rode on, leaving Smoke and Nicole alone. Preacher didn't return that winter of 1870–71, then one day Nicole came to Smoke.

The Last Mountain Man.

"We have to get married, Smoke," she said.

"We're going to get married. But didn't we say we wanted to wait until Preacher got back?"

"Have you considered the idea that he might not come back?"

"I don't like to think about it."

"How old is he?"

"In his seventies, I think. He's never really told me. I know he's too old to be spendin' another winter alone."

"Smoke, Preacher has spent a long, exciting, and very fruitful life. He wouldn't want to die in bed, would he? He would want to leave this life the way he has lived it, in the wilderness. And do you think he would really want you to be worrying about him?"

Smoke smiled. "You're right, Nicole, as usual."

"So, you don't think we have to wait for Preacher for us to get married? The reason I ask is, I'm pretty sure we're going to have a baby."

"What? No, Nicole, we can't! We're more than a hundred miles from the nearest doctor."

"There is nothing to having a baby, Smoke. That is a natural process that's been going on since the beginning of time. Besides, I went to nursing school. It's just that I want the baby to have a legal name. I want to be married. So, where can we go?"

"We're too far from Big Rock, wouldn't want you traveling that far. But Preacher told me there was a little settlement of Mormons just west of here, over in Utah Territory. We could go there."

* * *

It was still cool when they left the valley, heading for Utah.

"Smoke, do you think we'll see any Indians?"

"I don't know. I've never been this way before, I've never been in Utah. I reckon we'll just have to find out together."

On the fifth day of their travel they reached the settlement Preacher had spoken of, but all they found were half a dozen rotting and collapsing cabins. They found no sign of life.

"Preacher said there was a going settlement here back in '55. I wonder where everyone went?"

They saw an overgrown cemetery and going over to check it, saw a handful of rotting grave markers. The latest date they could find was fourteen years ago.

"Must've been some disease come to kill most of 'em off," Smoke suggested. "And the ones that didn't die, left."

They went back to explore the buildings, and finding a nail, Smoke built a fire, heated the nail, then with a hammer flattened the nail, then curled it into a crude ring. When the ring cooled, he showed it to Nicole. "Not much of a ring, I'm afraid."

"I would rather have this than a band of gold," Nicole said.

Smoke slipped it onto Nicole's third finger of her left hand.

"Nicole, I love you. And with this ring, I declare you to be my wife."

"And I declare you to be my husband," Nicole said.

They kissed.

Old Main Building

"That's when I learned that I had warrants out on me, and that there were bounty hunters on my trail, particularly Potter, Stratton, and Richards."

"I don't want to bring up unpleasant memories," Professor Armbruster said. "But weren't those men involved in Nicole's murder?"

Smoke's mouth tightened, and he nodded. "Yes," he said. "But you're getting a little ahead of the story."

"Sorry."

"That's all right. It's just that I haven't told this story, I haven't even thought about it, in many, many years. I think it might be good to get it all out of my system now. It started with Preacher."

CHAPTER EIGHTEEN

Del Norte, Colorado—Fall 1870

Preacher was walking toward a saloon when he saw a young man wearing a brace of pearl-handled pistols.

"Hey, grandpa! You a little old to be out by yourself, ain't you?"

Preacher didn't say a word in response to the young punk, nor did he look at him, or even change his stride. But as he walked by, he drove the butt of his rifle into the loudmouth's stomach. The young man bent over double, puking in the street. Unable to resist, Preacher pulled the two pistols from the loudmouth's holsters. He dropped the pistols into the horse trough, then went into the saloon, where he ordered a whiskey with a beer chaser.

A moment later the town marshal came into the saloon and stepped up to the bar.

"You're the one they call Preacher, ain't you?"

"Yes."

"You have a young friend, a gunman named Smoke, I believe. Thought you might like to know that the bounty's been upped. Someone's wantin' him real bad."

"Who is it that's a-wantin' him?"

"That would be Potter, Stratton, and Richards. Potter is into politics, Richards is in mining and cattle, and Stratton owns the town of Bury. They want the boy, and they got the money to get the job done. What did the boy do, to get 'em so mad?"

"He knows where a lot of gold is buried, gold that them three stole from the Confederacy, then the boy's papa stole back from them," Preacher said.

"I figured it had to be somethin' like that. There's a couple of gunfighters out on the front porch, Felter and Canning, and they got some more hardcases with them, camped just north of town."

"I thank you," Preacher said.

Preacher left town a short while later.

He knew he was being watched, but he thought it was Indians, and the Indians didn't worry him, because, for the most part, he and the Indians had gotten along well for the last fifty years. He was surprised when he felt a hammerblow to his shoulder, the heavy slug tearing through the tissue to come out his back.

"Get him alive, don't kill him! He can tell us where Jensen is!" someone shouted.

Preacher felt a second slug tear into his leg,

careen off his leg bone, then rip a big hole in his hip, taking a piece of bone with it. Now Preacher saw the three men who were following him. He snaked his Henry from the sheath, and began firing, jacking new a new shell into the chamber after each shot, getting off three rounds in less than four seconds. Two of the men were knocked from their saddles, and he knew that it had been killing shots that took them down. He shot the horse of the third man and it went down, crushing its rider beneath him.

With the three men down and Preacher badly wounded, he rode on, barely able to stay in the saddle. When night came he picketed his horse and wrapped himself up in a blanket, not sure if he would live through the night, but determined to do so, so he could warn Smoke.

Old Main Building

"Preacher did survive the night, and though I don't know how he did it, managed to stay alive long enough to get back to the cabin I had built for Nicole and me," Smoke said.

"He was badly shot up, his leg was infected, I don't know how he could stand the pain. Finally he put on his best buckskins, then telling us good-bye, rode off, presumably to die."

"But he didn't die then, did he?" Professor Armbruster asked.

"No. For the life of me, I don't know how he survived, but he did."

"Then, your baby was born?"

"Yes, the baby was born with the first snow that winter, and we named him Arthur, after Preacher. There was nobody there but Nicole and me. She told me how to cut the umbilical cord. I did that," Smoke chuckled, "then she sent me outside because she thought I was getting sick.

"We were taking a chance on staying there, but I knew that as long as the passes were filled with snow, that the bounty hunters looking for me wouldn't be able to get through. That meant that, for the time being at least, we were safe . . . but come spring we were going to have to move.

"Then, come April, just before we were going to leave, a really bad thunderstorm broke, and it scattered the herd of horses we were raising. I had to get them back. I hated leaving Nicole and the baby but . . ." Smoke stopped speaking for a moment, and waved his hand.

The professor moved the toggle switch on the speaker box. "Wes, hold it for a moment, would you?" Professor Armbruster said.

"Yes, sir," Wes replied, his voice coming back over the box.

"Take your time, Smoke."

"It's been fifty-two years," Smoke said. "You wouldn't think I would still feel it this intensely. I'm sorry."

"Nonsense, you have nothing to be sorry about," Professor Armbruster replied. "Some memories are so firmly embedded that they aren't just a part of our minds, they are also a part of our souls."

"Yes. I love Sally, very much, and we have had a wonderful marriage. But there will always be a part of me that loves, and misses, Nicole and our baby."

"Would you like a drink of water? A cup of coffee?"

"A cup of coffee would be good."

Again, Professor Armbruster spoke into the box. "Wes, we're going to take about a half-hour break."

"Very good, sir." Wes replied.

Smoke followed Professor Armbruster into the staff and faculty lounge, where there was a table on which stood a big coffeemaker and a large silver tray of doughnuts.

Professor Armbruster drew a cup of coffee and handed it to Smoke, then made another for himself. Smoke walked over to look through the window, out onto the campus. He saw half a dozen young men wearing raccoon coats, straw hats, and white spats, and he chuckled.

"Raccoon coats," he said. "They came along too late for the trappers of my generation. Beaver and marten, that's all anyone wanted then. About the only thing coon was good for was eating, and making caps. Now look."

"It started back East in the Ivy League schools," Professor Armbruster said. "Now, no college man is worth his salt if he isn't wearing a raccoon coat."

"Preacher and John would have had a big laugh over this."

"Have you ever seen a football game, Smoke?" Professor Armbruster asked.

"I've seen a few of the high school games in Big Rock. The Trappers, they call themselves."

"Yes, we've gotten some players here, from Big Rock. Have you ever seen a college game?"

"No."

"You absolutely have to see one while you are here. I do hope you and Mrs. Jensen will be my guests for the football game this weekend."

"Yes, we would be pleased to come to the game," Smoke said.

A car drove up in front of the building, a Model T Ford, sporting fox and raccoon tails and bearing painted signs: STRUGGLE BUGGY, 23 SKIDOO, IT'S THE BERRIES, IT'S A LOLLAPALOOZA, and of course, GO BUFFALOS, referring to the Colorado football team.

The driver, who was also wearing a raccoon coat, squeezed the bulb on the horn mounted on the door of his car, and several laughing young men and women hurried toward him.

Smoke shook his head as he watched them, and wondered how many of them could survive one year in the Rockies on their own. He finished his coffee, then took the empty cup back.

"Professor, I'm ready to go back, if you are."

"Absolutely," Professor Armbruster replied.

CHAPTER NINETEEN

"All right, Wes, we're ready to go again," Professor Armbruster said into the little intercom box.

"Very good, sir," Wes replied.

"Now, Smoke, if you are up to it, we'll continue with where we left off."

"Yeah," Smoke said. "I wasn't gone very long. By the second day I had found most of my herd and I closed them up in a canyon, keeping them there until I could find the rest of them. Then, late in the afternoon of the second day, I thought I heard gunfire. But when I stopped to listen, I didn't hear anything, so I figured it must just be wind blowing through the trees.

"I started back home on the third day and . . ." Smoke stopped and shook his head, "I don't know how to explain it, but I suddenly got the strongest feeling of dread. I knew something had happened.

"When I got there, I saw one of them, a man

named Grissom. I shot him. Then I saw someone just pushing open the door to the outhouse, and I shot him. The next one was a young punk, would-be gunman who called himself Kid Austin.

"When I ran to the back of the house I saw"— Smoke paused and took a deep breath—"I saw my baby, lying dead in the grass. He had just been tossed out like trash.

"Someone started taunting me from inside the house. I had Preacher's Sharps with me. I wasn't worrying about hitting Nicole; I knew she was dead. So I fired through the wall, and heard someone screaming. I found out later that the big Sharps had torn his arm off.

"A moment later, several men rode off at a gallop. But there was one left, a man named Clark. He was taunting me from the house, but he was crouching, looking out the back door, when I came in through the front. I got the drop on him, and when I saw Nicole, and what they had done to her, scalping her, partially skinning her, I felt an anger unlike anything I had ever felt before or since.

"Clark was on his hands and knees, begging me for mercy. I kicked him in the side of head, and knocked him out. Then I took him outside, stripped him naked, smeared his body with honey, and staked him out over a big hill of fire ants.

"I could hear him screaming the whole time I was digging a grave for Nicole and the baby. He was still screaming when I rode off, and I could hear him for at least half a mile."

"So you set things right. You avenged her murder."

"Nicole had been raped, murdered, scalped, and partly skinned. My boy was killed and tossed out the back door of the cabin like so much trash. There's no way you can make that right."

"I'm sorry, of course I didn't mean it like that. But you did kill the ones who murdered your family, did you not? I don't mean just the ones you killed at the cabin. I mean, one of the stories about you is how you tracked down and killed all the others as well. Is that true, or is it all a myth?"

"The story is true."

"Because of the research I'm doing, I have a repository of books about you, many of them pertaining to that very event. And of course, there is the Jack Holt movie about it . . . *Where There Is Smoke, There Is Fire.*"

Smoke chuckled. "It was Sally who came up with that title. A couple of the people associated with the film didn't like the title but Jack loved it, and he is the one that managed to get it through."

"It is a clever title," Professor Armbruster said.

"I think so," Smoke agreed.

"The problem with all these accounts, the movie, the books, the many articles, is that they vary so widely. Some say you killed fifty men that day, some say a hundred. I don't suppose anyone knows for sure."

"I know."

"Well, how many was it?"

"Eighteen."

"Eighteen?"

"I killed four of them there at the cabin. Then I went after the others and caught up with them at the silver-mining camp near the Uncompahgre. The four I killed at the cabin, and the fourteen more I killed in town, make eighteen."

"That's quite an accomplishment. I can see why so much has been written about it.

"After your wife and son were killed, you remarried though. I believe she was a schoolteacher?"

"Yes, but that wasn't for two more years."

"And you had two children?"

"We did. We had twins, Louis Arthur and Denise Nicole."

"I'm sorry to keep bringing up unpleasant memories, but they are both deceased now, aren't they?"

"Yes. They went to Europe to be educated. Denise died and was buried there. When Louis came back, he decided to stay East with Sally's family, where he became a lawyer. Sally and I didn't see much of him after that. We were never actually estranged, we just sort of went our separate ways. Ironically, Louis also died in France, and is buried there."

"Yes, I have done some research. He was a pilot who received the Medal of Honor."

[*I have located the citation which accompanied the Medal of Honor award, and post it here for the edification of the reader:*

"After having previously destroyed a number of enemy aircraft, Captain Louis Arthur Jensen voluntarily started on a patrol after German observation balloons. Though pursued by eight German planes which were protecting the enemy balloon line, he unhesitatingly attacked and shot down in flames three German balloons, being himself under heavy fire from ground batteries and the hostile planes. Severely wounded, he descended to within one hundred fifty feet of the ground, and flying at this low altitude near the town of Murvaux, opened fire upon enemy troops, killing six and wounding as many. Forced to make a landing and surrounded on all sides by the enemy who called upon him to surrender, he drew his automatic pistol and defended himself gallantly until he fell dead from a wound in the chest."—ED.]

"Do you know what I find particularly fascinating about your son receiving the Medal of Honor? I mean other than the obvious intrepidity he displayed."

"What is that?"

"There were no American witnesses to his action. All the facts of his heroism, including notarized eyewitness accounts, were from the Germans themselves. I find it fascinating that the details of his heroism were sent through the lines, along with his body, by the German army. They were that impressed with his bravery."

"I spoke to one of the Germans who was there that day," Smoke said.

"You did?"

"Yes. Last year Sally and I crossed the Atlantic on-board the ocean liner *Homeric.*"

"That must have been fascinating."

"It was. But, Professor, we are getting way afield here. Don't you think we should get back to John Jackson?"

"Yes, of course. Where did we leave off with Mr. Jackson?"

"He and Claire had just built themselves a cabin."

Upper Missouri River

John began chopping down trees and sizing the logs, and Claire debarked them, using a crowbar and a spud, which was like a hoe . . . but with a straight blade. John used ropes and his horse and mule to pull the logs into position, then, when he had the walls up, Claire chinked in between them with twigs and mud. While Claire was filling in between the logs, John made a roof of smaller-diameter limbs. When the roof was completed, it was covered with sod.

The cabin had a single room that was twelve feet square. The floor was dirt, but John promised that they would have a wood floor as soon as he could get around to it. There was only one door and no windows. John put the fireplace at one end of the cabin and built the chimney of wattle and daubed mud. Stone and clay were used for the hearth and the interior of the fireplace.

It took a lot of hard work, but two weeks after the first log was cut, they were able to spend the night in their own house. For the next month, John and Claire built furniture for their house, a bed, a table and some chairs, and some shelves.

By the time the first snows came, they were warm and snug in their house, and Claire announced that she was pregnant.

"Wow! Then we have to celebrate!" John said. "You know what? I think it must be nearly Thanksgiving. Yes, I'm sure it is. I'm going to kill us a turkey, and we'll have an old-fashioned Thanksgiving Day dinner, just the two of us."

John did kill a turkey and the aroma of it cooking filled the inside of the little cabin so that by the time it was ready to eat, they were both ravenous. John smiled as he carved up the turkey for them.

"Happy Thanksgiving," he said.

"What is Thanksgiving?"

"You've never heard of Thanksgiving?"

"No."

"Well, then I'll tell you the story."

For the rest of the afternoon John told the story of the Pilgrims, and their voyage to America on the small ship, the *Mayflower*. He told of the men and women who left England in search of religious freedom.

"They thought they were going to the Virginia Colony, where some Europeans had already settled, but in November, they reached Cape Cod, Massachusetts.

"There were a hundred and two passengers on the ship," John said. "And the ship remained at anchor while they built cabins where they could live."

"Like this," Claire said, taking in their cabin with a proud smile.

"That first winter was brutal, and more than one-half of them died the first year, from starvation and disease. The Pilgrims held secret burials for the ones who died, so that the Indians wouldn't realize how few were remaining."

"Indians?" Claire asked. She pointed to herself.

"These were Wampanoag Indians. And they eventually began helping the Pilgrims, because if they hadn't, I believe every one of them would have died. And think how that would have changed history."

"And they ate turkey?" Claire asked, not making the connection between the Pilgrims, half of whom had died, and the turkey they were eating now.

"Yes. You see, after almost dying of starvation, they had a good harvest, and to celebrate the harvest, and the fact that at least half of them were still alive, they held a feast. And the Indians came to join them," John said. He smiled, and made a motion with his hand to take in the two of them.

"It's like us," he added. "Indian and white man coming together to give thanks."

"The baby will be a Thanksgiving thing," Claire said. "The baby will be Indian and white," she added, touching John on the face, then putting her hand on her stomach.

"Yes, it will indeed be a thing for thanksgiving," John said.

John ran his traps every day that winter, beaver traps in the water, and marten traps hanging from trees near the water. The reason the marten traps had to be hung from trees was to prevent rodents from chewing on the martens once they had been caught.

The trapping was bountiful, much more even than he and Smoke had brought in the year before. He would skin the beaver, and hang the meat out so the wild animals couldn't get to it. Claire would scrape and clean the hides, then stack them. She also cooked the beaver meat, sometimes frying it, sometimes baking it, sometimes grilling it over the open flames of the fireplace. She also boiled the beaver and made a soup, cooked with wild onions, mushrooms, cattail, and sun root tubers.

John kept a close count of his furs and before

winter was half over, had over a thousand dollars' worth of pelts, based on the prices they paid the previous year. But he had also heard that the St. Louis market paid twice as much, and at that rate it would be worth his while to go there.

CHAPTER TWENTY

Boulder

"The team in red is the University of Denver," Professor Armbruster said. "So far this season, we haven't lost a game. As a matter of fact, nobody has even scored on us this year and . . . oh, oh, this isn't good."

On the field one of the players wearing red broke free from the rest and started a long run, with players wearing black chasing after him. There were loud cheers from the other side of the field, and groans from this side. "I spoke too soon," Professor Armbruster said.

"Why?" Sally asked.

"Denver just made a touchdown."

Despite Denver's score, Colorado won the game, twenty-one to seven, and there was much celebration on the campus that evening.

Smoke and Sally had been invited by Professor Armbruster to dine with him and his wife, as well as

Dr. and Mrs. George Norlin. Dr. Norlin was president of the University of Colorado.

"I have been listening to recordings of your account each evening," Dr. Norlin said. "And I must say that I am finding the story very fascinating. You will truly go down in history as one of our most valiant men."

"You are embarrassing me, Dr. Norlin," Smoke said with a smile. "I just spent most of my life trying to stay alive."

"Dr. Norlin won't say anything about it, but he has been in a fight as well, with the state legislature," Professor Armbruster said. "They have been taken over by the KKK, and they are demanding that he fire every Catholic and Jew on the campus. And to his credit, he has refused to do so."

"Good for you, Doctor," Smoke said.

"It has been at some cost, I must say," Dr. Norlin said. "The state has stopped all financial aid to the university. We are having to subsist on what income we can garner from tuitions, and such revenue-producing programs that we have, such as our football team."

"Sally, give me the . . ." Smoke started to say, but Sally had already gotten the checkbook from her purse and was handing it to him, with a smile.

"Would ten thousand dollars help?" Smoke asked, as he started writing the check.

"What? Why, yes, of course. But please, Mr. Jensen, I hope you don't think this was a request for a donation."

"It doesn't matter whether it was a request or not," Smoke said. "It's something I want to do."

"I'm serious," Wes said over Monday morning breakfast at the TKE house. He was talking to Philip McGrath, the Grand Prytanis of Tau Kappa Epsilon. "You come up with any name in the history of the American West, and this guy knew them. Wild Bill Hickok, Falcon MacCallister, Buffalo Bill, Monte Carson, Calamity Jane, Wyatt Earp, Doc Holliday. He knew them all! Not only that, he's lived the kind of life that you read about in novels. You need to meet him just so that someday, fifty or sixty years from now, you can tell your grandchildren that you met Smoke Jensen."

"I heard about what he did at the speakeasy, an old man like that," McGrath said.

"I tell you what, Phil. It might be that he's been around for a long time, but I wouldn't exactly call him an old man," Wes said. "No, sir, not by a long shot. And certainly, not to his face," he added with a laugh.

"I remember reading books about him when I was a kid," Phil said. "But they were all novels. I didn't know there really was such a person."

"When Professor Armbruster asked me if I would make the recordings, I tried to get out of it," Wes said. "I mean, who wants to sit around and listen to some old man mumble on with his stories. But I wouldn't trade what I'm doing for the world. Sixty, seventy years from now, if I'm still alive, I'm going to tell everyone I know that I met Smoke Jensen. Why . . . it's like meeting Abraham Lincoln, or Davy Crockett, or Andrew Jackson. I mean, you name someone from our history . . . anyone, and I wouldn't get any bigger a thrill meeting them than I have gotten by meeting Smoke Jensen."

"I can tell he's made quite an impression on you."

"Yes, he has," Wes admitted. "I'm telling you, Phil, you need to meet this man."

"Do you suppose he would come to dinner at the fraternity house and give us a little talk?" Phil asked.

"I don't know. That's all he's doin' all day long now, is just talking into the microphone. I wouldn't want to ask him to come give us a talk. But we might ask him to come have dinner with us."

"Good idea," Phil said. "All right, I will."

"Mr. Jensen," Wes said, greeting Smoke as he stepped out his car in front of the Old Main building. "I would like for you to meet Phil McGrath. He is the Grand Prytanis of the fraternity I belong to."

"He's the what?" Smoke asked with a chuckle.

"He's the president."

"Well, why didn't you say so? Hello, Mr. McGrath," Smoke said, extending his hand.

"Mr. Jensen, it is a great pleasure meeting you," McGrath said, taking Smoke's hand and pumping it enthusiastically.

"You are also on the football team, I believe," Smoke said. "I watched you play, Saturday. You played very well."

"Thank you," McGrath said, smiling in obvious pleasure at the accolade. "Oh, uh, I wanted to ask . . . that is, uh, I was wondering if you would have dinner with us tonight at the fraternity house?"

"Oh, I'd better not. My wife is here and I'm gone from her all day long. I don't know how she would take it if I left her alone in the evening as well."

"What about lunch?" Wes asked quickly. "You have to eat lunch somewhere, don't you?"

"I suppose I could. But today is Monday, isn't it?"

"Yes, sir, it is. Does that matter?" Wes replied, confused as to what difference it would make what day it was.

"Well, I always eat beaver on Monday, so if you would tell your cook to fry me up some beaver tail in a little bear grease, I'd be glad to join you for lunch."

Wes and McGrath looked at each other with a rather desolate expression on their faces.

Smoke laughed. "Well, I suppose I can make an exception. I'll be there and I'll eat whatever you have."

Wes and McGrath weren't the only ones who greeted Smoke that morning. There were even more students in front of the Old Main building today than there had been the morning after the speakeasy episode the night before. Several went out of their way to shake hands with him.

"What is all this about, Wes?" Smoke asked when, finally, they had run the gauntlet and were safely inside the building.

"It's you, Mr. Jensen. Everyone wants an opportunity to see history, firsthand."

"Boy, are you saying I'm history?" Smoke asked with a snarl.

"Oh, uh, no, I mean, uh, it's just . . ."

Smoke laughed. "I'm teasing you, Wes. At my age, I have seen a lot of history, so I guess, in a way, that does make me history."

"Uh, yes, sir," Wes said, somewhat awkwardly. "I'll, uh, just get everything set up for the recording session today."

"Good morning, Smoke," Professor Armbruster said when Smoke arrived, going directly to the recording studio.

"Good morning, Professor. Wes and a young man named McGrath have invited me for lunch at their fraternity house. Am I taking a risk by eating there?"

"Smoke, after everything you've been through, they could be serving bugs and I don't think it would bother you."

"Depends on the bug," Smoke said. "Grub worms can be quite tasty."

Professor Armbruster laughed. "I figured you

would say something like that. When we left off, I believe you said that John was considering a trip to St. Louis to sell his furs. Did he go to St. Louis?"

"Yes," Smoke said. "And it proved to be quite profitable for him."

[*After the Civil War, steamboat traffic on the Missouri River became a common sight. The boats were considerably different in design from the Mississippi River boats, with few of the fancy fittings. The most important feature of a Missouri River boat was that it be of light weight. From 140 to 170 feet long and 30 feet wide they had a shallow hull, and spoonbill-shaped bow. With this design they could carry two hundred tons of cargo through waist-deep water, safely navigating over anything from sandbars to whitewater rapids. In addition, this type of vessel was less expensive to fuel and much easier to steer.*

Steamboat captains in the late 1870s could charge as much as $1,200 every month for their services, an enormous sum, compared to the average income of $40 per month for the rest of America. They had to be extremely skilled captains and a good hand at striking a deal with merchants. The payoff was huge, however, since a steamboat could carry cargo worth a profit of up to $40,000.

A few words about the history of the city of St. Louis might enlighten the reader, and thus help in understanding the significant role the city played in

*the lives of not only the mountaineers and the fur
trappers, but all of the western frontier.*

*The first steamboat arrived in St. Louis on
July 27, 1817, which proved to be only the beginning of St. Louis as an important river city. By
1859, river traffic had increased to such an extent
that St. Louis took its position as the second-largest
port in the country, with only New York exceeding
St. Louis in total commercial tonnage moved.
Often as many as 170 steamboats could be counted
on the levee.*

*Because of the junction of the Missouri River,
St. Louis was uniquely positioned to truly become
the gateway city to the West. It was fed by boats from
the east, traversing the Ohio River, then entering the
Mississippi River at Cairo, Illinois, to beat their way
upstream to St. Louis. There was also a very busy
schedule of boats that plied the Mississippi between
St. Louis, Memphis, Vicksburg, and the seaport at
New Orleans.*

*By the time the construction of the railroads began
in the early 1850s, St. Louis had a population of
almost eighty thousand people. The first westbound
train left St. Louis in 1855. It was the railroads
that eventually led to the diminution of the importance of the riverboats in the city's economy.—ED.]*

Upper Missouri—1872

John built a raft, onto which he loaded his winter
catch of furs, then he, Claire, and their son, Kirby,

rafted downriver to Yankton. There, they boarded a Missouri riverboat, the *Nellie Peck*, for passage to St. Louis.

When John purchased the tickets, he was given a sheet of paper with the title, "Helpful Hints for Steamboat Passengers."

Welcome Aboard the Missouri River Steamboat, NELLIE PECK.

This guide is published as a service for the traveling public. Careful attention to its information and suggestions will insure the riverboat patron a memorable journey. This guide describes the many accommodations found on the boat, and gives warnings about possible unpleasant situations.

Departure Time

The NELLIE PECK will leave terminal ports on scheduled times. The arrival and departure times change at ports along the river. Your steamboat captain, Captain Milton Saddler, prefers early morning departures. This will provide the NELLIE PECK with as many daylight hours as possible. It is not feasible to operate at night unless the moon is very bright. There is too much danger in navigating in the dark, especially in low water.

Cabin Passengers

Enjoy the best of steamboat travel. Staterooms for the NELLIE PECK are on the cabin deck.

They are ten feet square with doors at each end, one to the interior passage and the other to the deck. The NELLIE PECK also provides clean mattresses and sheets on the berths. Curtains at cabin windows provide privacy to the passenger while dressing.

Toilet

Toilet facilities are vastly improved on the NELLIE PECK with a washstand and basin in each of the staterooms. For the deck passengers there are two washrooms, one each for ladies and gentlemen, located near the wheelhouse. Each deck washroom is equipped with a washbasin, one hair brush, a comb, a community toothbrush, and a roller-type towel. The crew keeps the pitchers filled with river water. The toilets are like the outdoor variety and placed next to the wheel.

Warning

Thieves, con agents, and gamblers ride the steamboats. Many of these undesirable citizens hang around levees, wharves, hotels, and taverns in the river towns. Travelers are advised to buy bank drafts. Some prefer letters of credit from their own bank. If you need to carry a large sum of money, wear a money belt. Avoid games of chance on the riverboats.

Wooding

A passenger can reduce his fare by wooding on a trip. However, the job of cutting and carrying wood is a hard one, and should only be attempted by those used to hard work.

St. Louis

The *Nellie Peck* approached the riverbank, then just before it got there, reversed the paddle, causing the water to froth at the stern. The boat glided in, until the bow bumped against the cobblestone levee. A crewman on the front of the boat tossed out a thick hawser, and someone on the bank made the boat fast.

The riverfront was alive with activity, not only the scores of other boats that were tied up, but the amount of traffic ashore: carriages, buggies, surreys, buckboards, coaches, and wagons of all sizes. There was noise from the steam relief valves of the boats, some of the venting sounding almost like cannon fire. Men were shouting back and forth to each other, and the air was rent with the clops of steel-shoed horses and mules on the paved streets.

Claire had never seen anything like this in her life, and she stood at the railing of the boat with her hand to her chest.

"Are you all right?" John asked.

"I . . . I have never seen so many people," Claire said.

"I should think not. If you put every person you had ever seen in your whole life, together, they wouldn't make but a fraction of what you are seeing right here, right now, just on the riverfront."

"How can so many people live so close together? Don't they step on each other's feet?"

John laughed. "I imagine they do," he said.

Claire reached out to grab John's arm. "John, do not leave the baby and me alone here. I am frightened by so many."

"Don't worry, Claire. I have no intention of leaving you alone."

"Mr. Jackson," the boat's purser said, approaching them then. "I have secured a wagon for your cargo."

"Thank you, Mr. Adams," John said.

John and Claire stood by, watching as bale after bale of beaver and marten pelts were loaded onto the wagon. Then, leaving the boat, John secured a cab, and they followed the wagonload of furs as it made its way through the city to the St. Louis Fur Exchange, on Lafayette Street.

Claire was in awe of the huge buildings, many of them five and six stories high. They passed by the Christian Staehlin's Phoenix Brewery, a huge building with towering smokestacks.

"Why don't I just let you and Kirby out here?" John suggested. "I'll come back for you later."

"No!" Claire said, grabbing his arm even tighter.

John laughed quietly, then kissed her on the forehead. "Don't worry, my sweet," he said. "I'm just teasing you. I have no intention of letting you go."

When they reached the fur exchange, John let the cab go, then he, Claire, and Kirby went inside to make arrangements to sell the pelts.

CHAPTER TWENTY-ONE

"I must say, Mr. Jackson," O. D. Clayton said a few minutes later as he examined the pelts. "These are in remarkable condition, much better condition than the ones I normally get. I think that's because the fur traders don't always take that good of care of them."

"How much are you willing to pay for them?"

"Five dollars apiece for the marten, three dollars for the beaver."

"Will you take all of them?" John asked.

"How many do you have?"

"I have six hundred beaver, and three hundred twenty-five marten."

O. D. Clayton did some figuring, then looked up. "That comes to three thousand, four hundred, and twenty-five dollars," he said.

"Three thousand, four hundred, and twenty-five?" A huge smile spread across John's face. "Claire!" he said, embracing her. "We're rich!"

"Do you want it in cash, or by check?" Clayton asked.

"I expect I'd better take it by cash," John said. "There aren't a lot of banks near my cabin."

Clayton chuckled. "No, I don't expect there would be," he said. "Is paper money all right?"

"Yes, where I do business, they take paper money."

"I'm never sure. Paper money is as good as gold all over St. Louis. But I've heard that there are some places where they won't take it."

Clayton counted out the money, and John, with a big smile, put it in his pocket.

"Now," John said. "Suppose you tell me where we can find an elegant place to eat in St. Louis."

"You might try the Delmonico on Olive," Clayton told him. "That's just three blocks over. Truth is, I've never been there, but I've heard it was an elegant place."

With his money in his pocket, John, Claire, and baby Kirby walked the three blocks to Delmonico. Smiling, they stepped into the restaurant.

"I'm sorry, but you aren't welcome here," a waiter said, stopping them just inside the door.

"Oh, I'm sorry," John said, touching his buckskin shirt. "I wasn't aware there was a dress code."

"No, sir, you are fine," the waiter said. "You can come in. It's the squaw and papoose who can't. They will have to wait outside."

John reached up and grabbed the man's collar

with his left hand, then he twisted it so that it was choking him.

"What did you say?" he asked. Though the expression on his face was fearsome, and he did have a tight grip of the man's collar, the question was spoken quietly, and coldly, the more frightening because of that. "Do you seriously think I'm going to leave my wife and child outside while I come in?"

"I . . . uh . . . the owner has a policy that only whites can come in. I'm sorry, sir, there's nothing I can do about it. No colored, no Indians, and no Chinamen."

"John, please, let's go," Claire said.

"Mister, I don't know who you think you are, but we don't want squaw men comin' in here," a man sitting at the first table said. He pulled a pistol and was about to point it at John, but before he could, John pushed the waiter away, drew his knife, and threw it. It pinned the man's sleeve to the table, and he dropped the pistol. John stepped over quickly, and picked up the pistol.

The man who had drawn the gun reached over with his left hand to pull the knife free.

"Leave the knife where it is," John ordered. "I'll remove it when I decide to." He pulled the cylinder from the man's pistol, dumped all the shells onto the floor, and kicked them away. Only then did he recover his knife, unpinning the man's jacket sleeve.

Then, doing it so quickly and smoothly that the would-be gunman had no time to react, John sliced through the man's septum. It started bleeding profusely.

"Ahhh!!" the man shouted out in pain, sticking his hand to his nose. "You cut my nose!"

"Yes, I did, didn't I? Well, that's just a reminder to make you think twice next time you want to stick your nose into somebody else's business," John said.

He used the man's shirtsleeve to wipe the blood away from his knife.

"If you good folks don't mind, I'll just find another place to spend my money," he said. "Let's go, Claire."

They started toward the door, but just before they left, John turned to address the others.

"By the way, if anyone so much as sticks a head out the door in the next minute, I'll shoot you dead."

Not one word was spoken by anyone in the restaurant, but all stared at him with expressions that ranged from curiosity, to shock, to outright fear.

The next restaurant accepted them without question, and not until they were seated at a table in the back of the room did Claire allow herself to laugh.

"Why are you laughing?"

"Did you see their faces? They were like this." Claire lifted her eyebrows, and opened her mouth, simulating an expression of shock.

"Yes, I suppose I did go a bit too far there."

Claire giggled again. "Yes, cutting his nose here," she put her finger to her nose septum, "is a bit too far."

"Claire, will you marry me?" John asked.

"What? But we are already married."

"No. I mean will you marry me by the law of the white man? My father is an Episcopal priest. I want to find an Episcopal church and I want us to get married. No, wait, if we do that, we'll have to post banns and that will take too long. I'll find us a circuit judge, he can marry us, then I'll get a priest to bless the marriage. When we go back, we will go back as legally married husband and wife."

Two hours later, having been married by a circuit court judge, John and Claire, with Kirby, stepped into St. Mark's Episcopal Church in south St. Louis. John dipped his fingers into the basin of holy water and crossed himself. Because he had taught Claire some of the liturgy of the church, she did so as well.

They walked to the front and knelt at the altar rail. They were there when the priest stepped out of his study and saw them. The priest waited until they both rose.

"Good afternoon," the priest said. "May I help you?"

"Yes, Father. We are married, but it was a civil ceremony. I would like to ask that you bless our marriage."

"You are Episcopalian?"

"Yes, my father is an Episcopalian priest back in Pennsylvania. His name is Nathaniel Jackson."

The priest's eyes widened. "Is he by chance the author of *A Book of Rites for the Use of Congregations of the Protestant Episcopal Church?*"

"He is," John said.

The priest smiled and extended his hand. "My name is Sharkey. Bill Sharkey. I am most pleased to meet you, sir."

"I am John Jackson, and this is my wife, Claire, and our baby, Kirby. I have baptized both of them, simply because we live so far from any church. I would like you to validate the baptisms as well."

"I would be happy to do so," Father Sharkey said.

It was as Mr. and Mrs. John Jackson that they, with their baby, boarded the train in St. Louis for the long trip back. Because he had enough money to do so, they took passage on the Palace Car.

For the first part of the trip, there were only six people in the car: John, Claire, and Kirby, plus one other couple, and a man dressed as a clergyman, who was traveling alone. The clergyman kept staring at Claire and the baby with an obvious look of displeasure on his face. Finally he spoke.

"You are in violation of God's law," he said.

"I beg your pardon, Parson, did you say something?" John asked.

"I said you are sinners, both of you. Cohabitation without marriage is a sin. Whoremongers and adulterers God will judge."

"Well, Parson, it's none of your business, but it so happens that we are married."

The parson shook his head. "No, that ain't possible. God don't hold with white men marryin' savages."

"Oh? Would you mind telling me where, in the Bible, it says that?"

"Ezra 10:2–3. 'We have taken strange wives of the people of the land, yet now there is hope in Israel concerning this thing. Now therefore let us make a covenant with our God to put away all the wives, and such as are born of them,'" the parson said, sanctimoniously.

"Colossians 3:11. 'There is no distinction between Greek and Jew, circumcised and uncircumcised, barbarian, Scythian, slave and freeman, but Christ is all, and in all.'" John replied

"How dare you, sir!" the parson said, pointing a long, bony finger at John. "How dare you quote scripture to a man of Gawd?"

"You call yourself a man of God. Yet 'you love all words that devour, oh deceitful tongue.' Psalm 52:4," John said.

"You . . . you know your scripture, sir," the parson said, surprised by John's Bible acumen.

"I do."

"Then why in Gawd's name would you marry an Indian whore?" he shouted at the top of his lungs.

"Mister, and I'm not calling you parson anymore, because by your words, you have proven yourself to be unworthy of that title. So I'm telling you now to leave this car, and don't come back in until either you, or we, leave this train. And we won't be leaving this train for a thousand miles."

"I will not leave this car," the parson said, angrily. "I paid for my passage."

"Here is ten dollars," John said, handing the parson a bill. "Now, get out of this car and stay out."

"You have no right to order me out."

"Oh, it isn't a question of whether I have the right," John said. He smiled, but it was a taunting smile. "It's a question of whether I am capable of grabbing you by the scruff of your neck and the seat of your pants and bodily throwing you off this train. And believe me, sir, I am. Now your choice is simple. Leave this car now, of your own accord, or I will throw you off the train."

"You wouldn't dare, sir!" the parson said, confidently.

"Shall we see?"

John walked over to him and grabbed him by his shirt and the seat of his pants and started moving him toward the door. "I wonder if you will bounce," John said.

"No! No! God in heaven, man, don't do it! Don't do it!"

"You'll leave of your own volition?"

"I will, I will!"

John took his hands away.

"Here's another thing," John said. "Don't let me see you again. When we are in the dining car, don't you come in. If we get off the train for a few minutes in some station, don't you be where I can see you. Do you understand that? I don't want to see your ugly face again, ever, anywhere."

"You . . . you have no right . . ."

"I thought we had already discussed that," John said. He shook his head. "I told you, I don't care whether I have the right or not. Now, get."

The preacher licked his lips a couple of times, then, turning, he hurried out through the front door of the car.

John looked at the other couple in the car, an older man and woman who had been watching the whole thing.

"Ma'am, sir, I'm sorry about that," he said. "But I've always believed that it was the duty of a man to look after his wife and family. And that means to shield them from all hostility, whether by word or action."

"Young man, you have nothing to apologize for," the elderly man said. "You had every right to protect your family."

"And your wife and baby are beautiful," the elderly woman added.

"Thank you, I think so myself. Of course, I might be just a little prejudiced," John said with a smile. "Would you care to join my family and me in the dining car for lunch? I would be delighted to have you as our guests."

"Why, yes, we would be happy to. Thank you very much, young man."

A few minutes later, John, Claire, Kirby, and the man and woman who had accepted John's invitation were enjoying their lunch in the dining car. Their names were Mr. and Mrs. George Upton. Mr. Upton was a retired college professor from Washington University in St. Louis. They were on their way to California because, as Upton explained, he had always wanted to see what was beyond the setting sun.

"I remember as a young man, seeing so many people coming through St. Louis, bound for California," Upton said. "That is how St. Louis acquired the name the Gateway City, you know."

"So I've heard," John replied.

"I almost joined one of the trains, but I was only fourteen at the time, and the wagon master would not let me come with them without my parents' permission. Oh, what an adventure that would have been."

"I have told him, many times, I am quite satisfied to be making the journey in the comfort of a Palace Car," Mrs. Upton said.

"Are you a . . . and please don't take offense, but my curiosity is piqued. Are you a mountain man?"

"No offense taken, Professor. I am indeed a mountain man," John said.

"But your language, your Bible acumen, that isn't something one would associate with a mountain man."

"I am a graduate of the University of Pennsylvania," John said. "But, I have taken a postgraduate course in mountaineering."

"My word, a postgraduate course in mountaineering? Where does one find such a course?"

"In Colorado and Montana," John said. "And I've had excellent professors, a man named Preacher, a man named Smoke, and a woman named Hanhepiwi."

Claire smiled.

CHAPTER TWENTY-TWO

Tau Kappa Epsilon Fraternity House

Smoke was given a position of honor at the head of the table in the dining room of the TKE house. Every member of the fraternity treated him with awe.

"Mr. Jensen, how many men have you killed?" a plebe asked.

"Booker! You are dismissed from the table!" McGrath said, angrily.

"No, please," Smoke said, holding up his hand. "It's a legitimate question, given the number of books that have been written about me, and many of them stressing only that part of the story. The truth is, Booker, I'm not quite sure how many men I have killed. It's not something I've ever wanted to keep a tally of, as some perverted badge of honor. But I will say this. I have never killed a man who didn't need killing."

"But what gave you the right to determine whether he needed killing or not?" Booker asked.

It was more of a challenge than a question, and everyone sitting around the dining room table looked toward Smoke to see how he would react.

"That is another good question," Smoke said. "For the most part, survival gave me the right to make the determination," Smoke said. "I killed men who were trying to kill me. But there have been times when I purposely set out to hunt men down for the sole purpose of killing them."

"There is no statute of limitations for murder," Booker said. "Are you afraid that some zealous prosecutor might bring charges against you today?"

Smoke chuckled. "Mr. Booker, do you, by any chance, plan to be a lawyer?"

"Yes, sir."

"Then, let's make a deal, right here. If some zealous prosecutor decides that he would like to try me for killing someone like oh, let's say, Ted Casey, I would like to hire you to defend me."

"Ted Casey is the one you lynched, isn't he?"

"Lynched?" Wes said. "Listen, I heard that story firsthand. If ever any man deserved to hang, it was Ted Casey."

"But he was hung without a trial, wasn't he?" Booker asked.

"He was."

"Looking back on it now, would you do things differently?" Booker asked.

"Yes."

"Ha! I thought so. What would you do differently?"

"I wouldn't have used a new rope," Smoke said.

The others laughed, then, when Booker started to speak again, McGrath held up his hand.

"Booker, Mr. Jensen has been more than generous with you. We'll have no more inquisition."

"Yes, sir," Booker said, contritely.

Old Main Building

"How was your lunch?" Professor Armbruster asked.

"Quite interesting," Smoke replied without further elaboration.

"Well, are you ready to resume the session?"

"I am."

"We left off with John and Claire going back home," Professor Armbruster said.

"Yes."

John's cabin

After John, Claire, and the baby returned from St. Louis they put in a garden. As John explained, "wild plants will do in a pinch, but there's nothing improves the table like fresh radishes, onions, tomatoes, lettuce, potatoes, carrots, beans, cabbage, and watermelon."

John worked hard on his garden, and soon he was raising a bountiful crop. Already they had radishes, and the tomatoes were coming along as well.

Because trapping was nonproductive in the

summer, John had a lot of time to work in the garden and he enjoyed it. He also enjoyed Claire's genuine enthusiasm at seeing the plants grow. She had no experience whatever with gardening, so it was all new and exciting to her.

John was also enjoying his son, particularly the infant's reaction to everything around him. Claire had made a flute from a sumac branch, and John was learning to play it.

"Now, listen to this, Kirby," he said, lifting the flute to his lips. He began playing, and to Claire's surprise, was actually playing a song.

"What is that song?" she asked.

"It is called 'Old Folks at Home.' Some call it 'Suwanee River.'"

"How can you do that? You have not played the flute before."

John chuckled. "Once you know how to play the scale, the rest is easy," he said.

He played a few more songs, then handed to flute to Claire, who played music from her background. The music was melodious, consisting of a lot of halftones, but there was a soulful, almost mournful quality to it.

"That was beautiful," John said when she finished. "What was it?"

"It is a prayer to the Great Spirit. It has words. Would you like to hear them?"

"Yes."

Claire sang the song, first in her own language, then again, this time in English.

"Oh Great Spirit whose voice I hear in the winds
Whose breath gives life to the world
I come to you as one of your many children
I am small and weak."

"Why, that is beautiful, Claire," he said. He embraced her. "I never thought, when I left Pennsylvania, that I would wind up with an Indian woman, let alone, that I would fall in love with her. I love you, Claire."

"I did not think I would ever love," Claire said. "It is only a word, I thought. But you have taught me that it is much more than a word."

John embraced her again, then he heard the sound of approaching horses, and he separated from her, and, picking up his rifle, stepped out in front of his cabin. It wasn't that he feared every sound, but the cabin was so remote that any visitor became suspect.

There was only one direct approach to the cabin, and he jacked a round into the chamber of his rifle and watched, and waited.

He saw a body of men approaching and he knew, immediately, that they were soldiers. He assumed they might be lost, and he put his rifle down, and waited until they approached. What he saw was eight soldiers, being led by a lieutenant.

"Excuse me, sir. Are you John Jackson?" the lieutenant asked when they reached the front of his cabin.

"I am. What can I do for you, Lieutenant?"

"Mr. Jackson, I am Lieutenant Murphy, from Fort Shaw. Major Clinton's compliments, sir, and he wonders if you and your wife would do him the honor of paying a visit to the fort?"

"Would this be anything more than a courtesy call, Lieutenant?" John asked.

"I believe the major has a favor he wishes to ask of you, sir. But I have not been made privy to what that favor might be."

"All right, Lieutenant Murphy, we'll join you," John said.

"What is it?" Claire asked when John went back into the cabin.

"Major Clinton wants us to pay a call on him at Fort Shaw," John said.

"Why?"

"I don't know, the lieutenant didn't say. I'm not sure he even knows. But, it's never a bad thing to have a good relationship with the military, so I think we should go."

"What about the garden?"

"It'll be all right for a few days."

With baby Kirby riding in a cradleboard hanging from the side of Claire's horse, John and Claire rode back to Fort Shaw with Lieutenant Murphy and his military detachment.

Fort Shaw was located on the south side of Sun River, constructed of palisade logs, and perched high on the end of a bluff that protruded over the water. There were projecting blockhouses on corners opposite each other, from which the soldiers had a good view of the approach.

The front gate to the post was tightly closed as Lieutenant Murphy and his party approached.

"Hello, the post!" Lieutenant Murphy shouted. "Open the gate!"

The gate was opened early enough so that there was no need for the group to break stride. They rode right through with Lieutenant Murphy returning the salute of the private at the gate. When they reached the parade ground, Lieutenant Murphy halted the detail.

"Dismount!" he ordered.

Claire looked John, and he smiled. "That's not us," he said.

The soldiers dismounted.

"Fall out!" Lieutenant Murphy ordered.

As the soldiers led their mounts to the stable, Lieutenant Murphy indicated than John and Claire should follow him. They rode to the headquarters building then dismounted, and tied their horses off at the hitching rail.

John took Kirby from his cradleboard, and handed him to Claire, then they followed Lieutenant Murphy inside.

"Sergeant Major, is Major Clinton in his office?" Lieutenant Murphy asked.

"Yes, sir," the first sergeant major answered.

Murphy went over to the door leading to the

commanding officer's office, tapped lightly, then pushed it open and stuck his head in.

"Sir, I have Mr. Jackson."

John couldn't hear the major's answer, but he did hear the lieutenant's response.

"Yes, sir, she is with him." The lieutenant turned toward John. "Come ahead," he said.

"John, the baby and I will wait here," Claire said.

"No," Lieutenant Murphy said, quickly. "The major wants to see both of you."

"Both of us?" John asked. He wasn't sure what this was about, but he wasn't sure he liked it. If the major planned to give him some trouble because he was married to an Indian woman, he wasn't going to put up with it. Taking Claire by the arm, he led her into the commanding officer's office.

"Mr. Jackson, Mrs. Jackson," the major said with a broad smile. He was standing and he came toward them with his hand extended. "I'm Major Clinton. Thank you so much for coming."

The major's demeanor allowed John to dismiss his apprehension. He wasn't acting like someone who was going to give him any trouble.

"Please," he said, "I know you have had a long ride. Have a seat." He extended his arm toward the side wall, where there was a sofa and a chair.

John and Claire sat on the sofa, and she held Kirby on her lap. Kirby stared at the major, his dark brown eyes open wide.

"I know you are wondering why I asked you here," Major Clinton said. "I have a favor to ask of you and, if you choose not to do it, I will certainly understand. In the meantime, I've made quarters available for you here, on the post, for the night, so you can start back, rested, tomorrow."

"What do you want, Major?" John asked.

"I want you and your wife to be an emissary for me," Major Clinton said.

"What sort of an emissary?"

"A peace emissary to the Crow Indians. I thought, with your wife, you would be an ideal ambassador."

"My wife is Lakota, not Crow," John said. "The Lakota and the Crow are traditional enemies."

"Can you speak the Crow language?" Major Clinton asked.

"I can speak," Claire said.

"It could save hundreds of lives," Major Clinton said. "All I need is for the Crow to understand that we will not encroach on their land, that we will in fact protect their land from any white men who try to violate their borders. Try and make her understand that."

"I won't try to make her understand anything," John said. "She will make her own decision, and I will honor it."

"I understand," Major Clinton said. "Well, I do hope you and Mrs. Jackson will be our guests for dinner this evening. And I promise you," he said, holding up his finger and smiling, "I will make no further petitions. As I said, whether or not you and Mrs. Jackson consent to do this, will be up to you."

"Thank you," John said.

The major's wife was a rather plump, blond woman with bright blue eyes. "Oh, it is so wonderful to have dinner guests," she said when John and Claire arrived.

"I must apologize for our dress," John said. "We had no idea we would be invited to your beautiful home."

"Oh, nonsense, you are dressed just fine. And what a lovely thing you are," she said, gushingly, to Claire. "Oh, may I hold the child for a moment? Our own son is back East, attending the Military Academy at West Point," she said. "It's been so long since I held a little one."

"Yes, you may hold him," Claire said, extending the baby to her.

"Oh, my, what a handsome creature you are," Mrs. Clinton said. "Yes, you are. Indeed, you are." Kirby smiled at her and a line of spittle trailed from his mouth.

True to his promise, Major Clinton made no more mention of the mission he wanted John and Claire to undertake. Instead they talked about St. Louis. John and Claire had just come from there, and Major Clinton had been stationed there at Jefferson Barracks.

After a pleasant dinner, and because Kirby had fallen asleep, John made his excuses, and said they needed to get the baby to bed.

"In regard to your request, Major, I will give you an answer in the morning," he said.

"Good, thank you, that's all I ask," Major Clinton replied. "I'm gratified that you are still thinking about it, rather than an outright dismissal of the request."

The empty quarters of what would normally be the residence of an unmarried junior officer, was for them. As they walked back to the quarters John heard the first note of the bugle.

"What is that music?" Claire asked. "It is so beautiful. But it is sad."

"It is called 'Taps,'" John said. "It is the bugle call that puts the soldiers to bed at night. Would you like to know the words?"

"Yes."

John sung the words, softly, as the bugler repeated the call.

> *"Day is done,*
> *Gone the sun,*
> *From the lakes, from the hills, from the sky.*
> *All is well, safely rest,*
> *God is nigh."*

"Those are good words," Claire said.

Looking around the garrison, John saw that

all the buildings, the officers' quarters, and the soldiers' barracks, were dark and quiet.

"Come," he said. "We must be to our bed."

Later, after Kirby was asleep, John and Claire lay together in bed, with Claire's head on John's shoulder.

"John, do you want to do what the major has asked us to do?"

"It is up to you, Claire. You are the one who will have to do the talking."

"Yes, I will do the talking, but you will give me the words to say."

"As I said, it is up to you."

"If it will make peace, I say we should go."

"All right," John said. "I'll tell the major in the morning. We'll go."

CHAPTER TWENTY-THREE

In the village of Iron Bull

When John, Claire, and the baby rode into the village, every villager crowded around them, men, women, and children. One of the older boys, who was about fourteen, ran up to touch John's leg. Then, with a loud shout he ran back into the crowd.

"I have counted coups! I have counted coups!" he shouted, proudly.

"Claire, where do we go now?" John asked quietly.

"They will lead us to the place of the village council," Claire replied.

Almost immediately, two men came up, and one took the bridle of John's horse in hand, as the other took the bridle of Claire's horse. The two men led them through the camp until they stopped in front of a teepee. There was a council fire and several men were sitting around the fire. One was sitting by himself, just in front of the teepee opening, making it obvious that he was the head.

"That is Iron Bull," Claire said.

John held up his hand. "I come in peace, Iron Bull."

"*Taŋyaŋ yahípi,*" Iron Bull replied.

"He welcomes us."

Iron Bull spoke again.

"He asks that you join the council, but I cannot, as I am a woman."

"Tell him I must have you beside me, because you are my words."

Claire translated John's words.

Iron Bull nodded, and made a motion indicating Claire could join them.

"*Philamayaye,*" Claire replied, thanking him.

"Tell him that we come from the soldier chief. That the white man wants to live in peace with his Indian brothers."

Claire translated, then Iron Bull spoke, and she gasped.

"What is it? What did he say?"

"He said that you have killed some of his people. That you, and one called Smoke have killed Crow."

"That is true, but only because we were attacked by Crow. That is why we are here now, to make peace so that our people will not kill each other anymore."

"You have come to me in peace, and you may leave in peace. But there can be no peace between us."

"What do you think, Claire? Do you think there is any chance in getting him to change his mind?"

"I will ask," she replied, then, to Iron Bull.

"Great Chief, how strong is your conviction that there can be no peace?"

"It is very strong. Why do you live with a white man?"

"I was sold to a white man, by my own people. It was not my choice."

"Were you sold to this man?"

"No. John Jackson is a good man. I came to him because I wanted to. This baby is our baby. I wanted to have our baby."

"The baby is white."

"The baby is white and Indian. It is a fine baby, and it is a symbol of peace between the Indian and the white man."

"You may leave the village in peace. But after you have left, there can be no peace."

Claire turned to her husband. "I think we must go now," she said. "We can do no more, here."

"All right," John said. "If that is what you think."

"Iron Bull, have we your word that we can leave without fear?"

"My word is good only as far as the village," Iron Bull replied. *"After you leave the village, there will be no peace."*

"Oh!" Claire said.

"Claire, what is it?"

"John, we must go, now."

John stood, then took the baby, and with Claire moved slowly and deliberately to their horses.

"Tie the baby in very tightly," Claire said. "For after we leave the village, we must ride as fast as we can ride."

"Claire, what is it? What did he say?"

"He said we are safe only until we are out of the village. Then we will be in great danger."

They rode quietly out of the village then, when they were clear of the village, someone shouted something.

"John! He said we must run!" Claire said.

Quickly they broke into a gallop, riding as fast as they could. Behind them they heard the cries and calls of Indians in pursuit, and when John looked around he saw several mounted Indians chasing them.

"In there!" John said, pointing to a narrow draw, as arrows flew by them.

The draw was so narrow that only one horse at a time could pass, and that was good, because that meant that only one Indian at time could be in pursuit.

Claire and the baby went in first with John behind them. He knew this draw well because he had been trapped here last winter. He knew where it came out, and he also knew that if they could make it out the other end, he could seal it off so that the pursuing Indians couldn't get through.

Pulling his rifle from the saddle sheath, John

twisted around in the saddle, raised the Henry to his shoulder, aimed, and fired at the horse the Indian was riding. The horse went down, throwing its rider over its head. The dead horse had the effect of blocking off the draw. That brought the Indians behind to a complete stop, enabling John and Claire to put a little more distance between them.

One Indian managed to get through, and he galloped after them. This time John shot at the rider, rather than the horse and that bought them enough time to make it all the way through to the other end.

"Keep going!" John yelled. "I'm going to stop them here!"

John dismounted, then climbed up to the top of the opening. There, using his rifle as a lever, he managed to roll a rock loose, which had the effect of starting others down, until there was a rockslide of sufficient quantity to block up the entire pass.

Climbing back down he stayed just outside the blocked-up pass for a few minutes to make sure none of the Indians were able to get through, then satisfied that he had stopped them, he remounted and joined Claire, who was half a mile away.

By now their horses were panting hard.

"We need to dismount and walk them for a while," John said.

"Do we go back home, now?" Claire asked.

"Yes, but first we should go by the fort to tell

Major Clinton that we didn't have any luck with our peace mission."

"But you don't need me," Claire said. "I want to go home." She smiled. "I want to make a soup with vegetables from our garden."

"All right, you and Kirby go on home. I'll stop by the fort to see Major Clinton, then I'll come on home."

"Tonight?"

"Yes, tonight."

"I will have soup ready for you. It will be a very good soup."

"I've no doubt but that it will," John said. He leaned over toward her, and kissed her. "Going to Rendezvous and finding you, is the best thing I ever did in my entire life."

By now the horses had resumed their normal breathing.

"I think we can ride them now," he said. "You go on home, I'll be back as soon as I can."

"*Thechíhila,*" Claire said.

"*Thechíhila.*" John replied. Lakota for "I love you," it was one of the first Lakota phrases John learned.

Fort Shaw, Montana

"Well, I'm very sorry to hear that, Mr. Jackson," Major Clinton said. "I was rather hoping that we might be able to come to some kind of an accommodation with them."

"I'm sorry as well," John replied.

"You can use the same quarters tonight and start home tomorrow."

"No, my wife and child have already gone home. I promised I would be back tonight."

Major Clinton laughed. "Well, I can't say as I blame you. I do thank you for your effort, even if it wasn't successful."

Before he left, John went into the sutler's store, where he bought a straw hat with a wide brim for Claire to wear as she worked in the garden. He was sure she would like it. He also bought some chocolate, and a small toy horse for Kirby. Kirby was too young to be able to appreciate it now, but he was sure that he would within another few years.

He thought about his friend Smoke, and thought he would be pleased to know that there was someone named for him.

[*Fort Shaw was established June 30, 1867. It was located on the right bank of the Sun River, some twenty-five miles above its junction with the Missouri, and five miles above the point where the Fort Benton–Helena stagecoach road crossed the Sun River. Fort Shaw was established to protect the route between Fort Benton and Helena and to prevent the movement of hostile Indians into the settled area to the south. Four companies, under the command of Major William Clinton, 13th U.S. Infantry, selected the site. First called "Camp Reynolds," the post was*

*designated "Fort Shaw" on August 1, 1867, in
honor of Colonel Robert G. Shaw, 54th Massachusetts Infantry, killed before Fort Wagner in 1863.
Abandoned on July 21, 1891, the military reservation was transferred to the Interior Department on
April 30, 1892. The former post served as an Indian
school from 1892 until 1910.—ED.]*

Boulder

Smoke couldn't believe he had let Sally talk him
into coming to the Jordan car dealership.

"Yes, sir," the slick salesman said. "There she is,
the Jordan Playboy. The niftiest car on the road
today."

"What do you think, Smoke?" Sally asked. She
got into the car, sat behind the wheel, and flashed
a big smile.

"Why don't I just buy you a jar of perfume?"
Smoke proposed.

Sally laughed. "A *jar*? A *jar* of perfume? Honey,
do you think they put perfume up in jars, like a jar
of pickles?"

"I know it comes in little bitty bottles, but for
what this thing would cost, I could buy you ten jars
of perfume."

"I can see that I'm getting nowhere with you,"
she said. She got out of the car. "Okay, take me out
to dinner. And if you aren't going to buy me this
car, then I want to most expensive dinner in town."

"That, I will do," Smoke replied.

Boulder's newest, and quickly one of its finest, restaurants was Summer's Sunken Gardens, a European-style eatery. The focal point was a large pool-like fountain in the center of the dining area.

"Please don't tell Pearlie or Cal that we ate lamb," Smoke said as they began on the entrée, crown roast of lamb. "I'll never live it down."

"How are your sessions with Professor Armbruster going?"

"It's funny," Smoke said. "But talking to him like this, I mean bringing things out in great detail, not just a quick story here and there, it's as if I am actually reliving it."

"Are you all right with that?" Sally asked as she carved off a bit of lamb.

"Yes, I suppose I am. Some of it, I'm actually enjoying. But some of it has been hard, much harder than I would have thought."

"I know you talked about Nicole and Arthur, and I know how difficult that had to be for you."

"Yes, it was difficult. And, it was also difficult talking about Denise and Louis, especially Louis, since it hasn't been that long since he was killed."

"At least we have our grandchildren, Frank and Elyse," Sally said.

"How old are they now?"

"Frank is eleven, Elyse is nine."

"They're living with their mother and her new husband, and we never get to see them."

"The trains run in both directions," Sally said. "We could go back East to see them easier than they could come here. They do have school, after all."

"Yeah, we can, can't we? Sally, what do you say that after I'm finished with this business with Professor Armbruster, that we go see the grandkids?"

"Oh, Smoke, I think that would be wonderful!" she said. "Yes, let's please do it!"

"We will," Smoke promised.

CHAPTER TWENTY-FOUR

Old Main Building

"Do you need to listen to where we left off yesterday?" Professor Armbruster asked Smoke the next morning when he showed up at the Old Main building to continue with the narrative.

"No, that won't be necessary," Smoke said. "I know exactly where I left off, and I know where it's going next."

Smoke was silent for a long moment.

"Is something wrong?"

"The part that is coming up isn't going to be easy," Smoke said.

"Do you want to take a few moments to compose yourself before we begin?" Professor Armbruster asked.

"I've had all night to compose myself, Professor. A few more minutes won't make any difference."

"No, I suppose not."

"Tell Wes I'm ready."

Professor Armbruster reached down to click the toggle switch. "We're ready, Wes," he said.

Through the window Smoke saw Wes nod, then bring his hand down. Smoke resumed the story.

John's cabin

Whips His Horses held his hand up as a signal for the others to be quiet. He didn't have to say anything, though, because they were all good warriors, and they well knew the value of stealth. Then, they saw the woman come from the house with a basket. She walked into the garden and began picking vegetables.

Whips His Horses signaled to three who were armed with bows and arrows. All three fired, and Whips His Horses watched the rapid and graceful flight of the arrows. All three arrows struck the woman and she dropped the basket, took a couple of stumbling steps, then fell.

"Ayiee!" Whips His Horses shouted, hoping the shout would bring out the man who had killed his brother.

But no one came from the white man's house.

They waited for a few moments, then they heard a baby crying. The baby cried for several minutes without letup.

"I think the man is not here," one of the others said. "He would not let the baby cry for so long. He would come for the woman, but nobody has come for the woman."

"We will see," Whips His Horses said.

There were six others with him. Eight had started in pursuit of the man and his woman when they left the village, but two were killed in the pass. Then, the rocks fell, and it took a long time to move the rocks so they could continue. Now they were here, and Whips His Horses did not think the man they had followed was here.

He started toward the cabin, moving in a crouch, and on the balls of his feet, ready to run if need be.

But the man did not appear.

One of the other Indians in the party darted quickly up to the cabin, stood with his back to the wall near the door, then, cautiously, looked inside.

"Only the baby is here!" he called back to the others.

"Bring the baby out," Whips His Horses said.

The Indian by the door went into the cabin, then came out again, carrying the baby upside down, holding him by his foot. The baby was still crying.

"What shall we do with the baby?" the man holding it asked.

"Throw it on the ground by the woman."

With a huge smile, the Indian holding the child swung his arm back and forth a few times to get the momentum he needed, then he let the baby go. It flew through the air, then landed, hard, on the ground, next to its mother. There it lay quiet and still.

"Shall we burn the house?" one of the other Indians asked.

"Yes," Whips His Horses said, then he changed

his mind. "No. Leave the house as it is. When the man returns, I want him not to know what has happened until he sees the woman and the baby."

"Will we wait for him?"

"No," Whips His Horses said. "If we wait for him, we will kill him, but he will die only one time. When he sees his woman and his baby dead, he will die two times. Then, we will kill him a third time."

"Yes, he will die three times. That is very good," one of the other Indians said.

"Let us return to the village now. It will be good to let him find his dead woman and child and weep over them."

It was dark by the time John returned to his cabin. All the way home he had been thinking about the soup Claire had promised him, and he thought it would be very good, with the vegetables grown in his own garden. He even thought he might be able to smell it when he got close enough.

He smelled nothing and was disappointed. Then, when he got to the little clearing where he had built a home for himself, Claire, and the baby, he was surprised to see no light shining through the window. Instead the cabin sat there, gleaming silver under the full, bright moon.

Why could he see no light from within the house?

Then he thought of what a hard ride it had been

for Claire and the baby, and with a smile, he realized they must already be in bed.

That was all right. The soup could wait until tomorrow. He was tired too, and it would be good to climb into bed beside his wife. And if she wasn't too tired . . . he smiled at the implications of that.

He took his horse around to the lean-to attached to the back of the house, unsaddled him, then tied him to the hitching rail alongside Claire's horse. The watering trough had water, and he pitched some hay into the feeding trough, then he went inside.

"Claire, I'm home," he said, speaking just loudly enough for Claire to hear, but not to wake the baby.

"Claire?"

John went over to the baby's crib and felt down inside. The baby wasn't there, and he realized that he must be in bed with Claire. He lit a candle. If he was going to move the baby back to his crib, he didn't want to trip over something.

"Claire, I'm going to put the baby back . . ." He stopped in mid-sentence. There was nobody in the bed, and in fact, the bed was still made.

"What?" he asked aloud.

She couldn't have gone anywhere, her horse was still in the lean-to.

John stepped outside. "Claire?" he called. "Claire, are you out here?"

John heard something from the garden, low and guttural, like the sound of wolves, feeding.

"Get the hell out of my garden!" he shouted loudly, and, with yelps, the animals ran.

John started out to the garden to see what kind of damage the wolves might have done. That was when he saw the two bodies . . . one large, and one small. Or at least, what was left of the bodies.

"NO!!!!!" The agonizing cry of horror and despair rolled back from the walls of the little canyon. "God in heaven . . . no!!!"

John fell to his knees in the garden beside the bodies of his wife and baby, and wept aloud as he hadn't done so since he was a small boy.

Old Main Building

"Please, stop the recording," Smoke said.

Professor Armbruster waved at Wes, who stopped the session.

Smoke sat there for a long moment, his eyes closed as he pinched the bridge of his nose.

"Are you all right, Smoke?" Professor Armbruster asked.

"I need to walk around a bit if you don't mind," Smoke said.

"No, I don't mind at all. Go ahead, walk around the campus all you want. I'll be in my office when you are ready to resume recording. You do intend to continue, don't you?"

"I don't know," Smoke said. "This has become . . . difficult," he said. "Much more difficult than I ever imagined it could be."

"I understand."

Smoke forced a smile. "I'm glad you understand, because I'm not sure that I do. In the first place, this happened many years ago. And in the second place, I've told this story before without it affecting me as it is now."

"But the way you are telling it now is different," Professor Armbruster said. "You have never before been as powerfully absorbed in the story as you are now. This intense immersion has heightened your reaction to the events so that you are, in effect, re-living, rather than merely retelling the details. There is a psychological explanation for this. It is called 'cognitive context-dependent memory.' You see, you lost your own wife and child by an act of violence, much in the same way as John Jackson lost his. And now, in the retelling of this story you are, in effect, redoubling and experiencing again, your own trauma."

Smoke smiled, wanly. "Yeah," he said. "Something like that."

As Smoke walked around the campus he heard the sound of an engine from above, and looked up to see an airplane passing overhead. Across a landscape covered with fallen leaves, and under a tree he saw a group of college students. They were listening to music on the radio, and two young girls, wearing bobbed hair and short skirts, were doing some sort of dance that seemed to require a lot of kicking.

He couldn't help but think what drastic changes there had been within his lifetime, and as he looked at the students, he wondered how many of them could have stood up to the ordeal of a two-month-long wagon train trip, or a winter in the mountains with nothing but their own wits for survival.

But even as he contemplated such patronizing thoughts, he recalled the Great War so recently concluded, and he realized that despite the outside trappings, nothing had really changed. The principles of courage, honor, and self-reliance were still present, and he was satisfied that these young men and women would be able to rise to whatever challenges they might meet in the future.

He wished he could go into Longmont's Saloon for a beer, but knew that, even if he were back in Big Rock, that option wouldn't be open to him. He wondered if the country would ever come to its senses and repeal the idiotic amendment that was prohibition.

Finally, the melancholy he had been experiencing since the moment he told of John finding the half-eaten bodies of Claire and Kirby passed. He turned and started back toward the Old Main building, the fallen leaves crackling under his feet.

When he returned to the recording room, he saw a glass of amber liquid sitting by the microphone, and he smiled.

"Something tells me this isn't tea," he said.

"I thought you might need a little . . . what is it you men called it in the old days? Snort?"

"Snort, yes," Smoke said. He picked it up. "And, yes, I do need a drink right now."

He tossed the drink down, wiped his lips with the back of his hand, and nodded.

"I'm ready when you are," he said.

On the other side of the window, Wes brought his hand down, and Smoke resumed talking.

CHAPTER TWENTY-FIVE

Montana

John carried Claire and the baby back into the house and he laid them both on the bed. The same bed that he and Claire had shared, the same bed on which Kirby had been conceived. He covered their bodies with a bright red blanket, then he pulled a chair up beside the bed and sat there, staring at the covered mounds on the bed.

As John sat there, unbidden, episodes of his past flashed through his mind. He saw himself as an acolyte in his father's church, and as a student at the University of Pennsylvania. Terrible images of the war tumbled by, as well as his difficulty in adjusting when he came back. He recalled his rejection by Lucinda, and his experiences in Annam.

But nothing, nothing in his entire life, had ever hurt him to the degree he was hurting now. The pain was unbearable, and he wanted to scream until he had no voice left.

"God, why?" he asked aloud.

He remembered asking that same question to his father after he came back from the war, when he was having such a difficult time adjusting.

"Why, if He is a just God, would He allow such evil things to happen?" John had asked.

"God allows things to happen for His reasons, whether or not we understand them," John's father had answered. "Above all, however, we must remember that He is a good, just, loving, and merciful God. I know that things have happened to you that are beyond your understanding. But you must trust in the Lord, and put aside all doubts."

Nathaniel's short homily had done nothing to ease John's inner turmoil then, and recalling his words was doing nothing toward easing his pain now.

"Why, God! Why?" John shouted at the top of his voice. Then, in an angry snarl he added, "Never mind. I'll set things right on my own."

When the sun rose the next morning, John went out into the garden where he gathered every flower that had been planted. Bringing them in, he spread them on top of the bed until the bed was covered with colorful blooms and petals.

That done, John emptied a container of kerosene, then he set fire to the house. He stood out front watching the flames leap up around the logs that he and Claire had cut, shaped, notched, and put into position to build the house.

He could feel the heat of the flames, and even though it was uncomfortable, he made no effort to back away. He stood right there, until the cabin was completely consumed by the fire, so that there was not one recognizable thing about it remaining. He looked where he thought the bed might be, but could see nothing but blackened ash. He made no attempt to look closer.

Not until the last wisp of smoke had died, did he mount his horse and ride away. In less than twenty-four hours, his life had taken a turn that closed off his previous thirty-five years, as if none of it had ever happened. He was now a man consumed with hatred, and a determination to avenge his wife and child.

Old Main Building

Smoke stopped talking and Professor Armbruster waited for a moment, then he reached down to flip the toggle switch on the intercom box.

"Wes, this will be all for the day," he said.

"Yes, sir," Wes replied.

"Are you okay, Smoke?"

Smoke nodded. "Yeah, I'm fine. I guess it's just a little more of this *cognitive context-dependent memory* you were talking about earlier."

"Yes, it can be very intense. Look, why don't you take off early today. You and Sally take in some of the sights of the town."

* * *

When Smoke returned to the hotel room, Sally was sitting on the sofa, her legs curled up under her, reading *Babbitt,* a novel by Sinclair Lewis. She looked up in surprise when Smoke came in.

"Hello," she said. "You're back early."

"Yes," Smoke said without further explanation. "Enjoying the book?"

"To be honest? Not particularly. There's no plot to the story, it's almost like a diary . . . we're just following him around, but he isn't going anywhere."

"Then if I suggested we go somewhere, you wouldn't necessarily be against it?"

"Where do you want to go?"

"You'll know when we get there."

Fifteen minutes later, Smoke turned into the large lot of the Jordan automobile dealership.

"Smoke, what?"

"Didn't you say you wanted a sports car?"

"Yes, but . . ."

"But nothing. You're my wife, I love you, we can afford it. So what is there to argue?" Smoke said.

Parking the Duesenberg, Smoke and Sally went inside, then walked over to stand beside a bright, shining, red car.

"Pretty car, isn't it?" a salesman asked, coming over to them.

"Beautiful," Sally said.

"It has a 127-inch wheelbase, a finely louvered hood, low-slung beltline, and steeply sloped tail."

"Where is the top?" Smoke asked. "If it starts raining, do you just get wet?"

"Oh, no, it has a top. But the top is completely re-movable. That way, you don't have a bulky folded top to spoil the car's lines."

"Is it fast?" Smoke asked.

"Fast? Mister, this car has a flathead six cylinder engine of sixty-five horsepower. Why, on a straight, flat road, you could get her up to seventy miles per hour, easily."

"We'll take it."

"Smoke! Are you serious?"

"Very serious," Smoke said.

Half an hour later, with the Duesenberg parked at the hotel, Smoke and Sally drove their new sports car up to the top of Flagstaff Mountain. There, they sat in the open-top car and looked down onto the blazing lights of the city of Boulder.

"Why?" Sally asked.

"Why what?"

"You know what I'm asking. Why did you come home early, with the sudden urge to buy this car?"

"Didn't you want it?"

"I had already put it behind me as a foolish notion. No, you bought this car, and it had nothing to do with me. I just want to know why?"

"It was a pretty rough day today," Smoke said. "I talked about John finding Claire and his baby, killed, and half eaten by wolves." Smoke half laughed. "I thought maybe buying this car, and driving it, might help me put it out of my mind."

Sally reached over to put her hand on his.

"Smoke, why don't you tell Professor Armbruster you've had enough and we're going home?"

Smoke didn't answer.

"I mean really, you've spoken about losing your father, about Nicole and Art being killed. And now this? It's too much. Your life was hard enough, and dangerous enough, Smoke. You've reached the point to where you should be able to just relax, and drive like a fool if you want to."

"What? What do you mean, drive like a fool?" Smoke asked with a chuckle.

"I mean you drove like a fool. Do you think you drove cautiously coming up here?"

"The salesman said it would do seventy miles per hour," Smoke defended.

"Yes, but just because the salesman said this car would go seventy miles per hour, that doesn't mean you should drive that fast on a winding mountain road."

"I'll be more careful going back down," Smoke said.

"I should hope so."

A meteor streaked across the sky.

"Look," Smoke said. "When you see a meteor, you're supposed to kiss a pretty girl."

"So now we're going to drive back in town so you can kiss a pretty girl?" Sally teased.

"I don't have to go to town for that. Don't you

know, Sally, that when I look at you, I see the same beautiful young schoolteacher you were when I first met you?"

"I'm an old woman, Smoke," Sally said. She put her arms around his neck. "But I'm glad you still see me that way."

They kissed.

Residence of the President of the University

"How are your sessions with Mr. Jensen going?" Dr. Norlin asked.

Once again Armbruster had been invited for dinner with the president of the university, but this time the invitation omitted Smoke Jensen. The reason Smoke was left out of the invitation was so Dr. Norlin could speak frankly with Armbruster.

"It's, uh, going fairly well," Armbruster replied.

"Fairly well? That's certainly a measured response. What is wrong?"

"There's nothing actually wrong, it's just that . . . well, some of the stories are very intense, and as Smoke shares them, it is as if he is reliving the experiences. And not just of his own life. He just told the event that started John Jackson on his killing spree, his coming home and finding his wife and child out in the garden. They had been killed by the Crow and half consumed by wolves."

"Would you mind a suggestion from me?" Dr. Norlin asked.

"No, I wouldn't mind at all."

"Take the conversation in another direction for a while. Then come back to Jackson."

"Yes," Armbruster said. "I was thinking about doing that. Your suggestion just reinforces it."

Old Main Building

"Are you ready to go on?" Professor Armbruster asked the next morning.

"As ready as I'm going to be," Smoke replied.

"I have a few questions, if you don't mind."

"I don't mind at all. That's why I'm here."

"This business with the Crow Indians, that was two years after you and John Jackson separated, wasn't it?"

"Yes."

"Just so we can fill in the gap, I'd be interested in catching up on what you were doing during that time."

"Besides marrying Sally, you mean?"

"Well, that's significant, yes. But more specifically, I was wondering if you might tell about Fast Lennie Moore. I've only read one account of it, and to be truthful with you, I don't even know if it really happened, or not."

"It happened," Smoke said.

[*On May 25, 1871, Lennie Moore (whose real name may have been Will Bachman) was drinking heavily in Tucson, Arizona, with his friend Larry Wallace, and eight or nine other cowboys. Wallace insulted Moore's friend Deputy Marshal Billy Baker.*

Baker ignored Wallace, but Moore took offense and insisted that Wallace accompany him and apologize to Baker. When Wallace refused, Moore threatened to kill him. Wallace complied, but Moore afterward heaped abuse on Wallace, announcing, "You son of a bitch, I think I'll just kill you anyhow."

Moore had already demonstrated his speed and skill with a pistol, and Wallace wanted no fight with him, so he left the saloon. Moore followed him. Feeling threatened, Wallace turned and shot Moore, wounding him in the cheek and neck. Marshal Baker arrested Wallace but the court ruled he acted in self-defense.

A Tucson doctor treated Moore, who had not been seriously wounded. When Moore recovered, he called Wallace out and killed him. Later he killed Michael and Isaac Paterson, cousins of Wallace who had come for revenge. Moore's reputation began to grow after that, and it is believed that he had killed nine men before his fateful encounter with Smoke Jensen in the small town of Perdition, Arizona.—ED.]

CHAPTER TWENTY-SIX

Perdition, Arizona—1872

When Smoke Jensen had ridden into town a few
minutes earlier, news of his arrival spread quickly.
Even though he was still a young man, his fame had
spread, and grandfathers held up their grandsons
to point him out as he rode by, so that the young
ones could remember this moment, and, many
years from now, tell their grandchildren about it.

Smoke had earned this not-always-welcome noto-
riety, because of his prowess with a Colt. He was in
the Rattler's Cage Saloon now, and had just ordered a beer. Picking it up, he looked around the
interior of the saloon. Half a dozen tables, occupied by a dozen or so men filled the room, and tobacco smoke hovered in a noxious cloud just under
the ceiling. It was now twilight, and as daylight disappeared, flickering kerosene lanterns combined
with the smoke to make the room seem even hazier.

Smoke had come to Perdition because he had

heard that his sister, Janey, was here. He and his sister had never been close, not since she ran away from home during the war, leaving a young Smoke to try and run the farm, and deal with their dying mother, all by himself.

He had encountered Janey again, briefly, in the town of Bury, Colorado, just before his showdown with Richards, Potter, and Stratton. Then, he had sent her away. But, at Sally's urging, he decided to make at least one more effort to find her, and to see if he could patch up things between them.

It had been a false lead though. She wasn't here and she hadn't been here, so his trip to Perdition had been a waste of time. He sent a telegram back to Sally, telling her that his search had been fruitless, and he was coming back home.

"Would you be the one they call Smoke Jensen? The famous . . . gunfighter?" It wasn't a friendly question, or even a question of curiosity. In fact, it was less a question than it was a challenge.

In Smoke's young life, he had already encountered dozens of men like this: angry, belligerent, challenging. He said nothing in reply to the question, but simply held his beer glass out in sort of a salute.

"You too good to talk?" the challenger asked.

Smoke sighed. "Mister, I've ridden a long way on a wild-goose chase. I hope you aren't going to make any trouble."

"Make trouble? Make trouble, you say?" the young man replied. He turned to address the others. The saloon had grown deathly still now as the patrons sat quietly, nervously, and yet titillated too, by the life-and-death drama that had suddenly begun to unfold in front of them. "You don't want me to make any trouble for the great gunfighter, is that it? Do you think I should just shut up and be scared of you because I am in the presence of the great Smoke Jensen?"

Smoke put his beer down with a tired sigh and turned to face his tormentor.

"What's put the burr under your saddle, mister? Have I killed someone close to you? A brother, perhaps? Or maybe your father or just a friend?"

"No, it ain't that. It ain't nothin' like that, at all," the young man answered. "I'm just a-thinkin' that if I killed the great Smoke Jensen in a fair fight, why, folks would be sayin' my name the way they say yours now."

"And is that what you want?"

"Oh, yeah," the man said with a sardonic grin. "That's what I want."

"What is your name?"

"The name is Moore. Lennie Moore, though you've probably heard of me as Fast Lennie. That's what most folks call me."

"Fast Lennie, huh?"

"Yeah. Have you ever heard of me?"

"As a matter of fact, I have," Smoke replied.

Moore's smile broadened. "So, you've heard of me, have you? What have you heard?"

"I've heard that you are an ignorant young punk, trying to pass yourself off as a man."

Moore's smile quickly turned to an angry snarl. "Draw, Jensen!" he shouted, going for his own gun even before he issued the challenge.

Moore was quick, quicker than anyone else this town had ever seen, and quicker even than anyone Smoke had encountered for some time. But midway through his draw Moore realized that he wasn't quick enough. The arrogant look of confidence on his face was replaced by the knowledge that he knew he was about to be killed.

The two pistols discharged almost simultaneously, but Smoke had been able to bring his gun to bear whereas Moore had not. Smoke's bullet plunged into Moore's chest. The bullet from Moore's gun smashed the glass that held Smoke's drink, sending up a shower of beer and tiny shards of glass.

Looking down at himself, Moore put his hand over his wound, then pulled it away and examined the blood that had filled his palm. By the time he looked back at Smoke the fear had been replaced by acceptance, and a little expression of surprise.

"Damn," he said. "You're good. I would have bet my life that I could beat you." Moore tried to chuckle, though the chuckle ended with a cough. "I guess I just did that, didn't I?" Moore fell on his back, his right arm stretched out, his forefinger still sticking through the trigger guard.

Moore had been wearing a black hat, with a silver

band from which protruded a red feather. The hat was upside down on the floor behind him. The eye-burning, acrid smoke of two gunshots hung in a gray-blue cloud just below the ceiling.

Smoke turned back to the bar where all that was left of his drink were pieces of broken glass and a small puddle of beer.

"Damn, he spilled my beer," Smoke said.

"Yeah, it looks like he did," the bartender said. Grabbing a new mug, he opened the spigot of the beer barrel, and a golden liquid began climbing the sides of the glass.

The saloon had grown silent in the moments just before the gunfight, but since the gunfight it had become a buzz of excitement as everyone shared with each other what all had just seen. Smoke was only halfway through his drink when the sheriff and one of his deputies arrived.

"What happened here?" the sheriff asked.

The question wasn't directed to anyone in particular, so everyone started answering at once, availing themselves of the first opportunity to tell a story they would be telling for the rest of their lives.

"Hold it, hold it!" the sheriff said, holding up his hands. "Don't everyone talk at once." The sheriff looked over toward the bartender. "Abe, what happened here?"

"Moore tried to brace Jensen."

"Moore started the fight?"

"Oh, yeah, Moore started it," Abe replied.

"Abe's tellin' it true, Sheriff," one of the saloon

patrons said. "All this feller here done"—the patron pointed toward Smoke—"was try 'n have hisself a drink in peace. Next thing you know, why Moore there, is gnawin' at 'im."

The sheriff stroked his chin as he looked down at Moore's body. Death had made the young would-be gunman's face appear slack-jawed and distorted.

"Let me guess," the sheriff said. "Moore recognized Jensen, and was trying to make a name for himself, wasn't he?"

"That's exactly what it was," Abe said.

The sheriff walked back down the bar toward Smoke, who hadn't spoken a word since the sheriff and his deputy came in. He was calmly drinking his beer.

"Mr. Jensen, I thought you told me when you found out your sister wasn't here, that you would be goin' back up to Colorado."

"I am going back," Smoke said. "Train's leavin' tomorrow."

"Too bad it didn't leave an hour ago," the sheriff said.

"I would have been on it," Smoke said.

"And Moore would still be alive," the sheriff said.

"For now. But with his attitude, he was sure to get himself killed, sooner or later."

"I expect you might be right."

"I know I'm right."

"I reckon you've run across people like Moore before."

"More often than I want to," Smoke said. "Most

of the time it's all jaw. Not ever'one has the guts to actually make the try, like Mr. Moore did."

"And you say your train leaves tomorrow?"

"That's right."

"What are your plans now?"

"My plans are to go back home."

"No, I mean from now until your train leaves tomorrow."

"I thought I might have supper and get a good night's sleep," Smoke said. "Unless you need me to stay around for an inquest or something."

"No, no, that won't be needed. Uh, but it would be good for all of us, if you'd maybe have your supper and turn in early. You wouldn't want to sleep late and miss your train tomorrow, would you?"

Smoke chuckled. "No, I don't think I would want to do that."

A tall, very gaunt-looking man dressed in black tails and a high hat came in then. Two other men were with him.

"Hello, Gene. I see it didn't take you long to get here," the sheriff said. "Gene Ponder is our undertaker," he added, speaking to Smoke.

"Oh, my, I do believe that is young Mr. Moore, isn't it?" Ponder asked. "He has given me business before, but always before it was the other gentleman I would be carrying away."

"Get him out of here," the sheriff said.

Ponder nodded toward his two associates, and they picked the body up and carried him out.

Immediately after the body was moved, one of Abe's workers began cleaning up the blood.

"Mr. Jensen, I apologize for this," the sheriff said. "And I do hope nobody else gets the idea to come after you."

"Yes, I hope so as well."

Sugarloaf Ranch

Smoke and Sally were sitting in a porch swing watching the light show on the mountains as the sun dipped lower in the western sky.

"And this man, Moore, just challenged you for no reason?" Sally asked.

"Oh, he had a reason all right. He wanted to be known as the man who had killed Smoke Jensen."

Sally shivered. "That's no reason."

"It was to Moore, and it is for other men just like Moore."

"Smoke, will you ever be able to just hang up your guns and become a gentleman rancher?" Sally asked.

"Oh, I don't know. That's pretty hard."

"What's so hard about it?"

"The 'gentleman' part," Smoke said, teasingly.

"Oh, pooh, you know what I meant," Sally said with a little laugh, hitting him playfully on the shoulder.

"To answer your question, truthfully, I don't know," Smoke said. "It seems to me like my trail has already been blazed. I don't know as I have any choice but to follow it."

"But wouldn't you like to see Sugarloaf become a productive ranch?"

"It will become a productive ranch, Sally, I promise you that. The day will come when Sugarloaf will be one of the biggest and the best ranches in all of Colorado."

"But if someone is always trying to kill you?"

"I'll deal with it," Smoke said, confidently.

CHAPTER TWENTY-SEVEN

Old Main Building

After Smoke finished with his account of the encounter with Fast Lennie Moore, he, Professor Armbruster, and Wes went into the faculty lounge, where they had coffee and freshly made bear signs.

Over coffee, Smoke told them about the Jordan automobile he had bought for Sally, and Wes, particularly fascinated by it, asked him all sorts of questions, most of which Smoke couldn't answer.

"I'm not all that familiar with modern gadgets," Smoke said. "For example, I'm barely able to understand how a telephone works, let alone a radio, or even how, when I speak into the microphone, you can play my voice back to me. All I know is that the man who sold the car said it had a sixty-five horsepower engine. But I don't understand that either, because even if you hooked sixty-five horses to the machine, they wouldn't be able to run at seventy miles an hour. The car will run seventy miles an hour though. I know this, because I drove it that fast."

Professor Armbruster and Wes laughed.

"Well," Armbruster said as he put his cup down. "Are you ready to continue the account of John Jackson?"

"Yes," Smoke said.

The three men returned to the recording studio, and as soon as Wes was ready, he gave the sign to Professor Armbruster.

"What happened after John burned the cabin, in effect cremating his wife and child?"

"John went on the warpath," Smoke said. "That's what happened."

Montana—1872

John saw smoke drifting up through the trees ahead, and he heard the sound of Indians talking. He had no idea whether these were the same ones who raided his cabin or not, but he didn't care. They were Crow, and it had been Crow Indians who had killed Claire and Kirby. And in John's anger and hatred, all Crow were the same.

Pulling his pistol, he urged his horse into a gallop, heading straight for the campfire of the Indians. He didn't know how many were there, and he didn't care. He intended to kill as many of them as he could before he was killed, and the idea that he might be killed disturbed him not in the least.

With a loud and enraged scream, John burst into the clearing. There were three Indians sitting around a fire, cooking some kind of meat. They looked around at John in shock and fear.

John began shooting. He killed two of them instantly, but the third managed to get to his feet and start running.

John put his pistol away and took out a hatchet that hung from his belt. Easily overtaking the running Indian, John swung his ax, blade first. He split open the fleeing Indian's skull, and his brains began pouring from the wound, even before he fell.

John left him where he lay, and he returned to the campfire to make certain than the two he had shot were dead.

They were dead, and John dismounted and stared at their bodies, wondering what he could do to send a signal to the other Indians, to let them know that this was more than just a random killing.

Then he recalled something Claire had once told him.

"To the Crow, the liver is the most important part of the body," she had said. "Without it, they don't believe they can make it to the afterlife."

John carved open the stomach of one of the Indians, then he cut out his liver. He did the same with the other two. Then, he skewered the three livers on a stick, and put them over the fire to cook.

Once they were cooked, he took a small bite from each of the livers, then cut the rest of them up in small pieces and scattered them about to be consumed by animals and insects.

The Indians had been cooking a rabbit, and he ate what he could, then wrapped the rest of it up in a piece of cloth and took it with him.

Two days later he saw a couple of Crow Indians hunting, and he rode quickly to be able to put himself in position in front of them. He waited until they were almost on him, then he suddenly jumped out in front of them, shooting them both.

Again, he carved out their livers, and again, he roasted them over a fire, taking but one small bite from each of the livers before carving them to spread them around.

Fort Shaw

"He's doing what?" Major Clinton asked, shocked at the report that had been delivered by two old mountain men.

"He's killin' Injuns 'n he's eatin' their livers," Emerson said.

"Who is doing that?"

"Whoever it is that's doin' it," Seth replied. Seth was one of the two mountain men who had come to the fort.

"You don't know who it is that's supposed to be doing this?"

"There ain't no supposed to be doin' it about this. Whoever it is, is actual doin' it," Seth said.

"You're telling me that someone is killing Indians, and eating their livers," Clinton said.

"Yep, but not all Injuns. From what we're a-hearin', it's only the Crow that's gettin' their livers et," Seth said.

"Is it supposed to be a white man who is doing this?"

"That's what the Injuns is sayin'," Emerson said.

"Well now, that just doesn't make any sense at all," Major Clinton said.

"Well, yeah, it does when you stop and think about it," Emerson replied. "You see, most Injuns don't pay that much attention to such things. Oh, they figure if they take a scalp, well you'll be wanderin' around in the Happy Hunting Grounds without your hair. But now the Crow, they figure you can't even get there at all if you ain't got your liver."

"Where did you hear about this?"

"It's all over the mountains," Seth said. "All the other trappers, all the peaceful Injuns, is all a-talkin' about it."

"An' here's the thing, Major, this has got all the Injuns spooked. So far whoever it is, is only killin' the Crow," Emerson said. "But what if he is somebody who's suddenly got hisself a big taste for Injun liver? 'Cause I reckon when you get right down to it, one Injun liver probably tastes pretty much like any other Injun liver. So if this here Liver-Eatin' feller can't get him a Crow, why, more 'n likely he'd settle for just any Injun."

"Leastwise, that's more 'n likely what all the other Injuns is thinkin' right now, the good ones an' the bad ones," Seth said.

"But so far he has just been killing Crow, right?" Clinton asked.

"That's right," Emerson said.

"There must be a reason."

"I figure it's revenge," Seth said. "Whoever it is that's a-doin' this was more 'n likely done wrong by the Crow. And he's doin' this to get back at 'em."

"You men have your ear to the ground. Have you heard about anything that the Crow may have done to get someone angry enough to do this?"

"Hell, Major, the Crows is always a-doin' somethin'," Emerson said. "I ain't got enough fingers and toes to cipher up how many men I know that's got a bone to pick with the Crow. Includin' me, but I ain't the one that's a-doin' this."

"I ain't either," Seth said. "But I don't mind tellin' you that whoever is doin' it, I say, good for him."

"We need to find out who this is," Major Clinton said. "And when we find out, we need to put a stop to it."

"What fer?" Emerson asked. "The Crow is some damn evil Injuns. And I figure whoever it is that's a-doin' this, is doin' us all a favor."

"No," Major Clinton said. "Don't you see? Whoever is doing this could set off a full-scale Indian war."

"Yeah, I reckon he could at that."

"You must do what you can to find out who this is, so we can find him and put a stop to it," Clinton said.

In the village of Iron Bull

"It is a ghost," Running Bear said. "It is a ghost and he can stay alive only as long as he can eat the livers of the ones he has killed."

"We must kill him before he kills any more of us," Iron Bull said.

"You cannot kill a ghost," Running Bear insisted.

"And so, what would you have us do, Running Bear? Would you have us continue to give him the liver of Apsáalooke to eat?"

"We must do something," Brave Horse said. "Our women and our children are frightened, and they cower and weep in the lodges."

"There will be much honor to the one who kills Liver Eater," Iron Bull said.

"There will be much honor to the one who kills Liver Eater." The words of Iron Bull resonated in Two Leggings's mind as he searched for Liver Eater.

"Hear me, people of the Apsáalooke!" Iron Bull would say at the council fire. "We are here to speak aloud the name of Two Leggings! Songs will be sung and his name will be spoken in all the lodges because of his bravery!"

Two Leggings composed Iron Bull's speech as he waited on the trail for Liver Eater. He had seen Liver Eater earlier, coming toward the mountain. He would have to come along this trail on the only pass that would let him through. And when he did, Two Leggings would be waiting for him.

Two Leggings began to chant, quietly, the song of a warrior.

"As a warrior I must go bravely into those dark places within myself. I must learn the truth of my being. It takes much courage to do this, and I have the courage within."

Two Leggings knew that in order to have the greatest honor in the campfire circle, he must kill Liver Eater with his own hands, and not shoot him from afar. He could hear Liver Eater approaching, and he climbed onto a rock and waited.

John saw several birds fly from the trees just ahead of him. Something had spooked them and though he knew it could have been a mountain lion, or a wolf, or even a coyote, it put him on guard. If it was a coyote he would run when John approached. And, more than likely, even a mountain lion or a wolf would give him room, if there was no food source to contend.

But John felt a tingling in his skin, an awareness that was beyond that of any animal. He had seen nothing more than the sudden flight of birds, but he had a distinct impression that someone was waiting for him in the path ahead. And, just as strongly, he believed that it was only one person.

John loosened the pistol in his holster. Unlike his friend Smoke, John had never mastered the art of the quick draw. But even as he thought about that, he chuckled, because he realized that no one was

Smoke's equal in the speed with which he could draw his pistol.

John was an excellent shot with pistol and rifle, and for his purposes, that was enough.

As John was deep in contemplation he rode by a large rock. Suddenly, and without warning, an Indian leaped down from the rock, grabbing John and knocking him off his horse. The horse whinnied and moved ahead quickly, its steel-shod shoes clacking loudly on the rocky pathway.

John felt a sharp pain in his shoulder as he, and the Indian who had a tight hold on him, hit the ground. He reached for his pistol, hoping to be able to pull it and shoot the Indian at point-blank range, but the pistol was no longer in his holster.

John and the Indian rolled around on the ground, each trying to get the advantage of the other. The Indian was holding a war club, but John was holding on to him so securely that he couldn't free his arm to use it. But if the Indian couldn't use his war club, neither could John free his hand long enough to get to his Bowie knife.

The two rolled on the ground for a moment, then John was able to bend his knees and get his feet into the Indian's stomach. Because he was on his back, beneath the Indian, it gave him leverage and he straightened his legs, throwing the Indian away from him.

Quickly, John got to his feet and pulled his knife.

The Indian had regained his own feet almost as quickly, and now the two men were facing each other. John was in a crouch and armed with a knife, which he was holding low with the blade parallel to the ground; the Indian was more upright, and he was holding a war club.

They moved around each other in a rather macabre dance, the Indian making a few motions with the war club, while John merely moved his knife back and forth like the head of a coiled rattlesnake.

Suddenly the Indian, with the club raised over his head, rushed at John. John leaned to one side so that when the Indian brought the club down, he missed. John counterthrusted with his knife, and the blade penetrated the Indian's stomach all the way to the hilt.

John withdrew the blade then, and as the Indian clamped both his hands over the belly wound, John made a slicing motion, cutting the Indian's throat. The Indian collapsed, and died quickly. John removed the Indian's liver, threw it away, then remounted and rode on.

CHAPTER TWENTY-EIGHT

Irwin, Colorado—1872

Smoke had come for Preacher, issuing him a personal invitation to come visit him so he could see the new house he had built for Sally at the ranch he was calling Sugarloaf. They were at least a day's ride away from Sugarloaf, and so stopped for the night in Irwin.

"Here's your food, gentleman," one of the bar girls said a moment later, carrying the two plates to the table.

"Thanks," Smoke said. He handed the young woman a quarter.

"Thank you, sir," she said, smiling broadly.

"How's your new ranch comin' along?" Preacher asked.

"It's coming along real good," Smoke said. "I've hired me a few hands to help out around the place."

"You goin' to raise cattle or horses?"

"Well, I tried raising horses when I was married to Nicole. They can be plumb ornery critters, there's no getting around that. I may raise some horses, but most likely it'll be cattle."

"I expect that's the best way to go," Preacher said.

Preacher's buckskins were nearly black, his long white hair and beard were matted and, no doubt, Smoke thought, filled with critters, and there was a leatherlike patina to his skin that Smoke knew was an accumulation of dirt. For himself, Preacher's appearance wasn't a problem. Smoke had lived with him for a long time and he knew there were many times when he looked just like Preacher did now.

But, he was taking Preacher home with him to see Sally. And Sally, coming from the East, and not only from the East, but from a fine family, was used to being around people who paid a little more attention to their personal appearance. Smoke himself had developed a habit of good hygiene, at least when he could satisfy that habit. And he knew that he had to do something about Preacher's appearance before they reached Sugarloaf.

"Preacher, what do you say we get us a hotel room and take us a bath after we eat?"

"I had me a bath," Preacher said.

"What? Just when did you have a bath?"

"I don't know . . . three, maybe four months ago."

Smoke laughed. "Four months ago?"

"All right, maybe it was six months ago, what difference does it make? I mean, just how many baths does a feller need in one year, anyhow?"

"I tell you the truth, Preacher, your stink don't bother me none at all. But Sally can be just real particular about things like being clean 'n smelling good, and all that. And she'd probably like it better if you took a bath, and got cleaned up some before we get there."

"Hrummph," Preacher grunted. "If I had known you was goin' to turn into such a fancy Dan about bathin' 'n all, I woulda never took you in to raise."

"Yeah, you would've," Smoke said. "You liked havin' someone to train and boss around."

"Boss around? When did you ever do anything I asked you to do?"

Leaving the café, the two men went into the hotel and walked up to the counter.

"Yes, sir, can I help you gentlemen?"

"We'd like a couple of rooms. And a bath," Smoke said.

The clerk looked at Preacher with an obvious sense of displeasure in what he was seeing. "Both of you will be wanting a bath, I take it?"

Before Smoke could answer, Preacher spoke up. "Yeah, both of us will be wantin' to take a bath. What do you think, that we're some kind of heathens what don't never bathe?"

"Very good, sir. That will be three dollars. A

dollar apiece for the rooms, and half a dollar apiece for the baths."

Smoke lifted a small buckskin pouch to the counter, then poured out a pile of gold and silver coins. He moved the coins, many of them twenty-dollar gold pieces, around with his finger until he found three silver dollars.

"Here you are," he said.

Sitting in the lobby of the hotel was a man named Angus Flatt. When he saw the sack of gold coins emptied on the check-in desk, he took in a deep breath. There had to be several hundred dollars there.

He left the lobby, then hurried down to the Hog's Breath Saloon, where he found Moe James, playing solitaire.

"Hey, Moe, how much money you got?" Angus asked.

"I ain't got no money a-tall, so don't be askin' me to lend you any."

"I ain't askin' to borrow any money," Angus said. "What I'm askin' for is, I just seen me a way to make two or three hunnert dollars real easy. And I was wonderin' if you wanted in on it?"

"If it's all that easy, why are you offerin' me a chance at it?" Moe replied.

"On account of because it would be a lot easier for the two of us to do it. And I'm tellin' you, there's enough money we could divide up, 'n still have more money than either one of us have had for a whole year."

"Where is this easy money?"

"Some man come into the hotel a little while ago, and when he paid for it, why, you shoulda seen all the gold coins that poured out of his bag. I'll bet there's three or four, or maybe even five hunnert dollars there."

"So we're just goin' to ask him to give the money to us?"

"Yeah," Angus said, as a big smile spread across his face. "We're goin' to ask him while he's takin' hisself a bath."

The hotel had a bathing room, complete with a large bathtub as well as a water-holding tank and a small wood-burning stove by which to heat the water. Smoke started the fire, then went back to his room to wait for the water to heat. He walked over to the window and stood there, just looking out over the town, watching the commerce for a few minutes. Leaving the window, he lay down on his bed for about fifteen minutes, until he was sure that the water would be warm enough for a bath. Then, taking a change of clothes, a bar of soap, and a towel with him, he started down the hall toward the bathing room.

Just before Smoke opened the door, he stopped. He had the soap and the water was hot. There was no excuse Preacher could come up with for not taking a bath now, so he was going to let Preacher go first. He walked back down the hall, then knocked on Preacher's door. "Preacher?"

The door opened. "Yeah?"

"I've filled the tub with hot water for you. Here's your soap and towel."

"What'd you do that for?"

"Let's just say I respect my elders," Smoke said.

"Do you now?"

"And I respect them more when they're clean," Smoke added with a chuckle.

"All right, all right, you don't have to hit me on the head with it," Preacher grumbled. "Your woman wants me clean, so I'll clean up. But it ain't for you, you understand. It's for your woman."

"I understand," Smoke said with a smile.

Preacher reached down to pick up his Sharps .50 caliber.

"You need a rifle in the bathing room, do you?" Smoke teased.

"I don't go nowhere without I have this with me. You know that."

Smoke held up his hands. "Take it. You never can tell but what you might run into a grizzly in there."

"It wouldn't be the first time I seen a grizzly while I was bathin'," Preacher said.

Smoke chuckled. "Considering where you do your bathing—that is, when you do bathe—that's not particularly surprising."

* * *

Angus and Moe were in the lobby of the hotel.

"I seen him headed toward the bathing room just a couple of minutes ago," Angus said. "By now he's prob'ly in the tub, and, more 'n likely, he took his money in there with 'im."

"How do you know he took his money with 'im?"

"You don't think he'd just leave it in his room, do you?"

"No, more 'n likely he wouldn't."

"That's why, it won't be nothin' to take it from 'im."

"You know he ain't goin' to just be quiet about it," Moe said.

"They's two of us, only one of him. He'll be nekkid in the tub. All we got to do is hold his head under water till he stops movin'. Folks don't make a lot of noise while they're drownin'. And once he's drowned, why we'll get his money and slip out just real quiet-like."

Angus and Moe looked over toward the check-in clerk, and when they saw him step away and walk into a room just behind the desk, they moved quickly to the steps and hurried up to the second floor.

The bathing room was at the back end of the corridor and Angus and Moe walked quickly down the carpeted hallway until they reached the door. They stood there for just a moment, listening.

"Yeah, he's in the tub, all right. I can hear the splashin'," Angus said. "Let's go in."

Angus tried the doorknob, found that it wasn't locked, then pushed it open and stepped inside.

"This ain't the one," Angus said when he saw the old, white-haired and white-bearded man sitting in the tub.

Smoke stepped out of his room just in time to see two men going toward the bathing room. He didn't know who they were, or what they wanted, but he was absolutely certain that Preacher wouldn't welcome their presence. And, because it was hard enough to get Preacher to take a bath anyway, he figured he had better see what's going on.

Smoke started toward them, and saw them open the door then step inside. He figured he would hear Preacher's bellow any moment now. And he wasn't disappointed.

"Get the hell out of here! Can't you see that I'm takin' a bath?" The words were loud and angry.

The two men who had stepped into the bathing room had their pistols in their hands, pointing them at Preacher.

"Where's the young one? The one with the gold?" one of the two men asked.

"That would be me," Smoke said from behind them.

Spinning around, they saw Smoke. They also saw that he wasn't wearing a gun.

One of the two men smiled. "Well now, Angus, look at this. Looks like these two men have got their selves into a situation. One of 'em is nekkid, 'n the other 'n ain't got hisself a gun."

"Tell you what, Moe. You go with this feller to get the money. I'll stay here and keep a gun on the old man," Angus said. "If you ain't back with the money in one minute, I'll shoot the old man."

"Yeah," Moe said. "Good . . ."

Whatever Moe was about to say was cut short by Preacher. While Angus's and Moe's backs were turned, Preacher had picked his rifle up from the floor, stood up quietly, then drove the butt of the rifle into Moe's back, between his shoulder blades.

The commotion distracted Angus and when he looked toward Moe, that gave Smoke all the opening he needed. He brought down the would-be thief with a hammerlike right cross.

"What do we do with 'em now?" Preacher asked.

Smoke took the pistols away from the two men and handed them to Preacher.

"When they come to, keep them covered until I get back. I'm going to get the marshal."

Sugarloaf Ranch

Unlike the cabin he had personally built for Nicole, Sally had wanted a house, and Smoke bought the material and hired two carpenters to build it for him. The main house, or "big house" as the cowboys called it, was a rather large, two-story Victorian edifice, white, with red shutters and a gray-painted porch that ran across the front and wrapped around to one side. The bunkhouse, which was also white with red shutters, sat halfway between the big house and the barn. The house was so new that it still had the smell of fresh-cut wood about it, though for the moment, the most predominate aroma was that of Sally's cooking.

"My, Preacher, I don't believe I have ever seen you looking so handsome," Sally said, greeting the two when they arrived.

"Hrrmph," Preacher said. "It ain't natural being all spiffed up like this."

"Oh, pooh," Sally said, kissing him on the cheek.

"'Course now, if I'm goin' to get a kiss from a pretty woman, and get fed to boot, why, it's worth gettin' unnatural ever' now 'n then," Preacher said. "Could that be apple pie I'm smellin'?"

"It could be," Sally said.

"I don't rightly recollect the last time I had me an apple pie. I hope you made one for you 'n Smoke too. I'd sure hate to be eatin' in front of you without you two didn't have no pie of your own."

Sally laughed. "Don't worry, I made more than one. How long will you be staying with us?"

"I don't know. Three, maybe four days. But if that's too long, why you can kick me out anytime you want . . . after the pie is all gone."

CHAPTER TWENTY-NINE

Arrow Creek, Montana

Whips His Horses gave the reins of his pony to another man, then he climbed to the top of the hill. He knew the warrior's secret of lying down behind the crest of the hill so that he couldn't be seen against the skyline, so he lay on his stomach, then sneaked up to the top and peered over. There, on the valley floor below him, he saw the three wagons. It was obvious that the whites had no idea they were in danger. It would be easy to count coups against them.

Whips His Horses smiled, then slithered back down the hill into the ravine where the others were waiting.

"Did you see them?"

"Yes," Whips His Horses answered.

"When do we attack?"

"Now," Whips His Horses replied. He pointed down the ravine. "We will follow the ravine around the side of the hill. That way they will not see us until it is too late."

For the moment the three wagons were stopped, because one of them had a broken front wheel. A long pole had been put under the front part of the wagon. Using a rock as the pivot, two men were using the pole as a lever to hold the wagon up. A third man had crawled under the wagon with a jack and, as soon as the wagon was high enough, he was going to put the jack in place.

"Can you get it, Dan?" James asked. His voice was strained because he and Steven were struggling at the end of the long pole.

"Just a little more," Dan said from beneath the wagon. He was in some danger at this point, because if James or Steven lost his grip, or if the pole should slip, the wagon would fall on him.

Straining hard, the two men lifted the wagon another couple of inches.

"There!" Dan called. "I think I can get it now."

"All right, slide out from under there so we can lower this thing down," James said, and his voice almost cracked under the strain.

Dan rolled over, then crawled out and, with a mighty sigh of relief, James and Steven set the wagon down on the rock.

"Whew," James said, wiping the sweat from his forehead. "I'm glad that part is over."

"You and me both," Steven said.

Dan started to remove the broken wheel. "I

appreciate you two holding up your wagons for us, it was . . ."

"Hush up! Listen," James said, interrupting Dan in mid-sentence.

"What is it?" Steven asked. "I didn't hear anything."

"Listen," James said again.

Not only the three men working on the wagon were quiet but, at the warning, so were the women and children. For a long moment there was only the sound of the ever-present prairie wind moaning its mournful wail. Then, they all heard what James had heard, the distant thunder of pounding hooves.

"Get the women and children behind the wagon," James said. "We've got company comin', and I don't think it's anyone we want."

The battle was short and violent. Whips His Horses had twenty warriors with him, which was more than the total number of people—men, women, and children—with the three wagons. Within a short time after the initial attack, the wagons were in flames and the men and women were falling, mortally wounded. The Indians galloped, whooping and shouting, through the remains of the wagon train.

Whips His Horses leaped over the rocks, and in and out of the gully, shouting with joy as he pursued the fight. The men, and even the women of the wagon train, fired at him, but it was as if he were impervious to their bullets. He leaped upon a burning wagon and looked at his handiwork, chortling in glee as the last white defender was put to the lance. Now that all the men, women, and children of the wagon train were dead, he and his warriors cut the livers from the body of everyone they killed.

Dog Runner, a Blackfoot Indian, was in the camp of Iron Bull when Whips His Horses and the raiding party returned from their attack on the wagon train. The raiders were excited by what they had done, and they began to dance around the council fire.

"Hear me!" Whips His Horses shouted. "Hear the victory song that I sing!"

The others of the village gathered around as Whips His Horses, dancing, and brandishing a war club began to sing.

> *"The white man who came for peace*
> *Now eats our livers.*
> *For every liver of the Apsáalooke he eats*
> *Our anger will grow."*

As Whips His Horses sang his song the others of the raiding party, who were dancing with him, suddenly pulled from pouches, the bloody livers of the white men, women, and children they had killed.

Waving the livers long enough for all to see, they threw them into the fire.

> *"With each white that we kill*
> *We will kill Liver Eater.*
> *We will kill many whites.*
> *Liver Eater will die many deaths."*

The singing, dancing, and celebration lasted far into the night. When Dog Runner left the next morning, many were still asleep. The campfire had burned down and was now only glowing embers, but the smell of the cooked human livers permeated the camp.

Dog Runner mounted his horse and rode away slowly. Not until he was far away did he urge his horse into a gallop. He rode hard all the way to Fort Shaw.

Fort Shaw

Dog Runner was held up at the gate.

"Where are you going, Injun?" the guard asked.

"Philbin," Dog Runner said. "Philbin." He then began talking rapidly in his own language.

"Corporal?" the gate guard shouted. "This Injun is talkin' about somethin', but I don't have no idea what it is he's a-talkin' about."

The corporal came over to the front gate.

"Philbin!" Dog Runner said, again following it with a long, excited stream in his own language.

"Philbin? Lieutenant Philbin?"

"Han, han!" Dog Runner said, at the same time shaking his head yes.

"Keep him here, McMurtry. I'll go get the lieutenant."

Dog Runner paced back and forth for a few minutes until Lieutenant Philbin arrived. Philbin was chief of the Indian scouts, and could speak to Dog Runner in his own language.

"Dog Runner," Philbin said, smiling with his hand up, palm out. "It is good to see you."

"It is not good," Dog Runner said. "The Crow have attacked wagons and killed many white people."

"What? Where? When?"

"Today," Dog Runner said. "I will take you."

An hour later Lieutenant Philbin and ten soldiers arrived at the scene of the massacre. They found five men, four women, and nine children lying in a pool of blood where they had fallen.

"Lieutenant, this don't make no sense," Sergeant Dawes said. "I mean, there ain't a one of 'em been scalped, nor cut up in any other way. But all of 'em's got their stomach cut open, even the kids."

"Yes," Philbin said. "I'll admit, that is quite odd."

Later that evening, with all the bodies returned to Fort Shaw, Major Clinton asked his post surgeon, Dr. Urban, to examine the bodies, to see if there was any pattern to all of them being cut open in such a way.

It was the next morning before Dr. Urban got back to Major Clinton.

"What did you find out?" Major Clinton asked.

Urban shook his head. "It's the damndest thing I believe I've ever seen," he said.

"What is?"

"The liver has been removed from every one of the bodies."

"What? From every one of them? Even the children?"

"Yes, sir."

"Well, that doesn't make sense," Major Clinton said. "Why would the Indians cut out their livers?"

"Major, I don't have the slightest idea. All I know is, the livers have been cut from all of them."

"Sergeant Major Porter?" Major Clinton called.

"Yes, sir?"

"Find Lieutenant Philbin and that Indian that told us where to find the bodies. Bring them to me."

"Yes, sir," Sergeant Major Porter replied.

Less than ten minutes later, Lieutenant Philbin and Dog Runner were in Major Clinton's office.

"Yes, sir?" Philbin asked.

"Lieutenant, the livers have been removed from every single body."

"Yes, sir," Philbin said.

"'Yes, sir'? You mean you knew that?"

"Yes, sir. Well, Dog Runner couldn't come up with the word in English, and I don't know the word in his language, but we finally managed to put it together enough that I understood what he was saying. I was just about to come see you, when Sergeant Major Porter found me, and asked me to come over."

Major Clinton shook his head. "Would you mind telling me why in the Sam Hill would the Indians be cutting out livers?"

"Because John Jackson is carving out the Indian livers and eating them," Philbin said, easily.

"What? Why, that is insane! Are you sure it's John Jackson?" Major Clinton asked, refusing to believe what his chief of scouts said.

"Yes, sir, I've talked with several of my scouts and they all say the same thing. It's out in every village in the territory. All the Indians call him Liver Eater, because after he kills an Indian, he cuts out, and eats, their livers."

"No, surely there is some mistake. They must be thinking of someone else," Major Clinton said. "I met the man, I was quite impressed with him. He is well educated, well spoken. And a finer gentleman I have never met. I can't imagine someone like John Jackson killing Indians and eating their livers. Why do you suppose he suddenly went on a killing binge like that?"

"It's because of his wife," Lieutenant Philbin said.

"What do you mean? I met her as well. She's

Indian, yes, but she isn't Crow. And her manners are such that I expect she would be welcome in just about any level of society, back East. Why would she want her husband to go on such an inhuman killing spree?"

"I didn't say she wanted it, Major. You said why would he do such a thing, and I said it's because of his wife. And his child. You see, the Crow killed them both."

"When?"

"As I understand it, they were killed shortly after Jackson and his wife visited Iron Bull's camp to talk peace with the Indians."

"After he visited their camp?"

"Yes, sir. Jackson delivered your message to Iron Bull, who granted them a pass only as long as it took them to get out of camp. Once they left the camp, Iron Bull sent Indians after them. According to Dog Runner, Jackson killed one of them in the chase.

"Then, Jackson came here to report to you, that he had failed. And while he was here, talking to you, Whips His Horses went to Jackson's cabin. There, he killed Jackson's wife and child."

"My God!" Major Clinton said with a gasp. "My God, that means I'm to be blamed! I'm not only to be blamed for Jackson's wife and child being killed, I'm also to be blamed for the attack on the wagons."

"Why would you say that, Major?"

"Because I am the one who sent them there!"

"I don't think there is anyone who actually blames you, Major."

"I don't care whether anyone else blames me or not," Major Clinton said. "I blame myself . . . not only for what he is doing now . . . but for what happened to precipitate this."

CHAPTER THIRTY

[*Warrior societies were an important aspect of the life of the Plains Indians. The tribes' fighting men were divided into distinct units which provided their members with prestige. They fell under two categories, graded and ungraded, and though the warrior societies of the Apsáalooke (Crow) were, theoretically, ungraded, there was, by recognition, a definite graduation among the three societies of the tribe. Those three societies were the Lumpwood, the Fox, and the Big Dog. There was a fierce rivalry between them and, in battle, each society strove to strike the first coup.*

There were, in addition, ranks within the individual societies which, while they conferred great honor, also demanded a personal sacrifice or commitment from the warrior upon whom the rank had been bestowed.

The Big Dog Warrior Society gradually emerged as the most prestigious. Members of this society would wear a belt of bearskin, complete with claws. They also daubed their bodies with mud, and rolled their hair into tight balls, imitating bear's ears. They made a commitment to walk upright straight toward the enemy, never to retreat, and to come to the aid of any tribesman in danger.—ED.]

In the village of Iron Bull

Stone Eagle wore two vertical stripes on his right cheek, one red and one black. The stripes ran from the bottom of his eye to the top of his lip, and they denoted his rank as chief of the warrior society known as the Big Dog Warrior Society. He had asked for a meeting of the council and now all were gathered before the council fire.

Stone Eagle pointed to Whips His Horses, and spoke derisively of him.

"Whips His Horses boasts of his feats," Stone Eagle said. "But what has he done? He has killed women and children. He has killed men who are not warriors. He has done this while Liver Eater continues to go free, to kill our braves."

"And what have you done?" Whips His Horses replied, angrily. "You have done nothing!"

"Liver Eater is but one man. I have thought, until now, that one brave warrior would be his equal, but ten have tried, and ten have died. And you," Stone Eagle said, pointing to Whips His Horses, "you have not even tried. You are afraid to fight Liver Eater, so you fight those who cannot fight back."

"Whips His Horses has asked a question that must be answered," Iron Bull said. "What have you done?"

"I have done nothing," Stone Eagle admitted. "But now I am ready to lead the Big Dog Warriors to find and kill this man who has killed so many of our own."

"How many will you take?" Iron Bull asked.

"He has killed ten. We will be two for every one that he has killed. We will be twenty."

"I will be one of the twenty," Whips His Horses said.

"You are not a member of the Big Dog Society," Stone Eagle replied.

"Then I will be a member."

"If you become a member, you must follow me. Do you agree to that?"

"I will also be a leader," Whips His Horses said. He pointed to his chest. "I am chief of the Fox Society."

"To be a Big Dog Warrior you must leave the Fox and become a Big Dog. You can be a member, but you will not be a leader," Stone Eagle insisted.

"I ask the council!" Whips His Horses said. "Hear me. I am chief of the Fox Warrior Society. Is it not fair that if I join the Big Dog Warrior Society that I shall be a chief, equal in authority to Stone Eagle?"

The members of the council discussed it among themselves, then Iron Bull spoke.

"Stone Eagle, would you agree to a test with

Whips His Horses to determine if he should be a chief?"

"Yes, I will agree to a test," Stone Eagle replied.

"Whips His Horses, will you agree to a test?" Iron Bull asked.

Whips His Horses looked at Stone Eagle with an expression of hatred on his face.

"If we are to test, then let it be a final test. Let us fight until the death," Whips His Horses said.

"Stone Eagle, you have been challenged," Iron Bull said. "You cannot deny the challenge and remain chief of the Big Dog Warrior Society. What is your answer?"

"I accept the challenge," Stone Eagle said.

Iron Bull held up both his arms and called out loudly so that all in the village could hear what he had to say.

"Hear me!" he called. "A challenge has been issued, and accepted. Whips His Horses and Stone Eagle are to fight. The fight must be until the death of one. The winner of the fight will be chief of the Big Dog Warrior Society."

A circle was drawn and the two warriors entered the circle, each armed with a knife. Facing each other warily, they held their arms crossed in front of them, the palm of their left hand open, while grasping the knife in their right hand. They moved around in the circle, first one, and then the other, leaning forward to make, mostly futile, downward stabbing motions with the knife.

On one of his thrusts, Whips His Horses made a slashing cut on Stone Eagle's arm. It wasn't a deep cut, but it did bring blood. A moment later Stone Eagle opened a cut on Whips His Horses' shoulder and now both men were bloodied as they faced each other.

Whips His Horses made another thrust but Stone Eagle stepped aside, then stuck out his foot, tripping Whips His Horses. Whips His Horses fell facedown and dropped his knife. Stone Eagle reached down and grabbed it, quickly, before Whips His Horses could recover. Now, with both knives, he reached down and laid the flat of the blade on the back of Whips His Horses' neck.

"I claim coup," he shouted, and turning his back to Whips His Horses' prone form, he held both his arms up over his head, his knife in one hand and Whips His Horses' knife in the other. "I have won!" he claimed, triumphantly.

Whips His Horses got to his feet quickly, then reaching out of the circle, grabbed a lance from one of the warriors who had been watching. With a shout of triumph, he rushed across the circle and thrust the lance into Stone Eagle's back, doing so with such force that the bloody point came through Stone Eagle's stomach.

Stone Eagle looked down in surprise, grabbed the lance point, then fell dead.

"Ayiee! It is I who have won!" Whips His Horses shouted.

There was some discussion among the elders of the council, but it was pointed out that the requirement was a fight to the death. And it was obvious that Whips His Horses had met that requirement. He was now the new head of the Big Dog Warrior Society.

"Will you now do as Stone Eagle would have done?" Iron Bull asked. "Will you take twenty warriors to kill Liver Eater?"

"I will do this," Whips His Horses said.

"Send runners to all the villages," Iron Bull declared. "Let the word go out to the Gros Ventre, the Piegan, the Lakota, and the Blackfeet, that twenty Big Dog Warriors of the Apsáalooke village of Iron Bull will avenge the death of our brothers!"

Fort Shaw

"What would you have me do about it?" Major Clinton asked the two civilian representatives from Helena. "Wage a full-scale war?"

"But don't you understand? The Indians attacked three wagons of whites. That is already an act of war," Babcock, one of the two civilians, said.

"From all that I've been able to learn, it was no more than a few renegade Indians," Major Clinton said. "It wasn't a full-blown war party. I have four companies of infantry here. And I stress that we are infantry, not cavalry. We are not a mobile force. I can detach one company of infantry and assign them to protect the town of Helena, but I don't really think the town of Helena is in any danger. Do you?"

"I don't know," Babcock said. "Is it true that what has gotten them all riled up is some crazy mountain man who has turned cannibal? He's actually eating the bodies?"

"From what I've heard, he's only eating their livers," Major Clinton said.

"Then I think if you can do nothing about the Indians, you should do something about this crazy mountain man," Jones said. Jones was the other civilian from Helena.

"Do something about the mountain man?" Major Clinton replied. "Do what? What are you suggesting?"

"I'm suggesting that you find him and kill him," Jones said.

"Definitely not!" Major Clinton said. "I'm appalled that you would even suggest such a thing!"

"It seems like a pretty good bargain to me," Jones said. "One crazy white cannibal against the lives of how many more whites will the Indians kill?"

"I'm going to ask you two men to leave this post, now," Major Clinton said, angrily.

"You've got no right to order us off this post," Babcock insisted. "We have come to seek army protection."

"You have two choices," Major Clinton said. "You can leave of your own volition, or I will have you escorted off this post under armed guard."

"All right, all right, we're going," Babcock said.

"But I intend to write a letter to the War Department protesting your refusal to protect us."

"Sergeant Major?" Major Clinton called.

"Yes, sir?" Sergeant Major Porter replied, stepping into Major Clinton's office.

"See that these"—Major Clinton paused, setting the next word apart from the sentence to show his disdain—"gentlemen . . . are shown safely off this post."

"Yes, sir," Sergeant Major Porter said. "This way, gentlemen."

Major Clinton walked to the front of the headquarters building and stood in the doorway as he watched the two civilians cross the quadrangle toward the gate. Lieutenant Philbin approached him with a salute.

"Do you know what those two men wanted?" Major Clinton asked.

"No, sir, not exactly. I know they were concerned about the people who were killed at their wagons."

"They wanted me to send the army out to kill Mr. Jackson. The very idea."

"Yes, sir, well, it might all be beyond our hands anyway," Lieutenant Philbin said.

"Why? What do you mean?"

"My Indians tell me that Iron Bull is sending twenty of his Big Dog Warriors out to find and kill Jackson."

"Do you think we should warn Jackson?"

Philbin chuckled. "In the first place, I'm damn sure Jackson already knows that he is the enemy of the Crow right now. In fact, I'm pretty sure he welcomes it. Major, he brought this war on himself, you know."

"No, he didn't," Major Clinton said. "I did, when I sent him and his wife to meet with Iron Bull."

"If he had just killed the ones who killed his wife and child, that would have been the end of it," Philbin said. "But he didn't stop there. He has made a personal war on all the Crow. And, don't forget, he is eating their livers. That is a slap in the face of every Crow alive."

"We don't know that he is actually eating their livers."

"It doesn't matter whether he is or not, now," Philbin said. "The Crow believe that he is, and that's enough."

CHAPTER THIRTY-ONE

[*One of the mysteries of the last century is how quickly information could spread from place to place. In a time before telephones were commonplace, before radio, and even when newspapers were few and far between, there was something referred to as the "underground telegraph." John Jackson's activities were limited to Montana, but word of his unique and very personal battle with the Indians spread quickly, from Montana through Wyoming, into Colorado, Utah, Nevada, California, and even down into Arizona, New Mexico, and Texas.—ED.*]

Buford, Colorado

The Pair of Tens Saloon in Buford, Colorado Territory, was already filled with customers, even though it was no later than three o'clock in the afternoon. A clean-shaven man whose eyes were enlarged by the thick lenses of the glasses he wore, was plinking away on a piano in the corner of the room while a glass of warm beer, its head gone, sat beside him. Two cowboys who were standing at the bar, were engaged in a vociferous discussion.

"They say the reason the Injuns attacked and kilt them folks in the wagons, is 'cause this feller, whoever it is, is a-killin' Injuns, then he's carvin' out their gizzards and eatin' 'em."

He put an exclamation mark to his statement by spitting out a large quid of tobacco into a nearby spittoon, making it ring with the impact. A soiled dove, whose profession had already caused dissipation beyond her years, had stopped making her rounds of the tables, just to listen in on the discussion the two cowboys were having.

"You don't mean he's actual eatin' human beings, do you, Pete?" she asked.

"Well now, I reckon that all depends on whether or not you call Crow Injuns human bein's. They's some that say that Crow ain't nothin' but heathens, through 'n through, 'n the words 'human bein'' don't quite fit with them. You take Ned, here. He don't hold much truck for Crow, do you, Ned?"

"I don't want nothin' to do with no Crows," Ned said. "Are you sayin' Crows is the only ones this here fella is killin' an' eatin'?"

Before the first cowboy could answer the question, two men slapped the batwings open, stepped into the saloon, and crossed over to the bar. Everyone in the place paused and stared at the pair as they made their way across the room. They looked

like before and after pictures of what life in the
mountains would do to anyone crazy enough, or
antisocial enough, to endure it. The older of the
two had fought in the Battle of New Orleans as a
fourteen-year-old boy. That was close to sixty years
ago, and he showed the effects of strenuous living
for all that time. The younger of the two was a boy
during the Civil War, which had been over now for
seven years. They were both dressed in buckskins;
the old one had a full beard and long hair that
hung down almost to his shoulders, the beard and
hair white as snow. The younger of the two was
clean shaven, with neatly trimmed hair.

Mountain men weren't all that rare in this part
of the Colorado Territory, but these two men did
capture the attention of all who were in the saloon.
They were both armed, as if they were about to go
to war. The older of the two was carrying a Sharps
Big Fifty cradled in his arms, and a Navy Colt .36,
not in a holster, but stuck down in his belt. The
younger of the two had a Colt .44 tied low on his
thigh in a right-hand rig. A matching Colt was butt-
forward in a high holster on his left hip, and a
twelve-inch-long Bowie knife rested in a scabbard in
the middle of his back. He was also carrying a rifle,
in this case a Henry repeating rifle.

When the older man sat his rifle down and they
both leaned on the bar, all the rest of the saloon
customers went back to what they'd been doing, ig-
noring the two newcomers.

"Seems to me like you two fellas stopped by here

not much more 'n a week or so ago, didn't you?" the bartender said as he slid down to wait on them. "You're Preacher, and you're the one they call Smoke."

"You got a good memory, pilgrim," Preacher said.

"Yeah, maybe, but it ain't good enough for me to 'member just exactly what it was you two fellers are likin' to drink."

"We'll both have beer," Smoke said.

"Two beers comin' up."

The two cowboys, after no more than a cursory glance at the two mountain men, resumed their conversation.

"They say the feller doin' all the killin' and the gizzard eatin' is doin' it 'cause the Injuns kilt his wife 'n kid," Pete said, continuing to impart the information as he had heard it.

"But they don't nobody know his name?" Ned asked.

"Nope. Don't nobody know nothin' a-tall about him. Onliest thing is, they say he's one of them mountain men. Up in Montana, he is."

"Hey, let's ask them two," Ned suggested. "They look like they're mountain men. Leastwise, the older feller looks like that."

"I wouldn't be gettin' them two men riled up if I was you," the bartender said. "Don't you boys know who they are?"

"Nope, ain't never seen neither one of 'em," Pete said. "They ever been in here before?"

"Oh, yeah, they been in here before. They stopped in here a week or so ago on their way to Big Rock. The young one has him a ranch there. The other 'n is pure mountain man, lives in the High Lonesome all by his ownself."

"That means you know them then, so who are they?" Pete asked.

"Well, sir, the young one there is Smoke Jensen," the bartender said.

"Smoke Jensen? Wait a minute! Are you talkin' about the gunfighter Smoke Jensen? The one that kilt Fast Lennie Moore a month or so back?" Pete asked.

"Yeah, that's who I'm talkin' about."

"Fast Lennie was supposed to be the fastest there was, couldn't nobody hold a candle to him, they said. But from what I heard, Fast Lennie started his draw first, and Smoke still beat him."

"That's true," the bartender said.

"But you just said he has a ranch near Big Rock," Ned said.

"That he does."

"What do you reckon he's doin' runnin' around with that old man?"

"You don't know who that old man is?"

"Can't say as I do."

"Well, I don't know his name. His real name, I mean. Long as I've known about 'im, I ain't never heard him called nothin' but Preacher."

"Preacher? Wait, are you talkin' about the old mountain man that's been here for, what? Forty, fifty years?" Pete asked.

"That's him."

"I'll be damn. I thought he was dead."

"Yeah, there's been two or three times I've heard he was dead too, but he's like a cat with nine lives or something. He always seems to show up again, to put to lie that idea."

"What I don't understand is how someone like Smoke Jensen would be runnin' with an old mountain man like Preacher," Pete said.

"Smoke is pretty much a mountain man his own-self," the bartender said. "You see, that old man most raised Smoke. Leastwise, that's what I've always heard. They're what you call tight, so I wouldn't be doin' nothin' to get airy a one of 'em riled," the bartender said.

"Ain't Smoke the one that kilt fourteen men at that silver mining camp near the Uncompahgre a couple years ago?" Ned asked.

"That's him, all right."

"Yeah, you're right, he ain't the kind of man you'd want to get riled up at you," Ned said.

"Well, come on, Ned, it ain't like he kilt all them men 'cause they got him all riled up by askin' a question, is it?" Pete asked.

"No. The way I heard it, them men kilt his wife 'n kid," the bartender said.

"So then he had hisself a good reason for killin' 'em. Sounds to me like they was needin' killin'. So how is it you think we're goin' to rile him just by askin' him if he's ever heard of some mountain man up in Montana that's killin' Injuns 'n eatin' their gizzards?" Pete asked.

"I don't know. If you want to ask him, you go ahead and ask, but I'm tellin' you, I ain't goin' to do it," Ned said.

"What do you think?" Pete asked the bartender. "You think a question like that would get 'em riled?"

"No, they're both good men. They sort of like their privacy, especially the old one. But I don't reckon there won't neither one of them get all riled up just from you askin' a question."

Pete looked down at the far end of the bar where the two men stood, talking quietly to each other as they drank their beer.

"All right," he said. "I'm goin' to do it. I'm goin' to ask 'em if they ever heard of this fella."

Pete fortified himself with the last of his beer, then, wiping his mouth with the back of his hand, moved down the bar to ask his question.

"Beg your pardon, gents, but I've got a question that I'm kinda hopin' you can answer," Pete said when he approached Preacher and Smoke.

"What is the question?"

"Well, sir, it's all over ever'where now, that there is a feller up in Montana, a mountain man like I expect you two is, who's killin' Injuns 'n eatin' their gizzards. And I was wonderin', that is, me 'n my friend"—he nodded toward Ned, who hadn't moved from the far end of the bar—"we was wonderin' if either one of you fellers had heard about it, and could maybe tell us who it is that's a-doin' such a thing."

"You're saying there's a mountain man killin' Injuns 'n eatin' 'em?" Preacher asked, his voice showing his incredulity.

"Yes, sir. Well, no, not quite. He ain't eatin' ever'thing of the Injuns he's kilt now, mind you. From what I hear, the onliest thing he's eatin' is their gizzards."

"People don't have gizzards," Smoke pointed out.

"They don't?"

"Nope."

"I'll be damn. Wonder what it is then, that that feller is eatin'?" Pete held up his hand, then turned toward his friend, who was sitting at the other end of the bar. "Hey, Ned, people don't have gizzards. So what is it this feller up there is eatin'?"

"Livers," one of the bar girls said. "He is eating their livers."

"Does folks have livers?" Pete asked Smoke.

"Yes, they do. But why would someone do something like that?" Smoke asked.

"Well, sir, from what I heard, the Injuns kilt his wife 'n kid, 'n he just kind of went crazy and is killin' as many of 'em as he can. Well, sir, I'm sure you can understand somethin' like that."

"Oh?"

"I mean, what with what happened at that silver mining camp near the Uncompahgre, 'n all."

Pete put his hand to his mouth as soon as he spoke the words, and his eyes grew wide in fear. Had he said too much?

"Yes," Smoke replied. "Yes, I can understand."

"Hope I didn't make you mad or nothin' by bringin' that up," Pete said, anxiously.

"No, why should I be mad? It happened, and just about everyone knows that it happened."

"Yes, sir, just so's you know I don't mean nothin' bad by it. Anyhow, what I've heard now is that Iron Bull, he's the chief of the Crow, has rounded him up twenty warriors from the Big Dog Warrior Society to hunt this feller down and kill him."

"But there is something I don't understand. If the Indians killed this man's wife and child, why isn't the army involved?" Smoke asked.

"I don't rightly know why the army ain't involved, but reckon it's 'cause it was a squaw and a papoose the Injuns kilt, bein' as that was who the mountain man was married to. And it's more 'n likely that the army don't really care that much about a squaw and a papoose, even if they are married to a white man."

"I see," Smoke said. He shook his head. "But I'm afraid I can't help you. I have no idea as to who it might be."

"The thing is, whoever it is, what I've heered now is that the Crow is out to kill 'im, and they're sendin' whole war parties out. It's come down to bein' purt' nigh that feller all by his ownself agin the entire Crow nation. Don't seem like no fair fight to me."

"Maybe he'll leave the country so's the Crow can't find 'im," Preacher suggested.

"No, sir, I don't think so. This here feller seems to have hisself a lot more guts than he's got brains, if you know what I mean. He's bound to just stay up there 'n keep on killin' Injuns an' eatin' their gizzards, till he gets kilt his ownself."

"I hope that fella didn't disturb you men none," the bartender said after Pete went back to join Ned.

"No, he didn't disturb us. What have you got in the kitchen?"

"Ham and beans."

Smoke pointed to an empty table. "Bring us some. We'll be back there."

"Yes, sir," the bartender replied.

Smoke and Preacher took their beer with them then walked back to the table in the far corner.

CHAPTER THIRTY-TWO

"It's him," Smoke said. "I know it is."

"Who are you talking about?"

"The man that's killing the Crow and eating their livers. That has to be John Jackson. Though, I'm not sure he is actually eating their livers."

"It's just like you told that cowboy back there," Preacher said. "You don't really have no idea who it is. It don't have to be John, why, it could be purt' nigh anyone."

"But I know that John took the Indian girl to be his wife. And there's been plenty of time for them to have had kids. But there's something else about it."

"What's that?" Preacher asked.

"I feel it."

Preacher made no teasing response to that. He well knew the value of intuition, though that wasn't a word he had ever heard. For him, it was best described as feeling it in his gut. And his life had been saved more than once because he had reacted to a feeling in his gut.

"Yeah," Preacher said. "Well, there is that."

"I think I'll just mosey on up there and see for myself."

"Do you want me to come with you?" Preacher asked.

"No, there's no need."

"Do you think I'm too old? Sonny, I was dealing with Injuns long before you were born. Even before your pa was born."

"Preacher, I don't doubt your courage, your skills, or your ability in dealing with, or fighting against Indians. But John and I may well find ourselves in positions where we have to move fast. You've slowed down a mite, and if you are honest with yourself, you'll admit that."

Preacher was quiet for a moment, then he nodded, and stood. "I guess I'd better get myself on back up to my cabin now. As old and as slow as I am, it'll more 'n likely take me a month or two to get there."

For just a moment, Smoke thought Preacher was hurt, then he saw the smile on the old man's face.

"You take care, young 'un," he said, grabbing Smoke's hand.

"I will," Smoke promised.

[*It was the underground telegraph I alluded to in my previous editorial insert that first alerted Smoke*

*Jensen to the fact that his friend was in a personal
struggle. Jackson had killed at least ten braves and
Iron Bull sent twenty of his most fearsome warriors
to kill Jackson.*

*Smoke valued friendship and loyalty above all
other personal traits, so he left Colorado to look for
Jackson, not to stop him, but to help him. He wasn't
sure he believed the part about John eating the livers
of the Indians he killed, but there was no doubt that
his friend was being hunted. Smoke rushed in to help,
knowing it wouldn't be easy.—ED.]*

Old Main Building

Professor Armbruster laughed. "Gizzards? Did
that cowboy really think that human beings had gizzards?"

"Well, you have to understand, Professor, most
cowboys had seen the innards of animals and
people, but except for the heart, and maybe the
lungs, most of them wouldn't know the difference
between a pancreas and a spleen." Smoke laughed
as well. "Hell, I'm not sure I could pick out a liver
from any of the other human organs. But at least
I've always known that we didn't have gizzards."

"What did you think when you learned that the
army had no intention of intervening on behalf of
your friend?"

"To be honest with you, Professor, I don't really
know that I gave it much thought at all. I just sort of
figured that this was a personal war between John

and the Crow, and I calculated that the odds were way against him, so I decided to go up and see if I could lend him a hand."

"Did you go up to Montana and look for John Jackson as soon as you heard that he was in trouble?" Professor Armbruster asked.

"Yes," Smoke replied. "Well, I say yes. I didn't actually leave until after I returned home to tell Sally what I was doing."

"How did she feel about that? I mean, you hadn't been married all that long then. Did she understand that this was something you had to do? And was she all right with that?"

"We hadn't been married too long then, that's true," Smoke said. "But Sally always was a very smart woman, and she knew, right away, what kind of man I was. From the very beginning she told me that she wouldn't get in the way if I had to do something that, in her words, 'was a matter of conscience or honor.' So, yes, she was all right with it."

Sugarloaf Ranch

Smoke and Sally were sitting on the front porch watching a couple of the cowboys pitching horseshoes.

There was a clang, then a yell of triumph. "Ha! I got me a leaner!"

"Yeah? Well watch this."

The next cowboy threw and his horseshoe knocked the leaner away, then fell down, ringing the stob.

The other cowboys yelled in approval.

"Look at that, would you? Mack is good!"

"He ain't good, he's just lucky," the first cowboy said, dejectedly.

"You've got something to tell me, don't you, Smoke?" Sally asked.

"What makes you think that?"

"I know you, Smoke. I can read you like a book."

Smoke chuckled. "I guess I better never lie to you, huh?"

Sally laughed. "You couldn't lie to me if you tried. Now, what is it you have to tell me?"

"You remember me telling you about John Jackson?"

"Of course I remember. You spent a year with him, teaching him how to become a westerner."

"I need to go see him."

"Well, why didn't you say so? I'd love to meet him. Didn't you say he got married? Oh, don't tell me," she added excitedly. "They have a child now. Of course you must go. We must go."

Smoke shook his head and put his hand out on Sally's hand. "It's not that kind of visit, I'm afraid. And we aren't going, I'm going."

"Oh," Sally said, obviously disappointed by the reply. "What is it? Is John in some sort of trouble?"

"Yes."

"What kind of trouble?"

"From what I can gather, the Crow killed his wife and child, and he has gone on a personal vendetta.

But now the Crow are fighting back. They've sent twenty warriors after him."

"I see," Sally said, quietly.

"Sally, I can't just . . ."

"I know," Sally said, interrupting him. She put her other hand on top of Smoke's hand. "I know that you have to do what you have to do."

Smoke lifted her hand to his lips and kissed it. "Thank you for approving."

"I'm not sure that I do approve," Sally said. "But I understand. God help me, I do understand."

It took Smoke two weeks to get to the upper Missouri River valley, but it only took him one more week to find John, once he arrived. That was because Smoke had spent enough time with John, right here, in this very location, that he had a pretty good idea as to where he should look. And once he got into the area, he was able to track him.

Smoke smelled the cooking meat, and he knew, intuitively, that it was John. He approached slowly, though not necessarily quietly. He wanted John to hear him approaching, and he wanted him to realize that it was a measured, rather than a secretive approach.

He found John squatting by a small fire on the banks of Porcupine Creek. He had a piece of meat on a green twig, leaning out over the fire.

"What are you cooking?" Smoke asked.

"Become finicky, have you?" John replied.

Smoke dismounted and walked over toward the

fire. "Well, when I come this far to be your dinner guest, I like to know what I'm eating."

"Something I found dead."

"Smells good, anyway."

John stood and stuck out his hand. "I guess you've heard about my particular situation." It wasn't a question, it was an observation.

"Hell, John, there isn't anyone between here and El Paso who hasn't heard what's going on."

"Yeah," John said. "I sort of thought it might be getting around."

"Let me ask you something . . ."

"No, I'm not eating livers," John said, answering before the question was completely asked.

"Why does everyone think that you are?"

"I took a bite of them, the first time. And I've been letting the Crow think that I'm eating the livers." John chuckled. "It seems to have gotten them a little upset."

"A little upset? You are their biggest enemy right now."

"Good. That's what I wanted. If you've heard about this, you also know what those bastards did to Claire and little Kirby."

"Yes, I heard," Smoke said. He smiled. "Kirby? Your baby's name was Kirby?"

"I didn't think you would mind."

"I'm honored," Smoke said. "But I'm also saddened that he had such a short life. And I'm saddened by what happened to Claire."

"Then you can understand why I'm doing, what I'm doing," John said.

Smoke sighed. "What do you know about the Big Dog Warrior Society of the Crow?"

John shook his head. "I don't know anything about it. I've never heard of it."

"Well, of all the Indians, the Sioux, the Cheyenne, the Apache, the Comanche, the Big Dog Warrior Society of the Crow is the most fierce. When they set out to make war against an enemy, they take an oath, to kill that enemy, or to, literally, die trying. John, twenty of them are after you."

"I may have already run across them; I've killed a few Crow, here and there."

"No," Smoke said. "If you've killed a few here and there, you have not encountered the Big Dog Warriors. They won't come after you, here and there. There are twenty of them, and they will all come after you all at the same time."

John carved off a piece of the meat and tasted it.

"It's done," he said, pulling it away from the fire. He carved it up, then gave a big piece of it to Smoke.

"Uhmm," Smoke said. "This is very good. You've come some distance from when I first saw you, losing a fight to a turkey."

"I've worked at it," John replied.

The two men ate in silence for a moment or two before John spoke again.

"If these fierce warriors are coming after me, en masse, as you say, I expect you had better put distance between you and me soon as you finish eating."

"Uh-uh," Smoke said. "I'm not leaving."

"Smoke, I'm the one they're after. There's no need in you getting yourself killed."

"Didn't you name your son after me?"

"I did."

"Then, like I said, I'm not leaving. I have a personal stake in this now."

"All right," John said. "I welcome your company."

"John, when we first met, I was the teacher, and I taught you everything I know about living in the mountains, trapping, hunting, and just generally surviving. But you are the soldier. You went through the same war my pa did, and you were over in Asia with the French Foreign Legion, so now, you are the teacher. We've got twenty armed men coming after us, and we are but two. Do you have any suggestions as to how we find them and deal with them?"

John smiled. "Yeah, I do. First of all, we let them find us. And I know exactly where we need to be found."

"Where?"

"It's a small cabin I discovered not too far from here. The walls are thick, we'll have good cover as long as we are in there."

Smoke shook his head. "I don't know as I want to be confined in a cabin," he said. "If they burn it down around us, we'll be trapped."

"Ah, my friend," John said, holding up his finger. "This cabin can't be burned down. It is made of adobe."

"Adobe? Up here, in the woods?"

"I know. I was surprised too, when I found it. But it's there all right. Now, all we have to do is leave a trail they can follow, so they'll come to us."

"I agree. But the trail can't be too obvious," Smoke said. "We have to make them think that we are trying to cover it up. We don't want them to know that we want them to find us."

John smiled and nodded. "You'd make a good army officer, Smoke. You catch on fast."

CHAPTER THIRTY-THREE

With the Big Dog Warriors at Elk Prairie Creek

Whips His Horses and the Indians in his raiding party had spent last night on the banks of Elk Prairie Creek. During the night Whips His Horses had gone off by himself to construct a sweat lodge. When he returned the next morning he called the others together so he could share with them what he had learned during his meditation.

"I have sought wisdom in the sweat lodge," he said when the others had gathered. "I asked for knowledge, so that I might know what to do, and that knowledge has been given me. I asked for a special power to guide me in finding Liver Eater, and that special power has been given me. I asked for the courage to face our enemy and to kill him, so we can remove his liver and bring it back to our village so that Iron Bull and the others can see what I have done, and know that Liver Eater is dead and can harm us no more. In the sweat lodge I was given the knowledge, the power, and the courage to do this thing before me."

[*It may give the reader some insight to understand something about the sweat lodge ceremony. It is, and has been for some time, central to most Indian cultures. It is a place to get answers and guidance by asking spiritual entities for wisdom and power.*

The entrance to the sweat lodge always faces to the east and the sacred fire pit. This is significant to the Indians, because each new day begins in the east with the rising of the sun, which the Indians see as the source of life and power.

Between the entrance to the lodge and the fire pit, where the stones are heated, is an altar upon which is often placed an animal skull atop a post. At the base of the post is a small raised earthen altar upon which are placed other items of significance, such as sage, grass, feathers, and, always, a pipe.

While subjecting themselves to heat intense enough to cause a sweat, the participant asks for such things as knowledge, power, courage, and endurance.

It is not at all unusual that Whips His Horses would have gone to the sweat lodge to seek such assistance as he searched for John Jackson.—ED.]

"We will find Liver Eater, this I know, for I was told this in a vision," Whips His Horses said.

The nineteen other men of the Big Dog Warrior Society who were with Whips His Horses became very excited, not only because Whips His Horses had shared his vision with them, but also because success seemed so assured. They began painting their bodies for the war party.

At the adobe cabin

Smoke and John had reached the cabin the day before. After they located a safe place for their horses that night, they brought into the little cabin everything they might need to withstand a prolonged siege. They filled two big earthen vessels, found in the cabin, with water from the creek. They had all their food, as well as what ammunition they had.

"If there is no set-piece battle, I think we are in an advantageous enough position to be able to defeat the Indians by attrition, if need be," John said.

There were two windows in front of the cabin, one on each side of the door. There was at least one window on all the other sides of the cabin, but it seemed unlikely that any Indian would approach them from the back, as the cabin was built so close to a sheer wall of a cliff, that there was no room for them to maneuver.

They had slept in shifts during the night, and now, early in the morning, Smoke stepped outside. That was when he saw a large dark mass advancing slowly out of the gray dawn. He realized at once that it was the Indians.

At almost the same moment he saw them, the Indians saw him, and a loud, collective war whoop emerged from their throats. They began riding toward the cabin, their horses thundering across the ground.

"John, here they come!" Smoke shouted at the top of his voice.

On came the Indians, their horses leaping, gliding over obstacles, the half-naked, painted bodies of the warriors shining in the first brilliant rays of the morning sun.

"Get in here!" John shouted, holding the door open.

Smoke dashed in through the door, then it was closed and bolted.

Smoke hurried to his window and looked outside. At that precise moment one of the Indians had ridden all the way up to the building. Smoke shot him, his bullet striking the Indian just under his left eye, killing him instantly.

The Indians greatly outnumbered the two defenders and, perhaps because they had such superior numbers, they were overconfident, and foolishly bold. They would ride all the way up to the walls of the building, then lean over and try to shoot through the windows, or they would dismount and run up to try and force the door open. Because of such foolish activity, they were making themselves very easy targets, and Smoke and John were cutting them down like a scythe through wheat.

The Indians withdrew, dragging their dead and wounded back with them. After what had been a thunderous roar of gunfire for nearly half an hour, there was absolute silence.

"You said only one man would be here. There are two," Swift Hawk, one of the Indians, said, protesting to Whips His Horses. "Where is your medicine?" He pointed to the dead and dying. "Do you see that your medicine does not work?"

"My medicine is strong," Whips His Horses insisted. "We will go again!"

"Here they come!" John said.

The Indians came again, three abreast this time, galloping through the dust, shouting and whooping their war cries. Again they charged all the way up to the little cabin The Indians fired from horseback, shooting arrows and bullets toward the open windows. Two of them jumped down from their horses and tried to force the door open by hitting against it with the butts of their rifles.

Again, the marksmanship of Smoke and John was deadly, and riderless horses whirled and retreated, leaving their riders dead or dying on the ground behind them.

"Damn," John said. "Is this to be *ngôi nhà trang trại*, again?"

"The Nogy what?"

"You remember, I told you about the business in Annam?"

"Oh, yes. Well, there the army came just in time," Smoke said. "We're on our own, here." He chuckled.

"Yeah, I guess we are," John replied with a laugh.

"The problem is, just like at the fight at *ngôi nhà trang trại*, I'm running out of ammunition."

"How much do you have left?"

"Five rounds for the rifle. Two rounds for the pistol. How about you?"

"I'm not much better. Three rifle rounds, one pistol is empty, four rounds in the other."

Throughout the rest of the day the Indians attacked several more times. But they prefaced each attack with loud screeches and war whoops, and that enabled Smoke and John to be ready for them. They made every shot count.

"If we can just hold on until dark, maybe they'll go away," John suggested. "I've heard that Indians don't like to fight in the dark."

"They may not attack, but that doesn't mean they are going to go away," Smoke said.

Smoke was right. The Indians didn't go away, and all night long Smoke and John—who took turns sleeping just in case—could hear singing, and see the campfires.

"I wonder how long they'll stay?" John asked.

"Hard to say," Smoke answered. "How many rounds do you have now?"

"Two. What about you?"

"One pistol round, one round in the Henry."

"Damn."

* * *

The next morning the Indians had pulled back, and were now milling around on top of a hill. They were making no attempt to conceal themselves, because they were well out of range.

"Bold bunch of bastards, aren't they?" Smoke asked.

John had a pair of binoculars and he used them to study the Indians, only one of whom was mounted.

"I'll be damn," John said.

"What is it?"

"The Indian on the horse. Take a look at him. Look at his face. Do you see the black and red vertical lines on his cheek?"

"Yes."

"Claire pointed that out to me when we visited Iron Bull's camp. That means this man is the leader."

"Is he now?"

"I wonder if we killed him . . ."

"Would the others leave?" Smoke finished.

"It's worth a try."

Smoke looked at him. "That's a hell of a long shot. Six or seven hundred yards, easily."

"But if we both shot at the same time?"

"I've only got one rifle round left," Smoke said.

"Then, one of us had better hit him," John suggested.

"Wait," Smoke said. "I'm going to try a trick Preacher showed me once. It might improve our chances of hitting him. But it's all or nothing, because if we miss, we are going to be in a bad fix."

"What do you have in mind?" John asked.

Smoke took out the bullet from his pistol, and the one from his rifle. Then he separated the two bullets from their casings. Looking down into the rifle casing, he saw that there was room to add more powder. He filled the rifle casing the rest of the way, with powder from the pistol casing.

"Good idea," John said, and he did the same thing, combining the powder from two bullets into one.

John chuckled. "But this is absolutely an all-or-nothing draw of the cards."

When both were ready, they rested the barrels of the rifles on the windowsills and took long and careful aim.

"I'll count to three," Smoke said. "One, two, three."

Swift Hawk was standing next to Whips His Horses when he heard an angry buzz, then a loud pop. Looking up he saw blood squirting from Whips His Horses' head, and from a wound in his chest. Whips His Horses fell at Swift Hawk's feet.

"How can this be? How can they kill from so far?" one of the Indians asked in awed fear.

The Indians were disoriented. Whips His Horses' medicine had not protected him, which meant it could not protect them.

"Swift Hawk, there are but five of us now. And surely the spirits are angry with us, for no ordinary man can kill from so far away."

"And the bullets of both men found their mark," another said.

"Their medicine is strong," another said. "Swift Hawk, what shall we do?"

"We will make peace," Swift Hawk said.

Swift Hawk mounted his horse then, slowly, very slowly, started riding toward the adobe cabin.

"Here they come," John said. "What'll we do now?"

"Wait," Smoke said. "Look!"

The approaching Indian held his hand up, palm forward, and he continued to ride.

"I believe he wants to make peace," John said.

"They don't need to know we are out of ammunition. Hold your rifle by your side in your left hand," Smoke said. "We'll go outside to meet him, with our right hands up in the sign of peace."

Swift Hawk rode to within twenty yards of the cabin, all the while holding his hand up. Smoke and John stood out front, holding their hands up as well.

"No more will the Crow make war against Liver Eater!" Swift Hawk said in English.

"No more will I will eat the liver of the Crow," John said.

Swift Hawk nodded, then turned and rode away.

EPILOGUE

Some may think, upon reading this study of two of Colorado's most colorful characters, that I have taken what might be considered a soft approach to history, using words that are more sensual than cerebral. And because of this, some readers might suggest that this is a substitute for academic research.

I assure you that nothing can be further from the truth. No amount of scholarly inquiry, particularly of the kind that requires poring over the printed word, whether it be the work of earlier scholars, newspapers, diaries, or letters, could be more accurate than getting the story directly from one of the actual participants. As of the time of this writing, Smoke Jensen is still alive, and still one of Colorado's living treasures.

The peace negotiated between Swift Hawk and John Jackson held up, and never again was there trouble between them. In fact, John Jackson eventually declared himself to be a brother to the Crow.

He never married again, so there are no direct descendants

of this storied legend. He was, during his lifetime, a soldier in the Union army, a soldier of fortune with the French Foreign Legion, a scout, hunter, and trapper. In the end, he returned to Pennsylvania where he died, alone, in a veteran's hospital on December 21, 1900.

> *Jacob W. Armbruster, Ph.D.*
> *Professor of History, University of Colorado*
> *Boulder, Colorado*
> *April 9, 1925*

J. A. Johnstone on William W. Johnstone
"When the Truth Becomes Legend"

William W. Johnstone was born in southern Missouri, the youngest of four children. He was raised with strong moral and family values by his minister father, and tutored by his schoolteacher mother. Despite this, he quit school at age fifteen.

"I have the highest respect for education," he says, "but such is the folly of youth, and wanting to see the world beyond the four walls and the blackboard."

True to this vow, Bill attempted to enlist in the French Foreign Legion ("I saw Gary Cooper in *Beau Geste* when I was a kid and I thought the French Foreign Legion would be fun") but was rejected, thankfully, for being underage. Instead, he joined a traveling carnival and did all kinds of odd jobs. It was listening to the veteran carny folk, some of whom had been on the circuit since the late 1800s, telling amazing tales about their experiences, which planted the storytelling seed in Bill's imagination.

"They were mostly honest people, despite the bad

reputation traveling carny shows had back then,"
Bill remembers. "Of course, there were exceptions.
There was one guy named Picky, who got that name
because he was a master pickpocket. He could steal
a man's socks right off his feet without him knowing. Believe me, Picky got us chased out of more
than a few towns."

After a few months of this grueling existence, Bill
returned home and finished high school. Next
came stints as a deputy sheriff in the Tallulah,
Louisiana, Sheriff's Department, followed by a
hitch in the U.S. Army. Then he began a career in
radio broadcasting at KTLD in Tallulah, Louisiana,
which would last sixteen years. It was there that he
fine-tuned his storytelling skills. He turned to writing in 1970, but it wouldn't be until 1979 that his
first novel, *The Devil's Kiss*, was published. Thus
began the full-time writing career of William W.
Johnstone. He wrote horror (*The Uninvited*),
thrillers (*The Last of the Dog Team*), even a romance
novel or two. Then, in February 1983, *Out of the
Ashes* was published. Searching for his missing
family in the aftermath of a post-apocalyptic America, rebel mercenary and patriot Ben Raines is
united with the civilians of the Resistance forces
and moves to the forefront of a revolution for the
nation's future.

Out of the Ashes was a smash. The series would continue for the next twenty years, winning Bill three
generations of fans all over the world. The series was

often imitated but never duplicated. "We all tried to copy *The Ashes* series," said one publishing executive, "but Bill's uncanny ability, both then and now, to predict in which direction the political winds were blowing brought a certain immediacy to the table no one else could capture." The Ashes series would end its run with more than thirty-four books and twenty million copies in print, making it one of the most successful men's action series in American book publishing. (The Ashes series also, Bill notes with a touch of pride, got him on the FBI's Watch List for its less than flattering portrayal of spineless politicians and the growing power of big government over our lives, among other things. In that respect, I often find myself saying, "Bill was years ahead of his time.")

Always steps ahead of the political curve, Bill's recent thrillers, written with myself, include *Vengeance Is Mine, Invasion USA, Border War, Jackknife, Remember the Alamo, Home Invasion, Phoenix Rising, The Blood of Patriots, The Bleeding Edge,* and the upcoming *Suicide Mission.*

It is with the western, though, that Bill found his greatest success and propelled him onto both the *USA Today* and the *New York Times* bestseller lists.

Bill's western series include *The Mountain Man, Matt Jensen, the Last Mountain Man, Preacher, The Family Jensen, Luke Jensen, Bounty Hunter, Eagles, MacCallister* (an Eagles spin-off), *Sidewinders, The Brothers O'Brien, Sixkiller, Blood Bond, The Last*

Gunfighter, and the upcoming new series *Flintlock* and *The Trail West.* Coming in May 2013 is the hardcover western *Butch Cassidy, The Lost Years.*

"The Western," Bill says, "is one of the few true art forms that is one hundred percent American. I liken the Western as America's version of England's Arthurian legends, like the Knights of the Round Table, or Robin Hood and his Merry Men. Starting with the 1902 publication of *The Virginian* by Owen Wister, and followed by the greats like Zane Grey, Max Brand, Ernest Haycox, and of course Louis L'Amour, the Western has helped to shape the cultural landscape of America.

"I'm no goggle-eyed college academic, so when my fans ask me why the Western is as popular now as it was a century ago, I don't offer a 200-page thesis. Instead, I can only offer this: The Western is honest. In this great country, which is suffering under the yoke of political correctness, the Western harks back to an era when justice was sure and swift. Steal a man's horse, rustle his cattle, rob a bank, a stagecoach, or a train, you were hunted down and fitted with a hangman's noose. One size fit all.

"Sure, we westerners are prone to a little embellishment and exaggeration and, I admit it, occasionally play a little fast and loose with the facts. But we do so for a very good reason—to enhance the enjoyment of readers.

"It was Owen Wister, in *The Virginian* who first coined the phrase *'When you call me that, smile.'* Legend has it that Wister actually heard those words spoken by a deputy sheriff in Medicine Bow, Wyoming, when another poker player called him a son-of-a-bitch.

"Did it really happen, or is it one of those myths that have passed down from one generation to the next? I honestly don't know. But there's a line in one of my favorite Westerns of all time, *The Man Who Shot Liberty Valance,* where the newspaper editor tells the young reporter, 'When the truth becomes legend, print the legend.'

"These are the words I live by."

TURN THE PAGE FOR AN EXCITING PREVIEW!

USA TODAY BESTSELLING AUTHOR
WILLIAM W. JOHNSTONE
with J. A. Johnstone

Present a Blazing New Series

FLINTLOCK

He is brave, tough as leather, takes no prisoners, and has left behind a trail of deadly enemies—outlaws he's hunted down or killed with the cold heart of a man used to violence. A feared bounty hunter and the scourge of bad men everywhere, Flintlock carries an ancient Hawken muzzle-loader, handed down to him from the mountain man who raised him. He stands as the towering hero of a new Johnstone saga.

BLOOD QUEST

Busted out of prison by an outlaw friend, Flintlock joins a hunt for a fortune—a golden bell hanging in a remote monastery. But between the smoldering ruin of his former jail cell and a treasure in the Arizona mountains there will be blood at a U.S. Army fort, a horrifying brush with Apache warriors, and a dozen wild adventures with the schemers, shootists, madmen, and lost women who find their way to Flintlock's side. From a vicious, superstitious half-breed to the great Geronimo himself, Flintlock meets the frontier's most murderous hardcases—many who he must find a way to kill . . .

On sale now, wherever Pinnacle Books are sold.

CHAPTER ONE

"I'm gonna hang you tomorrow at sunup, Sam Flintlock, an' I can't guarantee to break your damned neck on account of how I never hung anybody afore," the sheriff said. "I'll try, lay to that, but you see how it is with me."

"The hammering stopped about an hour ago, so I figured my time was near," Flintlock said.

"A real nice gallows, you'll like it," Sheriff Dave Cobb said. "An' I'll make sure it's hung with red, white and blue bunting so you can go out in style. You'll draw a crowd, Sam. If'n that makes you feel better."

"This pissant town railroaded me into a noose, Cobb. You know it and I know it," Flintlock said.

"Damnit, boy, you done kilt Smilin' Dan Sedly and just about everybody in this valley was kissin' kin o' his. Ol' Dan was a well-liked man."

"He was wanted by the law for bank robbery and murder," Flintlock said.

"Not in this town he wasn't," Cobb said.

The sheriff was a middle-aged man and inclined to be jolly by times. He was big in the belly and a black, spade-shaped beard spread over the lapels of a broadcloth suit coat that looked to be half as old as he was.

"No hard feelings, huh, Sam?" he said. "I mean about the hangin' an' all. Like I told you, I'll do my best. I've been reading a book about how to set the noose an' sich an' I reckon I'll get it right."

"I got no beef against you, Cobb," Flintlock said. "You're the town lawman and you've got a job to do."

"How old are you, young feller?" the lawman said.

"Forty. I guess."

"Still too young to die." Cobb sighed. "Ah well, tell you what, I'll bring you something nice for your last meal tonight. How about steak and eggs? You like steak and eggs?"

"I don't much care, Sheriff, but there's one thing you can do for me."

"Just ask fer it. I'm a giving, generous man. Dave Cobb by name, Dave Cobb by nature, I always say."

"Let me have my grandpappy's old Hawken rifle," Flintlock said. "It will be a comfort to me."

Doubt showed in Cobb's face. "Now, I don't know about that. That's agin all the rules."

"Hell, Cobb, the Hawken hasn't been shot in thirty, forty years," Flintlock said. "I ain't much likely to use it to bust out of jail."

"You're a strange one, Sam Flintlock," the

lawman said. "Why did you carry that old gun around anyhow?"

"Call me sentimental, Cobb. It was left to me as a legacy, like."

"See, my problem is, Sam, you could use that old long gun as a club. Bash my brains out when I wasn't lookin'."

"Not that rifle, I won't. Your head is too thick, Sheriff. I might damage the stock."

Cobb thought for a while, his shaggy black eyebrows beetling. Finally he smiled and said, "All right, I'll bring it to you. But I see you making any fancy moves with that old Hawken, I'll shoot your legs off so you can still live long enough to be hung. You catch my drift?"

"You have my word, Sheriff, I won't give you any trouble."

Cobb nodded. "Well, you're a personable enough feller, even though you ain't so well set up an' all, so I'll take you at your word."

"I appreciate it," Flintlock said. "See, I'm named for that Hawken."

"Your real name Hawken, like?"

"No. My grandpappy named me for a flintlock rifle, seeing as how I never knew my pa's name."

"Hell, why didn't he give you his own name, that grandpa of yourn?"

"He said every man should have his father's name. He told me he'd call me Flintlock after the

Hawken until I found my ma and she told me who my pa was and what he was called."

"You ever find her?"

"No. I never did, but I'm still on the hunt for her. Or at least I was."

"Your grandpa was a mountain man?"

"Yeah, he was with Bridger an' Hugh Glass an' them, at least for a spell. Then he helped survey the Platte and the Sweetwater with Kit Carson and Fremont."

"Strange, restless breed they were, mountain men."

"You could say that."

"I'll bring you the Hawken, but mind what I told you, about shootin' off a part of yourself."

"I ain't likely to forget," Flintlock said.

CHAPTER TWO

"Pssst . . ."

Sam Flintlock sat up on his cot, his mind cobwebbed by sleep.

"Pssst . . ."

What was that? Rats in the corners again?

"Hell, look up here, stupid."

Flintlock rose to his feet. There was a small barred window high on the wall of his cell where a bearded face looked down at him.

"I see you're prospering, Sammy," the man said, grinning. "Settin' all nice and cozy in the town hoosegow."

Flintlock scowled. "Come to watch me hang, Abe?"

"Nah, I was just passin' through when I saw the gallows," Abe Roper said. "I asked who was gettin' hung and they said a feller with a big bird tattooed on his throat that goes by the name of Sam Flintlock.

I knew it had to be you. There ain't another ranny in the West with a big bird an' that handle."

"Here to gloat, Abe?" Flintlock said. "Gettin' even for old times?"

"Hell, no, I got nothing agin you, Sam. You got me two years in Yuma but you treated me fair and square. An' you gave my old lady money the whole time I was inside. Now why did you do a dumb thing like that?"

"You had growing young 'uns. Them kids had to be fed and clothed."

"Yeah, but why the hell did you do it?"

"I just told you."

"I got no liking for bounty hunters, Sammy, but you was a true-blue white man, taking care of my family like that." Roper was silent for a moment, then said, "Sally and the kids passed about three years ago from the cholera."

"I'm sorry to hear that," Flintlock said. "I can close my eyes and still see their faces."

"It was a hurtful thing, Sam, and me being away on the scout at the time."

"You gonna stick around for the hanging, Abe?" Flintlock said.

"Hell, no, and neither are you."

"What do you mean?"

"I mean there's a barrel of gunpowder against this wall and it's due to go up in"—Roper looked down briefly—"oh, I'd say less than half a minute."

The man waved a quick hand. "Hell, I got to light a shuck."

Flintlock stood rooted to the spot for a moment. Then he yelled a startled curse at Roper, grabbed the rifle off his cot and pulled the mattress on top of him.

A couple of seconds later the Mason City jail blew up with such force its shingle roof soared into the air and landed intact twenty yards away on top of the brand-new gallows. The jail roof and the gallows collapsed in a cloud of dust and killed Sheriff Cobb's pregnant sow that had been wallowing in the mud under the platform.

A shattering shower of adobe and splintered wood rained down on Flintlock and acrid dust filled his lungs. He threw the mattress aside and staggered to his feet, just as Abe Roper kicked aside debris and stepped through the hole in the jailhouse wall.

"Sam, get the hell out of there," Roper said. "I got your hoss outside."

Flintlock grabbed the Hawken, none the worse for wear, and stumbled outside.

As Roper swung into the saddle, Chinese Charlie Fong, grinning as always, tossed Flintlock the reins of a paint.

"Good to see you again, Sammy," Fong said.

"Feeling's mutual, Charlie," Flintlock said.

He mounted quickly and ate Roper's dust as he followed the outlaw out of town at a canter.

Roper turned in the saddle. "Crackerjack bang, Sammy, huh? Have you ever seen the like?"

"Son of a gun, you could've killed me," Flintlock said.

"So what? Who the hell would miss ya?" Roper said.

"Somebody's gonna miss this paint pony I'm riding," Flintlock said.

"Hell, yeah, it's the sheriff's hoss," Roper grinned. "Better than the ten-dollar mustang you rode in on, Sam."

"Damn you, Abe, Cobb's gonna hang me, then hang me all over again for hoss theft," Flintlock said.

"Well, he'll have to catch you first," Roper said, kicking his mount into a gallop.

After an hour of riding through the southern foothills of the Chuska Mountains, the massive rampart of red sandstone buttes and peaks that runs north all the way to the Utah border, Roper drew rein and he and Flintlock waited until Charlie Fong caught up.

"Where are we headed, Abe?" Flintlock said. "I hope you've got a good hideout all picked out."

He and Roper were holed up in a stand of mixed juniper and piñon. A nearby high meadow was thick with yellow bells and wild strawberry, and the waning afternoon air smelled sweet of pine and wildflowers.

"We're headed for Fort Defiance, up in the old Navajo country. It's been abandoned for years but the army's moved back, temporary-like, until ol' Geronimo is either penned up or dead."

Flintlock scratched at a bug bite under his buckskin shirt and said, "Is that wise, me riding into an army fort when I'm on the scout?"

"There ain't no fightin' sodjers there, Sammy, just cooks an' quartermasters an' the like," Roper said. "All the cavalry is out, lookin' fer Geronimo an' them."

"We gonna stay in an army barracks?" Flintlock said. "Say it ain't so."

"Nah, me an' Charlie got us a cabin near the officers' quarters, a cozy enough berth if you're not a complainin' man."

Roper peered hard at Flintlock's rugged, unshaven face and then his throat. "Damnit, Sam, I never did get used to looking at that big bird, even when we rode together."

"I was raised rough," Flintlock said. "You know that."

"Old Barnabas do that to you?" Roper said, passing the makings.

"He wanted it done, but when I was twelve he got an Assiniboine woman to do the tattooing. As I recollect, it hurt considerable."

"What the hell is it? Some kind of eagle?"

Flintlock built his cigarette and Roper gave him a match. "It's a thunderbird." He thumbed the match into flame and lit his cigarette. "Barnabas wanted a black and red thunderbird, on account of how the Indians reckon it's a sacred bird."

"He wanted it that big? Hell, it pretty much covers your neck and down into your chest."

"Barnabas said folks would remember me because of the bird. He told me that a man folks don't remember is of no account."

"He was a hard old man, was Barnabas, him and them other mountain men he hung with. A tough, mean bunch as ever was."

"They taught me," Flintlock said. "Each one of them taught me something."

"Like what, for instance?"

"They taught me about whores and whiskey and how to tell the good ones from the bad. They taught me how to stalk a man and how to kill him. And they taught me to never answer a bunch of damned fool questions."

Roper laughed. "Sounds like old Barnabas and his pals all right."

"One more thing, Abe. You saved my life today, and they taught me to never forget a thing like that."

Roper, smiling, watched a hawk in flight against the dark blue sky, then again directed his attention to Flintlock.

"You ever heard of the Golden Bell of Santa Elena, Sam?" he said.

"Can't say as I have."

"You will. And after I tell you about it, I'll ask you to repay the favor you owe me."

CHAPTER THREE

"Are you sure you saw deer out here, Captain Shaw? It might have been a shadow among the trees."

"Look at the tracks in the wash, Major. Deer have passed this way and not long ago."

"I see tracks all right," Major Philip Ashton said. He looked around him. "But I'm damned if I see any deer."

"Sir, may I suggest we move farther up the wash as far as the foothills," Captain Owen Shaw said. "Going on dusk the deer will move out of the timber."

Ashton, a small, compact man with a florid face, an affable disposition and a taste for bonded whiskey, nodded. "As good a suggestion as any, Captain. We'll wait until dark and if we don't see a deer we'll leave it for another day."

"As you say, sir," Shaw said.

He watched the major walk ahead of him. Like

himself, Ashton wore civilian clothes but he carried
a regulation Model 1873 Trapdoor Springfield rifle.
Shaw was armed with a .44-40 Winchester because
he wanted nothing to go wrong on this venture, no
awkward questions to be answered later.

Major Ashton, who had never held a combat
command, carried his rifle at the slant, as though
advancing on an entrenched enemy and not a herd
of nonexistent mule deer.

Shaw was thirty years old that spring. He'd
served in a frontier cavalry regiment, but he'd been
banished to Fort Defiance as a commissary officer
after a passionate, though reckless, affair with the
young wife of a farrier sergeant.

Shaw wasn't at all troubled by his exile. It was
safer to dole out biscuit and salt beef than do battle
with Sioux and Cheyenne warriors.

Of course, the Apaches were a problem, but
since the Navajo attacked the fort in 1858 and 1860
and both times were badly mauled, it seemed that
the wily Geronimo was giving the place a wide
berth.

That last suited Captain Shaw perfectly. He had
big plans and they sure as hell didn't involve
Apaches.

The wash, dry now that the spring melt was over,
made a sharp cut to the north and the two officers
followed it through a grove of stunted juniper and
willow onto a rocky plateau bordered by thick
stands of pine.

In the distance the fading day painted the Chuska

peaks with wedges of deep lilac shadow and out among the foothills coyotes yipped. The jade sky was streaked with banners of scarlet and gold, the streaming colors of the advancing night.

Major Ashton walked onto the plateau, his attention directed at the pines. His rifle at the ready, he stopped and scanned the trees with his field glasses.

Without turning his head, he said, "Nothing moving yet, Captain."

Shaw made no answer.

"You have a buck spotted?" the major whispered.

Again, he got no reply.

Ashton turned.

Shaw's rifle was pointed right at his chest.

"What in blazes are you doing, Captain Shaw?" Ashton said, his face alarmed.

"Killing you, Major."

Owen Shaw fired.

The soft-nosed .44-40 round tore into the major's chest and plowed through his lungs. Even as the echoing report of the Winchester racketed around the plateau, Ashton fell to his hands and knees and coughed up a bouquet of glistening red blossoms.

Shaw smiled and shot Ashton again, this time in the head. The major fell on his side and all the life that remained in him fled.

Moving quickly, Shaw stood over Ashton and fired half a dozen shots into the air, the spent cartridge cases falling on and around the major's body. He then pulled a Smith & Wesson .32 from the pocket of his tweed hunting jacket, placed the muzzle against his left thigh and pulled the trigger.

A red-hot poker of pain burned across Shaw's leg, but when he looked down at the wound he was pleased. It was only a flesh wound but it was bleeding nicely, enough to make him look a hero when he rode into Fort Defiance.

Limping slightly, Shaw retraced his steps along the dry wash to the place where he and Ashton had tethered their horses. He looked behind him and to his joy saw that he'd left a blood trail. Good! There was always the possibility that a cavalry patrol had returned to the fort and their Pima scouts could be bad news. The blood would help his cover-up.

He gathered up the reins of the major's horse and swung into the saddle. There was no real need to hurry but he forced his horse into a canter, Ashton's mount dragging on him.

It was an officer's duty to recover the body of a slain comrade, but Ashton had been of little account and not well liked. When Shaw told of the Apache ambush and his desperate battle to save the wounded major, that little detail would be overlooked.

And his own bloody wound spoke loud of gallantry and devotion to duty.

Lamps were already lit when Captain Owen Shaw rode into Fort Defiance, a sprawling complex of buildings, some of them ruins, grouped around a dusty parade ground.

He staged his entrance well.

Not for him to enter at a gallop and hysterically warn of Apaches, rather he slumped in the saddle and kept his horse to a walk . . . the wounded warrior's noble return.

He was glad that just as he rode past the sutler's store, big, laughing Sergeant Patrick Tone stepped outside, a bottle of whiskey tucked under his arm.

"Sergeant," Shaw said, making sure he sounded exhausted and sore hurt, "sound officer's call. Direct the gentlemen to the commandant's office."

"Where is Major Ashton, sir?" Tone said, his Irish brogue heavy on his tongue. Like many soldiers in the Indian-fighting army, he'd been born and bred in the Emerald Isle and was far from the rainy green hills of his native land.

"He's dead. Apaches. Now carry out my order."

Tone shifted the bottle from his right to his left underarm and snapped off a salute. Then he stepped quickly toward the enlisted men's barracks, roaring for the bugler.

Shaw dismounted outside the administration building, a single-story adobe structure, its timber porch hung with several large clay ollas that held drinking water. The ollas' constant evaporation supposedly helped keep the interior offices cool, a claim the soldiers vehemently denied.

After leaning against his horse for a few moments, the action of an exhausted man, Shaw limped up the three steps to the porch, drops of blood from his leg starring the rough pine.

He stopped, swaying slightly, when he saw a woman bustling toward him across the parade ground, her swirling skirts lifting veils of yellow dust.

Shaw smiled inwardly. This was getting better and better. Here comes the distraught widow.

Maude Ashton, the major's wife, was a plump, motherly woman with a sweet, heart-shaped face that normally wore a smile. But now she looked concerned, as though she feared to hear news she already knew would be bad.

Maude mounted the steps and one look at the expression on Shaw's face and the blood on his leg told her all she needed to know. She asked the question anyway. "Captain Shaw, where is my husband?"

As the stirring notes of officer's call rang around him, Shaw made an act of battling back a sob. "Oh, Maude . . ."

He couldn't go on.

The captain opened his arms wide, tears staining his cheeks, and Maude Ashton ran between them. Shaw clasped her tightly and whispered, "Philip is dead."

Maude had been a soldier's wife long enough to know that the day might come when she'd have to face those three words. Now she repeated them. "Philip is dead . . ."

"Apaches," Shaw said. He steadied himself and

managed, "They jumped us out by Rock Wash and Major Ashton fell in the first volley."

Maude took a step back. Her pretty face, unstained by tears, was stony. "And Philip is still out there?"

Boots thudded onto the porch and Shaw decided to wait until his two officers were present before he answered Maude's irritating question.

First Lieutenant Frank Hedley was in his early fifties, missing the left arm he'd lost at Gettysburg as a brevet brigadier general of artillery. He was a private, withdrawn man, too fond of the bottle to be deemed fit for further promotion. He'd spent the past fifteen years in the same regular army rank. This had made him bitter and his drinking and irascible manner worsened day by day.

Standing next to him was Second Lieutenant Miles Howard, an earnest nineteen-year-old fresh out of West Point. His application for a transfer to the hard-riding 5th Cavalry had recently been approved on the recommendation of the Point's superintendent, the gallant Colonel Wesley Merritt, the regiment's former commander.

Howard had a romantic view of the frontier war, his imagination aflame with flying banners, bugle calls and thundering charges with the saber. He'd never fought Apaches.

"Where is the major?" Hedley said.

"He's dead," Shaw said. "We got hit by Apaches at Rock Wash and Major Ashton fell."

Hedley turned and saw the dead officer's horse. "Where is he?"

Shaw shook his head and then stared directly and sincerely at Maude. "I had to leave him. The Apaches wanted his body but I stood over him and drove them away. But I was sore wounded and could not muster the strength to lift the gallant major onto his horse."

Lieutenant Howard, more perceptive and more sympathetic than Hedley, watched blood drops from Shaw's leg tick onto the timber.

"Sir, you need the post surgeon," he said.

"Later, Lieutenant. Right now I want you and Mr. Hedley in the commandant's office," Shaw said, grimacing, a badly wounded soldier determined to be brave.

GREAT BOOKS,
GREAT SAVINGS!

When You Visit Our Website:
www.kensingtonbooks.com
You Can Save Money Off The Retail Price
Of Any Book You Purchase!